completely
LOST

completely LOST

jessica swan

Odette Books

Published in the United States by Odette Books, Oakland.
www.odettebooks.com

Publisher's Note: This is a work of fiction. Names, characters, places, and incidents are a product of the author's imagination. Locales and public names are sometimes used for atmospheric purposes.

Library of Congress Control Number: 2016901095

Completely Lost/ Swan, Jessica.
ISBN 978-0-9972069-3-7

Typeface: designed by Antonio Rodrigues Jr.

10 9 8 7 6 5 4 3 2

First Edition

for Auggie

contents

THE NINE EXPERTS OF JULIA CLARK

The Psychologist

The Ballerina

The Chef

The Monk

The Musician

The Astrophysicist

The Billionaire

The Diplomat's Daughter

The Artist

THE NINE MUSES OF ANCIENT GREEK MYTHOLOGY

Melpomene, the Muse of tragedy

Terpsichore, the Muse of dance

Thalia, the Muse of comedy & pastoral poetry

Polyhymnia, the Muse of meditation

Euterpe, the Muse of music

Urania, the Muse of astronomy & peace

Clio, the Muse of history & heroism

Kalliope, the Muse of eloquence & epics

Erato, the Muse of love

Part 1 The Psychologist

But oh Melpomene! thy lyre of wo—
To what a mournful pitch its keys were strung,
And when thou badest its tones of sorrow flow,
Each weeping Muse, enamoured, o'er thee hung:
How sweet—how heavenly sweet, when faintly rose
The song of grief, and at its dying close.

~James Gates Percival, "An Ode to Music", 1823

one

THE EMOTIONAL MINEFIELD of these early years of marriage is all the more difficult without the advice and wisdom of my mom. I wish I had her here to tell me the little things. How to cook meals on a shoestring budget and host dinner parties and what linens I should use and all the things a wife is expected to know and do. I haven't the faintest idea which pots and pans I'm supposed to buy. I don't know how to iron Leo's dress shirts properly or when to use that mysterious blue can of starch. And I don't have a clue about sewing or how to mend a rip with a needle and thread. I don't even know how to make a roast. Isn't that what wives are supposed to cook on Christmas Day?

Sometimes I ache to just ask her a question. *What was that tea you always made for me when I was sick? Why does my tomato sauce taste different from yours? Am I doing this right?* Just a question. Or just to feel her arm around me to show her support. Even though I tell myself again and again that she's looking down on me from heaven, I feel terribly alone. And I have to reassure myself that I have my family. I have Leo. And I've also gained someone else. A mother-in-law…

Her name is Lilly. She is perpetually cheerful and well-groomed, with detective-like eyes of green that never let her miss a thing. And she's a lovely woman who doesn't understand why in the world her youngest son's wife spends her days writing and not making grandbabies. By the bundle. Or the batch. Or whatever made-on-the-assembly-line groups of babies are called.

Once I accompanied her on a quick shopping trip for a new handbag. I had just picked up a satchel when she let out a long sigh.

"What is it?" I asked.

"Oh…nothing. It's nothing," she replied.

I made the mistake of thinking that "nothing" actually meant "nothing" and continued hunting for a bargain.

"Do you…eat?" Lilly said. She shook her head as she looked at my waist disapprovingly.

That must have been bait, because I definitely got hooked.

"We just had pancakes and bacon before we left, remember?" I replied, confused.

Then she leaned forward and said, "You know, I *really* don't want to be the sort of mother-in-law who asks, but…"

"But?"

She leaned in even more. Side nose to side nose.

"When *exactly* are you two planning on having children?"

2

I nearly swallowed my tongue. At that time, Leo and I had been married for only two months.

"Well," I began, uncertain how to answer.

"I don't want to pry, of course," Lilly quickly added.

"Oh. Good."

"But how much longer?"

And she stood there with those penetrating green eyes that most certainly did not match her polite smile.

"Well, I think we'll probably get a pet monkey first and see how that goes," I said. Her jaw dropped faster than I could say, "Just kidding." I tried to come up with a safely vague answer. "I think once we move out of our studio apartment and into a…well, slightly bigger apartment, we'll be better prepared for kids," I said as confidently as I could. *There*, I thought, *I'm off the hook*. She wouldn't dare ask a follow-up question to that. No way. And I watched as Lilly's blonde brow furrowed the way a tank rolls determinedly over delicate terrain. "And when will that be, my dear?" she said in her sweetest, most motherly voice.

I never did tell her the truth. The real, honest-to-goodness truth. I never dared. Secretly though, it's always been my goal that I get at least one novel published before I have children. But that's a tough answer to offer to a woman who thinks *female writer* is just a fancy term for *lazy housewife*.

"What *do* you do all day?" she'll often ask me.

"I write," is my usual response.

"But, what do you *do*? Walk me through your day. You wake up, you get dressed (I would imagine), you eat…something…and then? And *then*…?"

And though I hate to admit it, Lilly's circular arguments always leave me feeling a little, well, bothered. Why is it so hard for her to believe that I'm a writer? Maybe it's because I don't sound like a writer in our conversations. I'm not confidently verbose even on a good day. Or maybe it's because I don't indulge in season-long bouts of depression. Mine last only a few hours.

I suppose I'm not a typical writer. I don't swig vodka martinis when I get a new deal. I don't go through a pack of cigarettes in an hour when I'm working on a manuscript. But I do go through a pack of gum. That's right, a whole pack of gum. And yes, a pack an hour. It's disgusting, as Leo repeatedly reminds me. It's my secret shame. I do it when I'm alone, flying through pages upon pages, with words oozing out from my head and dripping down to my fingertips. Writing is what gives me pleasure. Delight. It enchants me. It keeps me up at night. Late, late, late into the night and well into the bird-chirping hours of dawn.

I've been consumed with getting my latest manuscript, *Alice's Dream*, off the ground. No such luck just yet. Despite months and months of casting query letters out into the vast sea of literary agents and publishing houses, I can't seem to get a worthwhile bite. So in the meantime I ghostwrite.

No one really knows who the ghostwriters are. No one talks about them. And for the most part, no one cares. And yet ghostwriting—or ghosting, as it's usually called—offers endless oceans of alluring, albeit ego-bursting, anonymity. Perhaps it's the mystery of it that fascinates me. I feel like a spy. An agent. Someone with top secret clearance who is knee-deep in some spectacular covert operation. *Psst…will you write this book? Yes, of course. Will you*

4

write it for me? Certainly. And will you swear on your life that you will never, ever, ever tell another living soul that you wrote it? Definitely!

That's the hard part for most people to grasp at first. How can someone spend so much time and energy writing a book and then let someone else take the credit for her hard work? Tough question.

But here are the facts. There are usually three types of people who depend on ghostwriters. Experts are the first. They're the ones with inside information on the hot and sexy topics of the headlines and the watercooler discussions. They're scientists or doctors, business professionals or politicians. But these kinds of experts need ghostwriters because they are too busy spending their days acting difficult and making the lives of those around them miserable to take the time out to write a book. Well, maybe not *every* expert. But certainly most.

The second type are the survivors. Survivors of anything, really. Of war, of drugs, of psychoses, of illness, or even of kidnapping or cults. Anyone who has been somewhere absolutely dreadful and lived to tell about it. And surprisingly enough, survivors are the ones who usually could do a better job writing the book themselves if they wanted to. These people have stories that are raw. Gritty. Real. But survivors are often just too traumatized or too fatigued to sit down and write it out.

The last type are the celebrities. Most famous people live surprisingly uninteresting lives and need someone to help "beef up" or "fill out" or "fluff up" their personal stories so that the public will not be disappointed. And sometimes the celebrity has lived a notoriously rich and exciting life but lacks the writing skills to create an equally compelling story.

Yet despite these important categorical differences, publishers will invariably lump everyone together and refer to each of them as the expert. And the brave soul who takes on the role of the ghostwriter without looking back is referred to only as the "agreed party." Plain. Simple. Elegantly understated and adequately elusive. It's the publisher's diplomatic way of getting around calling anyone "the author."

But really, a ghostwriter is more like a translator. She extracts information and transforms conversations with the expert into a narrative that has a natural, controlled ferociousness—it screams authenticity in a loud whisper.

And so the ghostwriter's task is simple: Waltz quietly into someone else's life, try on his or her shoes for a while, and try to discover things about the expert that even the expert didn't realize. Ask questions that have never been asked before. Draw wild conclusions that have never been drawn before. Explore. Delve. Investigate. And live. A ghostwriter must drown her own self and let her imagination live a completely different life. A ghostwriter lives many, many lives and must adapt as quickly and as smoothly as possible.

But the most important qualification of a ghostwriter is that she must find some thrill, some excitement, in taking on the expert's voice and life and experiences as her own, all while absorbing the expert's distinct style and nuances. And then, when the book is finally finished, the ghostwriter must surrender the expert's identity and life back to the expert and pretend that none of it ever happened. What could be more exhilarating, more adventurous, than living other lives besides your own without anyone ever finding out?

And so I can't help but be grateful for the nondisclosure agreement. The NDA. That little paragraph that always shows up in the middle of every one of my contracts with a publisher. That tiny indented section that tells me that no one must ever know of my involvement in the project.

Of course, I do enjoy a good round of gossip. Maybe it's the French in me. Or maybe it's because I was the youngest in my family. The youngest is always a tattletale. And as long as I don't "name names," I'm free to say what I please to whom I please when I please. Or at least I think I am. I've never asked anyone. But maybe a ghostwriter who talks about her secrets is no better than the magician who reveals his secrets—the trick mirrors and phony swords—and ruins his audience's enchantment. Or maybe it's different. Maybe I'll open the doors to a secret world that has never been exposed to the light of day before. And maybe, for the first time ever, a ghostwriter will finally emerge from that hidden universe, remove the veil of obscurity, and proudly claim her role in all those deliciously secret lives.

two

LEO CALLS ME A LITERARY chameleon because, for some strange reason, I have the ability to mimic anyone's writing voice. In high school this helped me tremendously with making friends (or so went my plan), as I could write my classmates' English essays for them and still make each one sound unique to the person whose name was on the paper. It's not so tough, really. Some people are naturally long-winded in their speech, and usually their writing follows suit. Others indulge in dramatic pauses or "ums" and such when they talk, which translates well into short, punchy writing.

Now I mostly write autobiographies, which are really just ghosted biographies. For the past two years, I've been ghosting exclusively with the same editor at the same publishing house in New York. It's not a big house, or small—it's more of a medium size, like my medium-size editor. We've met only once, and I can never remember his last name. His signature on the last page of our NDA is indecipherable. So let's just call him Mister X.

He likes me because I have a freakish pair of abilities: I can dependably write in hyper-speed while surviving on less than four hours of sleep. That's about it. Most ghostwriters take anywhere from six months to several years to complete a manuscript. I take three months from start to finish. Three and a half, tops. That's a new manuscript every season, more or less, at about eighty hours a week. I am perpetually oversensitive and overtired with dark under-eye circles to show for it, along with nearsightedness that is so extreme that technically I'm legally blind. I know I won't be able to keep this up much longer, but for now it's paying off my student loans. Still, I'm not exactly writing poetry or world-saving prose. It's pretty light stuff, really. Last summer it was a tell-all for an unsavory yet charismatic New England woman who may or may not be disowned from the Kennedy bloodline. And the spring before that, it was an autobiography for a tween Hollywood star who thought it finally time to sell her memoirs.

I'm not sure why I feel that I have to change something about myself when I start a new manuscript, but I do. I dye my hair. Chocolaty brunette in the spring. Honey blonde for summer, and then jet black for autumn, and auburn or crimson for winter. It makes me feel as though I'm somebody new, somebody to get to know and figure out. Somebody exciting and unpredictable. Maybe it keeps a certain part of me free to channel any new "expert" who gets thrown my way.

I've learned that just about every ghostwriter has a weird quirk of identity. Some will go by the first name of their expert for the duration of the project—except with the expert, of course. Others will change their walk or their fashion style. One ghost I know changes his accent for every project. Irish when he works with male experts and Italian when he works with female experts. He's still single.

It's September now, so every super-straight strand on my head is ink black and looks a little blue in the sunlight. Leo tells me it's the color of a beetle and that he feels as though he's having an affair. He says that whenever I'm not strawberry blonde, my hair color when we married in July.

"You look like a completely different woman," he tells me in bed. It's morning, and the fresh autumn air is blowing through our open bedroom window. His green eyes always look blue in the early light. We hear the crinkled leaves falling from the branches of a nearby sycamore. The morning air smells fresh and clean, and it's still too early to enjoy being awake. But there's a dim glow in our room, and I see that Leo is smiling at me. I find him very handsome when he looks at me like that.

He gently slides my thick, razor-sharp bangs off to the side of my forehead and kisses me. Never mind that his leaning arm is painfully tugging on my hair or that his chin stubble is grazing my cheek like sandpaper—it's not every day that a wife gets kissed unexpectedly by her husband. And just as I start to savor the moment, the phone rings. Leo jumps out of bed with a start. He answers and then sighs an exaggerated sigh from his nose.

"I guess it's that time again," he says as he hands me the phone. "I'll be in the shower."

The only thing more predictable than the seasons or my ever-changing head of hair is the phone call. *The* phone call. It usually lasts under a minute and always ends with a yes instead of a good-bye.

"This is Julia," I answer.

"Julia, it's me," replies Mister X. He sounds even more rushed than usual. "Do you know any psychology?" he asks.

"Sure," I lie. "I majored in psych in college," I lie again.

"Great. I got one for you. It's in Palo Alto. A psychoanalyst. Can you do it?"

"Of course," I reply as I struggle with my contact lenses in the mirror. "What's the story?"

"I'll send over the details. From what I hear, it's a bit of a tightrope. Try not to be so flippant. She's fired the past three ghosts. Tough personality or something, I don't know," he says.

"I'm flippant?"

"Are you even listening? I'm just saying she can be a little dry, so if I don't get this thing ghosted, it's gonna read like a goddamned textbook," he says quickly. I can hear the smack of his doughnut chomping in between his words, and I can almost see the puff of powdered sugar. "And she's really, really *connected*," he adds in a hushed, secretive voice, "so do what she wants, Julia!"

"I know, I know," I reply.

Mister X pauses. "Sure you can handle this?"

"Don't worry," I reply. "I get it."

three

MOST EVERYONE TAKES Highway 101 all the way down from San Francisco to Palo Alto. But I don't. The 280 is just too gorgeous to pass up. With its green hills that melt seamlessly into even greener mountains, this scenic route is the most relaxing way to drive through the Peninsula. Every shade of green paints the earth out as far and as infinitely as blues do the ocean. There is also a natural rhythm to those rolling hills as you drive them—smooth and slow, one by one, like still, massive waves suspended in time.

Yet despite the calming scenery, I'm a complete mess.

I know I shouldn't be nervous right now. But I am. I feel so jittery. I always get a little anxious whenever I'm about to meet anyone new, especially the new expert—and most especially a psychologist. My hands get clammy, and my heart begins to race, and I start to wonder what she is assuming about me and what she is inferring about my personality. Or if she is thinking anything at all about me. And if not, why not?

I take a big gulp of green tea while I drive and ponder my new expert. Let's call her Dr. Eleanor B. I swerve a little as I skim the dozen pages Mister X faxed me this morning. Thanks to her groundbreaking research in the 1970s, Dr. Eleanor B. is Stanford's pride and joy in the Psychology Department. She needs help writing a more lighthearted book, and she doesn't want some grad student hungry for a byline. She wants an outsider—Damn it! Spilled the tea all over everything—who doesn't know her well. Someone who isn't scared of her and who can keep her on track. Well, this is going to go great.

After an hour of driving and another half hour of getting lost and found again, I finally arrive at the psychologist's home. It's nestled at the end of a long boulevard of impressive, ivy-covered *Gatsby*-esque mansions. They're all grand and four or five stories high. And all are surrounded by tall and elegant gardens, stately iron gates, and a sparkling parade of newly waxed, vintage Porsches.

The psychologist's house looks surprisingly plain in comparison, with its single-story design. It stands rather unassuming on a corner, just around a bend. White camellia bushes that look more like trees cover most of the front of the home, and two simple rows of meager-looking marigolds line the short path to the bright-white wooden front door. I'm reminded of going to my piano teacher's home for lessons when I was seven.

I ring the doorbell and a loud, alarm-like buzz sounds. Several moments go by. Nothing. I cringe as I dare to ring it again. The heavy block of a door finally opens quickly and quietly, without the slightest creak. Yet to my surprise, it opens not to the inside of her house but to an enchanting shaded courtyard.

Cascading branches of lavender wisteria sway against the walls, above a hundred different types of immaculately potted flowers and lacy ferns. Planters of white gardenias and pink azaleas sit beneath a flourishing bush of orange trumpet-shaped blooms. Sweet-smelling honeysuckle vines climb the walls and cover them completely.

As I step into the courtyard, the air immediately feels cooler. Fresher. The fragrance puts me at ease. I feel as though I've just discovered a miniature flora paradise. A pair of plump robins swoop down and land in the middle of a small but perfectly trimmed lemon tree and look at me suspiciously, as if I were an intruder in this special place of theirs.

And still there is no one to shoo me away or even greet me. I wander around a little for another door until I find one behind a scarlet-colored Japanese maple. This door looks much more ornate than the first. It's painted pearl white, with beveled bevels and decorative glass trimmed with even more decorative glass. But there's no doorbell. At the center, there is an engraved brass knocker, taunting me, daring me to crack the glass. I take my chances and just barely tap it down. Within seconds, a petite Vietnamese woman wearing all white quietly opens the door and motions me inside.

She whispers her name (let's call her Lottie) and says that she is the maid. She looks young for her voice, but the tired lines around her eyes tell me she's a mother.

"Miss Eleanor will be with you in a few moments," Lottie says slowly and very softly, as if she's trying her best to camouflage her accent. "Won't you follow please to library?"

The inside of the psychologist's home has a scary sort of elegance. The air is stagnant and thick—as if the door and windows were rarely open. The place is silent. Hanging from the foyer's vaulted, stained-glass ceiling are various oversize chandeliers dripping with enormous teardrop crystals. Each one is sparkling and dangling, almost trembling, as narrow rays of colored sunlight pierce their surfaces.

Beneath them, giant white floral arrangements tower over their marble pedestals. Calla lilies and tulips, mostly. And other imposing, waxy flowers as well; their petal'd faces staring ominously toward the door. Watching. Waiting. A grand piano stands guard nearby in the adjacent living room; its rich, onyx-like finish shines with such a lustrous sheen that even the most innocently floating dust particles would fear landing on its lid.

As I walk with Lottie the maid, I notice several oil paintings on the walls, all of them looking very English, with scenes of fox hunting or stuffy portraits of men with curled mustaches. One painting in particular catches my eye. Its frame is the same as the others, intricately ornate and gold, but it holds a painting of a young woman.

She is dressed like a Greek goddess, loosely draped in gold and silver robes that are wrapped with several strands of garland. Her hair is pulled back in a loose bun, and a crown of ivy sits atop her head. She is sitting in front of a red curtain of silk. And her face is strangely expressionless. Her mouth is neither smiling nor frowning. It isn't content or serene or even bored. And yet it looks purposeful in some way, as if the mysterious woman is trying to hide any and all emotions.

If I look carefully, however, I can see how her eyes are shifted slightly to the left instead of forward. They give her equal parts of suspicion and fear. One of her hands is raised and curled slightly as her temple is resting on it. The other hand is inconspicuously off to the side, all the way in the bottom corner of the painting, and tightly clutching a long knife. Her knuckles are white. She's holding the dagger in an unnatural way, as if she doesn't know how. On the bottom edge of the frame, I see an inscription engraved in a bronzy gold. It reads,

MELPOMENE, THE MUSE OF TRAGEDY

Lottie the maid continues to guide me through the house until we reach the library. This room is much simpler than the others yet more uncomfortable. A large, white lambskin rug covers most of a creaky hardwood floor. Even though I'm not eating or drinking anything, I just know I'm bound to spill something on that. I'm nervous just looking at it.

"Won't you please take chair?" Lottie the maid says.

Two wingback chairs sit at one side of the room, facing a long desk. Behind it are wall-to-wall, floor-to-ceiling rows of books. Beautiful, leather-bound books.

In between every ten or so there sits a large, framed photograph of a peculiar pair: a celebrity stands arm in arm with an elderly woman. There must be more than a hundred of these photos in this room, scattered among the books, and each with a different celebrity—Harrison Ford, Jimmy Carter, Roger Federer, Celine Dion, and even one of the 1980s *American Gladiators*—standing next to the same tiny woman with oversize glasses and wispy white hair.

In each photo, the subjects hold the same awkward pose: the white-haired woman is on her tiptoes and has her arm around the shoulder of the celebrity, and both of them are smiling a painfully wide smile and holding their opposite arms high in the air in a "thumbs-up." Who is this woman? And why does she insist on making these famous people give the thumbs-up to the camera?

Ten minutes go by, and I'm getting more nervous by the second. Sometimes I wish I never had to go through this part. Sometimes I wish there were another way to absorb and learn all there is to know about the "expert"—but there just isn't. The dreaded face-to-face, although agonizing, is unfortunately the quickest way. Sort of like getting your legs waxed.

I'm hit with a peculiar fragrance. It's leather and potpourri mixed with tobacco. Cigars, perhaps. I see a figure approaching. She looks much older than I had expected, although I hadn't thought about it much beforehand. Eighty. Maybe eighty-five. She's wearing a wool suit in royal-blue and a necklace of large pearls, which match her curly chalk-white hair. She looks more like a former First Lady than a psychologist. She's walking slow and unevenly with a brass cane. Right away I recognize her as the smiling woman from the photos, even though she's walking toward me very slowly with a solemn, sour expression on her wrinkled face. She certainly doesn't look like she wants to give me a thumbs-up.

I walk toward her, extend my hand, and say, "It's wonderful to meet you, Dr. B. I'm Julia Clark." But instead of a reply or even the remaining half of the handshake, Dr. Eleanor B. looks me up and down slowly. I stand nervously as she studies me.

"Hmm," she finally utters in what could only be disappointment.

"Is something wrong?" I ask.

"No, no. Nothing at all, nothing at all," she replies coldly. "It's just that when we spoke on the phone, I *assumed* that you were the writer's secretary or assistant." She stops to laugh a bit, but instead of laughter her small shoulders shake a little. "You see, I was expecting a *man*."

"Didn't the publisher tell you my name?"

"Yes, of course—it's Julian, isn't it? That name can go both ways."

"Well, actually, it's Julia."

"Yes, of course, Julian," she says with a sigh before switching to a high-pitched squeal of a call: "Lottie? Can you bring us some chilled water, please? I'm sure Julian here must be thirsty after her drive. Evian for me, please, and tap will be fine for Julian here."

four

I WALK IN THE FRONT DOOR and see Leo sprawled out on the sofa watching television. Monkeys? He's watching a show about monkeys?

"Hey, honey! Look at this documentary—these chimps are amazing!" he says.

"No, I think I'm going to take a hot bath. I'm pretty beat."

"But you've got to see this!"

I shake my head and walk into the bathroom, but Leo follows me.

"These chimps. Holy cow. You gotta watch it with me—they are so smart!"

"Yeah, I know, honey," I reply as I turn on the water.

"OK, so they showed these male monkeys photos of female monkeys. And the male monkeys loved it!"

"Uh-huh," I reply. I start the water.

"No, really! The researchers were giving them snacks—sodas and Pixy Stix and stuff like that—and the monkeys would trade them in to ogle the photos of the females! It was *hilarious*!" he says.

"OK, honey, I'm really tired. I just want to take a bath now."

"You know, you should put that in your next book. About the monkeys. You should totally do it," he says.

"OK, sweetie, yeah. Monkeys."

"Well?" he asks.

"Well, what?"

"Well aren't you gonna write that down? It's really funny!"

"Why don't *you* write it down for me." I slide into the tub, but Leo's still standing there, looking puzzled.

"Is something wrong, Julia?"

"No. Well, yes. I mean, it was just a really long, weird day," I reply as I sink under the water to get my hair wet.

"But isn't the worst part over? The meeting?"

Leo is right. Sort of. The worst part really should be over. But the psychologist wasn't just another expert for a ghostwriter. Dr. Eleanor B. was the rare "I-want-to-be-involved-at-every-stage-of-my-book-which-you-happen-to-be-writing" expert. Most experts insist that their time is too valuable to spend chatting with the ghostwriter and usually have to be dragged by the publisher to meetings, and rarely even return phone calls. But Dr. Eleanor B. was different. Dr. Eleanor B. is a control freak. Although she did insist that her time was beyond invaluable, she asked that I do most of the writing for the project when I was *with* her. Side by side. Shoulder to godforsaken shoulder.

And yet the first meeting was cut short and not nearly as helpful as first meetings usually are for me. After Lottie brought me the glass of water, Dr. Eleanor B. promptly handed me an eight-inch-high pile of her "notes" and told me to transcribe them by tomorrow so that I would, as she put it, understand her "unusually high level of sophisticated thought."

And then she looked at me with a wrinkle between her brows and asked, "Julian, you will tell me, won't you?"

"Tell you what, exactly?" I replied.

She paused for a moment to yawn and then said, "Tell me why in the world you wanted to ghostwrite for a psychologist? You know, I really was expecting a young man to do this."

"Well," I began, "it just interested me and—"

"It would be quite a switch for me, you know. A young man working for me. The old Madame Psychologist." And then she laughed.

"Why would that be a switch?"

Dr. Eleanor B. leaned forward but kept her eyes down at her desk. "Psychology has changed a lot, you see. It used to be a man's world. Leadership positions were for men and only men. I had a professor once who—well, there's no need for us to get into that now."

Dr. Eleanor B. stopped abruptly and started adding more papers to my pile. "Perhaps we'll use them in the project," she said after a long sip from her crystal goblet of Evian water.

"Uh-huh," I replied slowly, "and you want me to transcribe these notes by tomorrow?"

"You *are* a writer, are you not? I imagine you know how to type. Don't you know how to type? Do you even own a computer?"

"Yes, but—" I tried to reply.

"Then it's settled! I'll see you tomorrow morning at six," she said quickly as she walked toward the door.

"Wait—six?"

"Do try to be punctual this time, Julian. I have an important phone meeting with a colleague from the East Coast at seven, which I absolutely must make. You're not bipolar, are you? Writers are usually bipolar, you know. Hmm, no. I suppose you're not."

And before I knew it, I was standing alone in her enchanted courtyard again. The robins had flown away, and the flowers turned their droopy-petaled heads away from me.

But I don't feel like telling Leo the whole story right now, and I just say, "It's not a big deal, honey. So tell me more about those monkeys."

five

I'M SITTING ACROSS FROM DR. Eleanor B. for our second meeting—
back in her library. The room feels much colder today. I already
regret taking off my coat. I feel terribly uncomfortable and secretly
manic inside. It's been an entire five minutes, and she hasn't said a
single word to me. She's looking at me. Studying me, just as I
dreaded.

"I don't know why writers insist on being late all the time," she
finally says in a cool, nonchalant tone as she reads over some of my
papers. She's the only person I've ever met who somehow manages
the discipline to speak without using any hand gestures whatsoever.
It's as if she just absolutely refuses to do so. Even the slightest raise
of the finger is only engaged if it's to signal me to remain silent, so as
not to disturb the quietness that surrounds her careful train of
thought. Dr. Eleanor B. always speaks calmly and purposefully, as if

she were reciting Shakespeare for the first time from a book. Her words are emphasized by the raise of her sharp chin, which in turn narrows her eyes and raises her already upturned nose a bit more.

She's wearing another tweed suit, this time in plum, with a large ruby and emerald dragonfly brooch pinned to her lapel. Her pearls are dark gray this time but look like a lustrous vine of grapes draped ever so carefully around her droopy neck. There are matching earrings as well, with pearls so perfectly plump and heavy that her already sagging earlobes prominently droop down even farther. Perhaps those pearls are filled with extra pomp and circumstance in case she runs out, although I can't imagine that happening.

Still, she seems comfortable in her attire, as if she'd wear it anytime and all the time, even on a lazy Saturday afternoon in the backyard by herself. Or perhaps she's just comfortable no matter what. Just completely comfortable in her own well-worn skin.

"But I walked through your front door at five minutes *before* six," I reply as I point to my watch, reluctantly omitting the part about how I had to leave San Francisco when it was still pitch-black, at four-thirty, to beat traffic. As I talk, I notice that she doesn't look me in the eye: she focuses instead on my forehead or sometimes my nose, and I'm afraid I'll go cross-eyed trying to find her gaze.

"You were nearly *thirty* minutes late!" she announces. "Julian, I clearly stated yesterday that you were to be here at half past five and no later. Well, let's not dwell on it. The Past has passed and there isn't anything that you, I, or anyone can ever do about it, is there? Ah, I see you've finished transcribing my notes. Well done."

And just like that, her criticism takes a sharp left turn into a compliment. She leans over her desk and, for the first time, smiles at me. I didn't really look at her face closely until now. Her wrinkles are mostly around her mouth but they disappear when she smiles. Everything about her has softened, in a way. Her wispy white hair seems a bit tousled today. Her eyes are a light brown, almost amber, and have an openness to them. She seems more approachable and less intimidating. The room feels a little warmer. And I finally feel at ease.

Before anything else is said, Lottie the maid walks into the library. She's so quiet that we barely notice. She is wearing all white again, and her thick, dark hair is swept up in a tidy bun, except for a few stubborn pieces at the sides. She walks lightly through the library, as if the floors were made of glass.

"Miss Eleanor? There's a telephone call for you. It's Mr. Marsalis."

"Thank you, Lottie. Excuse me for a moment, won't you, Julian? This won't take but a few minutes." As Dr. Eleanor B. and her cane rush out of the library, I'm left alone with Lottie the maid. I smile politely at her as she swoops down to pick up a single fallen flower petal from the floor.

"Would you like more water?" she asks as she delicately clasps her hands in front of her crisp white apron.

"Oh no. Thank you," I reply. "Lottie? Can I ask you something?"

"Yes?"

"Do you like working here?" I ask.

"For Miss Eleanor? Oh yes, she very kind to me," she replies with a smile.

"That's nice, that's nice. How long have you worked here?"

"Oh…many, many years. Miss Eleanor is very kind. She paid for me and my family to come here all the way from Vietnam. She paid for all of us. She is, yes, very kind," Lottie replies. Her mouth makes a smile, and her voice becomes loud and proud when she says "family."

"You came here straight from Vietnam?"

"Oh yes. It took fourteen days for all of us squeezed in that tiny boat. It was dark, very dark, and I had to sit down holding my knees close to me, day and night. No food. No water. And now I live here in beautiful mansion, and I have every Sunday off to be with my family. Miss Eleanor is very kind."

"And you learned English here?" I ask.

Lottie the maid nods. "Miss Eleanor paid for a tutor for me. She even paid for my eldest to go to college. She is a very, very kind woman," she says.

"You really think so?"

We hear the triple echoes of Dr. Eleanor B.'s footsteps and her cane taps drawing near.

"Lottie? I noticed that the piano needs another dusting. And I saw through the window that the dead blooms need to be plucked from the camellias out front again. They're looking dreadful," the psychologist says. "I absolutely detest seeing dead things."

"Yes, Miss Eleanor."

I half expect Lottie the maid to curtsy, but instead she just lowers her head and walks silently out of the library, her eyes on the floor.

"Now then, where were we?" Dr. Eleanor B. asks as she sits back down behind her desk.

"We were just about to figure that out," I say.

Surprising me, Dr. B. lifts one eyebrow in a high arch and says, "You know? I think I like you, Julian. I'm almost sure of it."

"Almost?" I dare to ask. To avoid further eye contact with her, I look around her office for something. Anything. I notice a small framed drawing on her desk. It's an ink sketch of a man's profile. I can't tell if it's of Sigmund Freud or John Lennon. It looks like a peculiar blend of both. Sort of like a weird, fragmented, psychoanalytical Beatle. I've forgotten what we were talking about.

"There is a certain something askew inside you, I suspect," Dr. Eleanor B. says as she stares off into the distance. "A strong tendency toward depression, I'd say."

I haven't a clue how to reply. Baffled, I just continue to sit and pretend to be unruffled and unaffected.

"You're a complete mess," Dr. Eleanor B. continues. "It's written all over you. The dark circles under your eyes. Your stooped shoulders. The way you speak, the way your eyes search desperately for a sign of acceptance. Even your walk is dismally depressed!"

I make some stuttering noises in an attempt to defend myself to no avail.

"Did you lose someone?" she asks bluntly.

I try to straighten up the papers in front of me. I bite my tongue down hard to keep myself from crying. My cheeks are turning red. I can feel them. My skin is scorching hot. *I will not cry in front of her*, I keep telling myself. I feel tears welling up inside me, about to explode, but instead I just say, "I think we should get back to the project. I, um, have an outline to show you—"

"Someone you loved very much, perhaps?" she presses on.

And there it is. In a few minutes, the psychologist has chipped away at my carefully constructed professional facade until she has stripped away everything there is but my grief. My lonely, miserable grief.

The tears are escaping. I feel them racing down the sides of my cheeks. I turn away and wipe my face with my hands, but the tears won't stop. There are too many. My eyes burn and my shoulders start to tremble and I can't make them stop, no matter how embarrassed I feel. The dam has broken. And there's a flood.

"How old was she?" she asks in a tone that is more curious than moved, "How old was your mother when she died?"

I can't figure out how she knew that, yet somehow I find a breath in between the sobbing to reply, "Fifty-seven. She was fifty-seven."

Dr. Eleanor B.'s jaw drops open. She dry-gasps the words back to me, "Fifty-seven? My word, that's young!" Her face looks upset now and even more wrinkled. Frustrated. She pulls her chair out and starts shaking her head in disbelief as she and her cane walk out of the room, murmuring, "Fifty-seven…fifty-seven…oh, my…"

And now I am alone. I press my red, swollen face into my hands. My muffled cries echo and echo and echo some more in the library until they start to sound like a sad song that someone is singing in the distance. It hurts so badly to remember. And it hurts even more when my emotions are out of control. I close my eyes as tightly as I can to squeeze the tears out, but there are just too many to force them out all at once.

I feel a hand on my shoulder. "Shh, shh, shh," says a whisper. I look up and find myself wrapped in a hug. It's Lottie the maid, or at least I think it is. All I can see is her white apron.

"You'll be OK," Lottie the maid says. "Take deep breaths."

"That woman," I begin, "she just says whatever the hell she wants," My tears dry. Anger rises up inside me to replace my sadness.

My lips curl back to my teeth, and even my hands cramp into furious fists.

"Shh, shh…Miss Eleanor doesn't mean to be like that. Sometimes she just say the wrong thing. Shh, shh…it not her fault. Really."

"But how can she say such things and then just leave?" I ask.

"Shh," Lottie the maid whispers. "Miss Eleanor is a nice lady. Very nice lady. She likes you. She does. She told me. She's just very afraid of dying." Lottie the maid clenches her teeth over the word "dying" and says it very slowly to make sure I understand.

"What? How do you mean?" I ask as I sniffle away tears.

Lottie the maid puts her head down near mine and whispers even lower, "Every morning, before Miss Eleanor wakes up, my job is to go over to the side of her bed and take a tiny mirror—"

"A mirror?"

She nods. "And I have to put the mirror next to Miss Eleanor's mouth to see if she has a breath."

"But why?" I ask.

"Because she want me to wake her up every day and say, 'Good morning, Miss Eleanor, you are alive today!' Because Miss Eleanor tell me that she afraid that one morning she will wake up and be dead."

"She makes you do that every morning?"

Lottie starts dusting every visible surface in the library with a pink feather duster and whispers, "Shh…she's coming…shh."

A faint triple footstep resonates down the hall, and Lottie the maid quietly leaves the library through a side door that I hadn't noticed before. Dr. Eleanor B. returns and makes her way back to her desk. She looks calmer now, more subdued. She watches me for a moment and then turns away.

I shuffle through some papers in front of me and pretend to be working. I keep my head down so she can't see my swollen eyes.

"Psychology has changed a lot, Julian," she finally says as she looks out a window. "Everything is rather upside down and sideways now."

"Is that a bad thing?"

"No. Goodness, no! It's a remarkable thing."

"I'm sorry, Dr. B., I'm not following," I say.

"It was a curious time when I was studying psychology back at Harvard. It seems so long ago now. So different."

"In what way?"

"Men dominated the discipline then. I was one of three women studying psychology in my graduating class—did you know that? And that, you see, makes for a very curious working relationship."

"Dr. B., I still don't really understand."

"Think about it. Here is a discipline of study—psychology—that has been pioneered mostly by men for decades. And then all of a sudden, women start to appear. Here and there at first. Studying. At the bottom of the ranks."

"But how is that bad?" I ask.

"It's not *bad*. It's awkward. Imagine a young girl, such as yourself, trying to break into a new field," she replies.

"OK," I say. I'm trying my best to follow.

"The only people you can go to for help or guidance are these very old *male* psychologists. It's very awkward indeed! Old men who have been cooped up in basements for God only knows how long, paired up with young, naive girls! Working side by side…"

Dr. Eleanor B. pauses briefly to take more papers from a desk drawer. She hands a single page to me. It is yellowed and wrinkled slightly at its edges. It's a title sheet for a research project: "The Flaw of Genius: A Case Study."

"Is this yours?" I ask.

She nods. "This was my thesis prospectus for my doctorate. Or rather, it was supposed to be mine."

"Supposed to be?"

"It was such a marvelous idea, really," she replies. "I was exploring the manic side of genius. The link between creative genius and mental illness. Nietzsche had dementia. Van Gogh suffered from bouts of madness and depression. Beethoven had bipolar disorder. So did Schumann. Even Charles Dickens was clinically depressed! It was my belief that creative genius is really just another variation of psychosis. You see, the creative genius is not bound in any way by the ordinary standards of reality. Just like the madman."

"Why didn't you finish the project?" I ask.

"I most certainly did. I just failed to receive credit for it. Something happened. Well, I don't have time to explain that now—"

"Please, Dr. B., continue. What was it?"

"Well, it was my grandmother, on my mother's side. She was very sick and…and…" Dr. Eleanor B. pauses, as if she's lost her train of thought.

"And you left school to take care of her?" I ask.

"I don't need you to finish my sentences for me, young lady! I'm perfectly capable of finishing my own sentences, thank you *very* much!" the psychologist blurts out. She turns her head and crosses her arms like a stubborn child.

I go back to my mound of papers and start looking busy again. Ten minutes of awkward silence go by, and Dr. Eleanor B. is fidgeting in her seat and looking out her window. Abruptly she gets up and walks around my chair. The soles of her pumps slam against the hardwood floor with each step.

"Is that damned tape recorder on right now?" she asks.

"No, it's still in my bag," I reply.

"Very well. I don't want this in the book," she says as she returns to her chair. "I left school—just temporarily, you see—for my grandmother's funeral. She died when she was seventy-nine."

"Oh, I'm sorry," I begin. "Were you close with her?"

"No. No, I wasn't," Dr. Eleanor B. replies sharply.

"OK…"

"She was seventy-nine!" the psychologist repeats.

"Did she pass unexpectedly?" I ask, confused.

"Seventy-nine…seventy-nine," she says again. "That's the age my great-grandmother died as well. And her mother, and her mother before that."

"Really?"

"My own mother died at seventy-nine as well. I was in Switzerland for a conference at the time. In Geneva. And my sister, my only sister. She died just a few years ago. She was seventy-nine. Not one woman in my family has lived to be eighty."

The psychologist gets up and again walks around my chair.

"You're sure the tape recorder isn't on?" she demands.

"Yes, I'm sure."

Her eyes stare deep into mine, as if I were trying to pull the wool over her own eyes. Apparently she doesn't like what she sees in my eyes because abruptly she lifts my bag up from the floor with just one of her gaunt arms and empties its contents dramatically on her desk. My makeup bag flies out, along with my keys, wallet, and everything else I had in there. Including the damned tape recorder.

"See?" I say. "It's off. It doesn't even have batteries in it yet."

The psychologist says nothing. She just grabs the recorder and throws it in one of her desk drawers. She sits back down and looks pleased with herself, though still anxious. She motions for me to come closer. I scoot my chair closer to her desk, and Dr. Eleanor B. leans as far forward over her desk as she can. Her eyes bulge out of their sockets. She takes a deep breath and whispers, "I turned seventy-nine last month, Julian. Death could take me at *any* minute. Any minute! Do you realize that?"

"Isn't that just, well, I mean, it's uncanny, but, still...isn't it just a superstition?" I ask.

I could have said anything. Anything at all. And it wouldn't have made a difference. The psychologist doesn't answer me or even acknowledge that I said anything. Her mind seems to just shift gears as she leans back in her chair.

"Julian," the psychologist begins harshly, "I'm hoping you can wrap up the project in two months. I'm quite busy and I'm afraid that's as much time as I can allot to this. Dear me! Why are you sitting so close? Give me some space, for goodness' sake. We have this entire room, you know."

"I usually take three," I reply as I scoot my chair back to where it was.

"Th-r-ee?" she asks in a peculiar, multi-syllabic way that I've heard only in musicals.

"Three months is pretty good. Most ghostwriters take at least six months or a year. And Dr. B., you really don't need to be *with* me, side by side. I mean, the whole point of having a ghostwriter is—"

"Julian, I think two months will be quite sufficient," she says. And all at once, she turns away from me and pulls something out of her desk drawer. I think I smell cedar. Her back is turned away from me now, but I can see her fiddling with something in her lap.

My eyes return to the weird ink portrait that stands in a crystal frame on her desk. I wonder if it's one of those ink-blot tests that psychiatrists administer just to mess with your head. Rorschach. "Raw-shock."

Dr. Eleanor B. slowly turns her chair back toward me, only now she's puffing on a cigar. It smells old and interesting. Sort of like a dense, smoky vanilla mixed with a tinge of metallic cherry. And wet. It most definitely smells wet, like rain falling on a burning fire. The aroma fills the library room and suffocates everything in it.

It's funny to watch her. I wasn't expecting it. Her tiny, wrinkled mouth quivers as she dangles the cigar in her hand, knuckled between her tiny, knobby fingers. I can't help but laugh a little as she stops and leans back in her leather chair to blow a ring of smoke up in the air as dramatically and emphatically as Fidel Castro might.

"You know, Julian," Dr. Eleanor B. begins thoughtfully, "a famous clinical psychologist once said that there are two types of people in the world." She pauses to free an atrocious-sounding cough from her throat and continues. "There are those who are prone to depression and those who are prone to paranoia."

"It's just that simple, is it?" I ask, still raw from her nonchalant cruelty in our last meeting.

Dr. Eleanor B. leans over her desk toward me and smiles at me again. I look away, fearful that she might uncover yet another secret about my personality or trick me into a maddening hypnosis session. But instead she just takes another ponderous puff.

"Well, you see, it *is* that simple. It's all a matter of blame, really."

"How so?" I ask.

She stops smoking and looks at me intently yet distantly, as if she were staring right through me and watching the grandfather clock that ticks and tocks behind me. Never have I felt so transparent.

"With depression," she says, "you blame the bad things that happen in your life on *yourself.*"

"And with paranoia?"

"Ah. Paranoia. It's so marvelous. You blame all those bad things on everyone else." She stops to take another puff from her chocolate-colored cigar. "Isn't it a grand theory? I've always been fond of that one."

"I'm not so sure," I say.

"That's where we differ, you see," the psychologist continues with her impeccable chin raised. "You prefer depression…while I…I prefer the company of paranoia." She punctuates this notion with a rather smug sort of smile, curved ever so slightly.

six

WHEN I WAS LITTLE, I loved to be sick. Well, not *really* sick, but ill enough to convince Mom that I needed to stay home from school. I'd call her into my bedroom, wave my hand over my stomach, and feebly utter, "I don't feel so good." And she'd look at me with her immediately understanding eyes and check my temperature with the back of her hand. Thanks to her poor circulation, her hands were always freezing and so my forehead always felt hot by comparison.

"Oh!" she'd exclaim, "you're burning up! I think you had better stay home with me today. I'll call the school secretary."

And then I'd pull the sheets up to my nose, turn over, and give a weak moan until I could hear her pick up the phone in the next room. Her excuses to the school office were always fantastic, each one more creative and urgent than the one before: "Something just cracked in her back, and now she can't move her neck!" or "I'm quite sure her chicken pox has returned!" or the very impressive "Her contact lens just exploded in her eye! I must take her to the eye doctor this instant!"

"Hmm, it's getting tougher with that lady," Mom would say to herself after hanging up the phone, "I shouldn't have said Julia's appendix was about to burst. She sounded suspicious. Didn't I tell her that she had a stomach thing last time? Darn it, I should have said something about her braces getting caught on the banister. Oh well. Next time."

And then she would float back into my bedroom, still in her long pink bathrobe, with a tray prepared just for me. There would be an ice-cold washcloth (always folded lengthwise three times), which she would place gently across my forehead. A cup of tea with milk and just the right amount of honey. A pretty saucer (taken from her good tea set) of Ritz crackers arranged in a circle, with apples sliced so thin you could see through them, piled high in the center. And a couple of little See's fancy Bordeaux chocolates placed on the side, "Just in case you start to feel better," she would say. But the best part was that she would sit on the edge of my bed, gently rub the tops of my feet, and talk to me. Not about school, or problems, or how I was feeling, but about funny things like how she let my large pet rabbit, Thumper, loose in the backyard the day before and how he tried to mate with the dog. And how the dog spent all day trying to avoid the overweight-and-overeager bunny until she finally had to jump in the swimming pool to escape. "Poor Thumper," she said, "we really need to find him a girl bunny. Brandy can't hide in the pool all day...the weather's starting to turn!"

I think Mom always knew when I wasn't really sick. But she seemed to understand that I just needed to stay home sometimes. No matter if it really was a flu or just me being overwhelmed by teachers or kids in the schoolyard, she was always ready to be my refuge.

It was a treat to have her all to myself. Dad would be at work. My two older sisters at school. It was just us. She'd spend the whole morning taking care of me and then, around lunchtime, she'd say, "How are you feeling, my love? You look a lot better. You have a lot more color in your face now. I think you're still too weak to go back to school. Now you need to recuperate. But…I do think it would be a good idea if you got some fresh air. Want to come downtown with me for some errands?"

I would always nod yes. None of her errands were ever downtown. "Downtown" meant "fun." Plain and simple. It meant strolling through a near-empty avenue on a school day and window-shopping in quirky antique stores. It meant giggling together at the funny mannequins wearing mottled fur stoles and lopsided wigs. It meant a giant root beer float on Thirty-Fourth Street and learning that Mom's favorite ice cream was one scoop of vanilla and one scoop of chocolate together. As I got older, the afternoon "errand" would change. In junior high, it was horseback riding. In high school, it was long drives to see the green foothills change to gold. It never really mattered what we did. Just so long as she was there to make me feel better.

Of course, all of that changed when I was sixteen. Mom was no longer able to call the school office or cut the apple or make the tea. Everything became different. Mom had cancer. No longer could she take care of me. It was I who took care of her. The daughter was now the mother.

I was good at taking care of her. I just pretended I was her. I put an ice-cold washcloth on her forehead when the cancer gave her 105-degree fevers in the middle of the night. Folded lengthwise three times, just as she had done for me when I was little. I brought her paper-thin apple slices when her swollen lymph glands made her throat too tender to swallow real food. I gently rubbed her feet in the evenings, after the chemotherapy had made them so swollen that she couldn't squeeze into any of her shoes. And just as Mom had always made me feel better when I felt overwhelmed, so too did I know precisely how to distract her when she got scared whenever the doctor would enter the room with news to match his frown. "Mom, I forgot to tell you something. The neighbor's fat tabby cat got stuck in that hole in the fence again yesterday. The one in the side yard. Boy, was Thumper ever happy!"

In place of errands, I'd take her shopping through the mail-order catalogs. I'd flip through the magazine pages with her, help her pick out a wig when her hair fell out. "Oh, this one looks just like Jaclyn Smith from *Charlie's Angels*, doesn't it? Hmm, I didn't know Raquel Welch had her own line." I remember laughing with her when it finally grew back in, in tight little curls like a lamb. And then consoling her when she had woken one morning, looked at her pillow, and realized her hair had fallen out all over again: "Maybe this time you can go short and blonde!"

She needed me. And it felt good to take care of her. It gave me control over that terrible disease, which wanted to take her. I wasn't scared because it never entered my mind that she would die. I always told myself that she would get better. "I won't let her die," I remember telling myself. "I won't let anything happen."

seven

I'M STANDING OUTSIDE ON OUR balcony. The phone is ringing but I don't care. I just want to stand out here and feel what's left of the autumn afternoon air. I remember when Leo and I first moved into this apartment. We were so excited about this balcony. It seemed chic and European. We gleefully filled it with a big barbecue grill, a cute wrought-iron café table, coral-colored geraniums, and giant climbing vines of bougainvillea. My mom used to call them Chinese lanterns. For years, that was what I thought they were called. It wasn't until Leo pointed out their little fuchsia-leaved heads in Home Depot that I saw their true name for the first time. "Bou-gain-ville-a?" I could barely pronounce it.

I think I liked them better when I thought they were Chinese lanterns. They seemed magical then, as if they held flickers of light inside their fragile, boxy blooms. Lights that would never go out. She gave those flowers a story. That was what my mom did. She gave everything a dash of mystery and whimsy. Flowers had feelings, feet were tootsies, and clouds were tragic dramas set in the sky.

Right now, I see great art in the sky. The winds have created an autumnal masterpiece with every shade of blue in the spectrum. The clouds are a still photograph of ocean waves, with dramatic curves that delicately dip and crescendo into one another. Sunlight weaves in and out of these swells, casting spectacular shadows in their arcs. I wonder what heaven looks like.

It feels lovely to stand on the balcony. We barely come out here anymore. And when we do, it's usually to just water the plants or shake out a rug. Or sometimes Leo comes out here by himself when he's mad at me for getting mad at him. But right now it's just me.

I hear the ring again. I'd better get it. Might be Dad. I rush inside and look for the cordless phone. It's ringing and ringing and ringing, but I can't even tell where the damned thing is. Leo loves leaving it wherever he pleases; he gets me so mad sometimes! More ringing. I finally find it on my dressing table. Hmm. I must have left it there when I was taking off my earrings.

"Hello? Hello?" I ask in a huff. But there's nothing. I'm too late.

I walk over to check our answering machine and nearly fall over when I see that there are eight messages. Whenever I see that little red light blink, I always worry a little. And then I worry a lot. I'm always afraid that when I press play, I'll hear a nurse's voice from a hospital in Santa Barbara telling me that my dad was just in an awful motorcycle accident and that I need to get there right away. Dad's been racing those dirt bikes since long before I was born, but I've seen enough of his cracked ribs, broken collarbones, and injured legs and arms to know that his Honda CRX 250 is a demanding mistress.

I grew up around motorcycles. Hondas. Triumphs. Even his dusty Honda Magna he never rides but keeps in the garage for nostalgia. Motocross is his passion.

He used to ride every single Sunday, while Mom took my sisters and me to Our Lady of Perpetual Help Catholic church down the street. Now that Mom is gone, he rides whenever he gets the chance. Three, sometimes four times a week if he can get his friends together for a play ride in Gorman, just over the Grapevine. I don't think I'd worry so much if he didn't live alone now. But he does and so I do. I can't help but flinch a little when I press play. Thankfully, it's not Dad. And it's not a doctor or even a nurse. It's Lilly…my mother-in-law.

Message one, 11:04 a.m.: "Hi Jules! Hi Leo…This is Mom… Jules, I have a question for you, so please call me back if you get this message before three… I hope you both are well, and God bless the both of you. Bye!"

Message two, 11:15 a.m.: "Jules… this is Mom. I still haven't heard back from you. I really need to ask you something. Call me on my cell. God bless. Bye."

Message three, 11:18 a.m.: "Jules? If you're there, please *pick up*! I know you like to screen your calls, but please… Pick up the phone! I *really* need to ask you something! OK… bye. Oh, and this is Mom!" There was a sigh followed by inaudible muttering.

Message four, 11:21 a.m.: "You two *never* answer your phone! Leo, if you get this message, please have Jules call me. I can't find her cell phone number. I need to ask her something very important."

Message five, 11:45 a.m.: A hang-up.

Message six, 12:02 p.m.: Long sigh followed by a long pause. "Well, I still haven't heard from you, Jules." (Another pause.) "I don't know why you are avoiding me, but..." (Extra-long pause.) "Please call me. I really must speak with you. G—" (Machine cuts off.)

Message seven, 12:24 p.m.: "Well... I can take a hint! I'm not stupid! I just had *one* question. I wasn't going to take so long out of your precious time! Just call me back! Is that so hard? Are you so busy that you don't even time to call your own mother-in-law? I used to call my mother-in-law every single day! And I had children to take care of! Dinners to cook! I had to feed a family! You know what? Just *forget* it! Don't even call me back! Just... forget it! Don't bothe—" (Machine cuts off.)

Message eight, 1:19 p.m.: "Um...this is Mom. Listen, about earlier... I just wanted to apologize to Jules. Leo, if you're listening to this, I'm sorry. I just sort of got carried away. It's been a long day. Call me back. Bye."

I always feel strange when I hear Lilly say, "This is Mom." I don't know if I'll ever get used to it. More important, I don't know if I'll ever *want* to get used to it. And it feels even weirder for me to even try to call her Mom. She's not my mom. *My* mom is in heaven. But I know that me calling her Mom is number one on her agenda. She made that abundantly clear the moment she found out Leo and I were engaged.

Leo proposed to me on New Year's Day. Just an hour after the countdown. We were so excited that we stayed up the entire night, laughing and kissing and being in love. We waited until morning to call our families.

"Mom?" Leo cheerfully said. "I did it! I asked Julia, and she said yes! We're getting married!" After answering a few "How'd you do it?" questions, Leo handed the phone to me. "She wants to say hi," he whispered.

"Can you believe it?" I said into the receiver, "I'm so excited!"

"I'm so happy. For you both," Lilly replied. "I mean, I don't know how you two will make it. I...I don't know how you'll survive—I mean, you two are *just* out of college, and neither of you are working and—"

"Well," I said, "Leo is interviewing with IBM next week, and I have my ghostwriting job... Aren't you going to congratulate us, Lilly?"

"Oh," she replied. "Yes, yes, yes. Of course. I'm very happy for you. For both of you. Listen, I want you to know that you're part of the *fam-i-ly* now," she said, carefully enunciating each syllable, "and I'd really like it if you started calling me *Mom*."

I couldn't believe my ears. I wanted to just pass the phone off immediately to Leo, but he was in the bathroom brushing his teeth.

"Well," I began slowly, not sure how to answer without hurting her feelings. "I know that's important for you, but...I mean, it would be pretty difficult for me right now and—"

"Difficult? Why would it be difficult? Just call me Mom."

"It would be hard for me because I just lost my own mom last year and all—"

"But I've *always* wanted my daughters-in-law to call me Mom. And Leo's ex-girlfriend, Belinda, always called me Mom. Belinda was a really very nice girl. She and I are still very close. She calls me often. Just to see how I'm doing. Such a nice girl that Belinda. Leo treated her so badly in the end. He's *just* like his father. Breaking up with her like that when she was doing my grocery shopping for me! I said to him, 'Couldn't you just keep her around for the summer when it's so hot out?' But no, he said no, he just wouldn't. Poor Belinda. With all that beautiful hair. And the one before that, what was her name? She called me Mom too." She rattled it all off so quickly. Had she heard a word I'd said?

"I just don't think—"

"Listen, I gave birth to five boys—five!—and I've always wanted a daughter, Jules. When he was born, I really wished that Leo were a girl. So, just call me Mom."

"It's still very painful for me," I tried again, afraid of upsetting her.

"It would mean a lot to me," she shot back sweetly.

Leo grabbed the phone away from me and cupped his hand over the receiver.

"What did she say to you?" he whispered. "You're crying... shh, shh... honey, what did she say?" He cradled his other arm around me, and I didn't know that I was even crying until I pressed my cheek against his and felt my tears—cold—between us.

Since then, I've tried hard to avoid the subject altogether and instead just string my salutations together so fast that maybe she won't miss it or notice it at all: "Hi-this-is-Julia-how-are-you-is-everything-good?" But Lilly always manages to interrupt me in her singsong voice and say, "Ah-ah-*ahh*...what do you call me? *Mom*...call me Mom."

But right now I'm gonna forget all that and call her back. She did sound pretty agitated in those messages, after all. I hope she's OK.

"Hello?" Lilly answers in a voice I almost don't recognize.

"Hi-it's-me-Julia-I-just-now-got-your-messages-I'm-so-sorry," I say as fast as I can, but Lilly interrupts halfway through.

"Jules, why don't you ever pick up your phone? I'm *so* tired of hearing Leo's greeting!" Her voice is cheerful and jokey.

"But," I begin in my most apologetic tone, "I wasn't home." *Oh, how silly she'll feel now!*

"You could at least have picked up your phone," she suggests. Her tone is more serious now and strangely martyr-like. "I was beginning to worry about you!"

"But I was *gone*. I was in Palo Alto for that psychologist I told you about, remember?" Maybe she didn't hear me.

"Oh," she says flatly, "so you were just out shopping? You were shopping?"

"No, no—I was working. With the psychologist. I didn't get home until fifteen minutes ago. I just checked the machine. I just now got your messages, all of them, and—"

"Well, I don't know why I'm surprised. You and Leo always screen your calls."

Time to cave in. It's a losing battle and I just sigh to signal defeat.

"I'm sorry," I say. "So, what was your question?"

"Oh. Right. The question. Well, I was planning to go to Macy's later this afternoon—for their big bra sale—and I thought you might need some underwear. What size do you wear?"

"I'm sorry, what did you say?" All that calling, all those messages. For underwear? Is she crazy?

"Well, they're having a big sale—40 percent off. And does Leo need socks? Oh, and you don't wear those wedgie things, do you? What do they call them? Thongies? Thongs? Something like that?"

"No, no, no," I say as fast as I can, "we're fine, we're fine. We don't need anything. Thank you but no. *Really.*"

Lilly is silent, and I'm feeling beyond uncomfortable and trying to figure out how I can get out of any more panty questions. She sighs briefly and says, "Well, it would just be nice if you answered your phone once in a while. That's all."

"I'm sorry, but if I'm not home, you should really just try me on my cell. I always have that with me," I reply.

"But if you're at home all day," she says sharply, "why don't you just answer your phone? Geez!"

"OK, well, I have a lot of writing I need to finish for tomorrow, so I'd better let you go," I say gently.

"*Writing?* Aren't you going to get dinner started? It's nearly three!"

Part 2 The Ballerina

And when Terpsichore, with iris-plume,
Bade o'er her lute her rosy fingers fly;
'T was pleasure all—the fawns in mingled choirs,
Glanced on the willing nymphs their wanton fires.

~James Gates Percival, "An Ode to Music", 1823

eight

IT NEVER FAILS. I'M ALWAYS wearing the wrong thing. No matter the occasion, no matter the weather. I'm always either too dressed up, too casual, not wearing enough, or wearing too much. I can't get it right. All I can do is lower my head, raise my hand, and admit that I'm one of those girls who perpetually falls backward in a fashion-forward world.

When I was little, I was too dressy. Mom loved to make sure I was always wearing white tights and white patent-leather Mary Janes, along with a lace-trimmed pinafore over a ruffled dress—even when the other kids in my elementary school were wearing cool faded and perfectly-frayed jeans and even cooler wrinkled T-shirts. I used to beg her to let me attend the private Catholic school down the block instead, where everyone wore the same thing, so no one could make fun of your outfits.

"Please let me go to Our Lady of Perpetual Help. You don't understand," I would plead. "My life would be so much easier!"

"Oh no," she'd always reply, "that's where both your sisters went and they were so unhappy there. What's wrong with Longfellow?" Despite the fact that she was a devout Catholic, Mom was much happier seeing me attend a school named after an American poet than one with strict, no-nonsense nuns. But I would gladly have taken a thousand nuns armed with rulers if it meant that I never had to worry about planning an outfit again.

I remember my worst day at Longfellow. And it wasn't the day that I tripped on my last lap around the asphalt track and injured my knee so badly that you could see the bone. Or that day when I accidentally knocked the tray of milk cartons over onto the classroom's rack of coats one winter morning in front of everyone. It wasn't even the day that I was sent to the principal's office for the first and only time (for throwing rocks at Tommy Setzer while chanting, "Seltzer water! Seltzer water!").

Oh no.

My worst day at Longfellow Elementary was the day in fourth grade that started with Mom spending an hour with me in the bathroom trying to convince me that yes, green does indeed go with purple. "They complement each other, Julia," she reassured me as she brushed my hair. "Trust your mother. You look very pretty in this outfit. Besides, didn't you tell me that you didn't want to wear dresses anymore? Hmm?"

But the 1980s weren't about complementary colors. They were about matching. Plain and simple. Belts. Watches. Swatches. Bracelets. Socks. Shoes. *Everything* had to match. It was a hard-and-fast rule. Everyone in school knew and understood it. I can remember just standing there in front of the mirror with my jaw dropped in despair. And as I stared hopelessly back at the lime and emerald-green floral-print shorts and the bright purple tank top in the reflection, I knew it was going to be a bad day. I shuddered as Mom tied a neon-pink ribbon in my hair. "There," she said in a proud voice. "The pink adds…pizzazz."

Pizzazz? I don't want pizzazz! What kid wants pizzazz? Doesn't she know that I just want to blend in? But no, she didn't. She was French. Everything had to be unique and chic. I tried so badly to trust her. I looked up at her in the reflection and thought that maybe…just maybe…she was right.

Unfortunately, she wasn't. Within minutes of arriving at school, Delia walked over to me. "Gee-ew-lee-ah!" she squealed. I froze. Mom had already driven off, and I had already made eye contact with Delia, the most fashionable fourth grader at Longfellow Elementary. Pastel-pink pierced hoop earrings. White Swatch. Pastel-pink tank top, layered perfectly over a white, off-the-shoulder tank top. White denim shorts. Pastel-pink barrette in her hair. She knew the rules. Oh yes, she knew them well.

I stood there nervously in front of her. My knees wobbled as I felt her serious brown eyes studying me. Her cruel little mouth twisted as she maintained her most thoughtful expression. Her eyebrows were furrowed in careful concentration. She worked in silence except for the rhythmic smack of her strawberry Bubble Yum. She walked completely around me once and then twice. I pressed my lips tight together and prayed for her eyes to be blind.

"You know, Julia," she finally said, one hand at her hip, "you *really* don't match today."

"Well, actually, see, the green and purple, I mean...everything sort of complements...each other," I said.

"Um...," she said and smacked her gum in my ear. "I'm trying to find a nice way to say that you look *ugly* today." And before I could say anything, Delia smiled a warm, lovely smile at me and happily skipped away, as if she had just accomplished her good deed for the day. Looking back, I should have been better prepared for Delia's criticism. After all, she found something wrong with me each and every day that school year. More often than not, however, she was generous enough to point out to everyone how terribly skinny I was. Thanks to Delia, I was The Toothpick. The Stick. Chicken Legs. Spider Legs. Every day she found something new about my looks to make me feel like the strangest girl in Longfellow. And every day after school, I would spend the entire car ride home sobbing and wishing as hard as I could that I would look like Delia, with normal legs and normal arms and nothing too lanky or long.

Little did I know that someday that awkward lankiness would be "in" or even desired. But here I am on a December afternoon, standing backstage at a San Francisco Ballet rehearsal on Franklin Street—where three or four creatures called ballerinas barely equal one of me.

And of course, I'm wearing the wrong thing. My navy skirt and ivory sweater set belong at an entry-level job interview, not backstage with the chicest ballet company in America. Everyone else here is wearing skinny black trousers and long, fitted black tees. The artistic director. The choreographer. The choreographer's assistant. The wardrobe staff. The crew. Everyone but the dancers. They're in pale leotards and mismatched leg warmers.

I spot Anastasia M. at the center of the stage. She looks as if she's twirled right out of a Degas sketch. Her dark hair is slicked back tightly in a trim, braided bun that accents her long, swan-like neck. She's getting propelled by a male dancer up into the air for a lift. Three turns and already she's flying. Her willowy arms arc gracefully above her as she lands ever so gently on the tips of her toes. She's beautiful. Her porcelain body bends with such fluidity and ease that I can't help but wonder if the poor girl has any bones at all. But up close, her body looks far from frail. Daintiness is only a disguise. Long, tight muscles span every inch of skin for those leaps, jumps, and spins. Even her muscles have muscles, yet they move with ease. I watch her soar through the air. Her arms beautifully cascade and droop in turn to express the slightest change in emotion.

Anastasia M. is a famed ballerina from Saint Petersburg who left Moscow's Bolshoi Ballet to escape her last lover in a string of lovers. Mister X's employer is publishing the memoirs of her scandalous, fast-paced life, so Anastasia M. is my latest expert. And I couldn't be more excited. I started working for the dancer about two weeks ago, at the start of December. We hit it off right away. I loved hearing her stories. And she loved telling them.

I watch with wonder as she walks carefully across the stage in her pointe shoes and then, in one motion, rises up to the tips of her toes like a spring. The lean muscles in her calf contract as she lifts her foot against gravity. She holds her pose, silent and still, as she creates the illusion of weightlessness. There is a lightness about her. An airy, ethereal quality. Dancing might as well be floating.

"Do you grasp the difficulty of this art?" a raspy voice behind me says. "Do you know the years of patient study, the hours of painful labor it takes to become even average?"

It's the choreographer.

"It's amazing," I reply, "it's all so amazing."

The choreographer folds his arms across his chest. He's a short, stocky man with tanned skin and wild, wavy white hair in need of a trim. He's the portrait of eccentricity. He's also the famous artistic director of a ballet troupe that often appears on PBS.

"So you're the ghostwriter, aren't you?" he says in what can only be described as a shouting whisper. "Anastasia told me to look for a redhead. You're the only one!"

I nod.

"And you have to follow our girl around for three months?"

"Just now and then," I reply as I smile. "How could I miss *Swan Lake*?"

"Good, good. Write well!"

We stand together watching the routines. Ordinarily I would be nervous, but I'm not. I should be shaking as I stand next to the man who won the Tony Award for Best Choreography this year and two Emmys the year before. But I'm too engrossed in Anastasia M.'s performance to worry.

Even though it's only a practice routine, it's as if she's the words to a wonderful and mysterious poem of ballet. But not a ballad or blank verse. No, Anastasia M. looks as though she's performing a sonnet: lyrical and precise. Her intricate steps count out the meter in between various series of perfectly spun pirouettes. There is a pathos that surrounds her as she dances. At this moment she is a living, breathing metaphor, representing all that is mythical and magical in the world.

"You see her shoes?" he asks me.

"Her toe shoes? Yes."

"Handmade," he says. "All her pointe shoes are handmade. All are from Freed of London. *Nothing* else. She goes through roughly seventy pairs in a month. *Seventy!* Can you *believe* that?"

"Incredible," I reply as I stare at the curiously square tips of Anastasia M.'s ballet shoes. There is no right or left with toe shoes— they are straight-lasted and made individually.

"You should know," he says, "a ballerina is not just a dancer. She must be an actress, a storyteller. A song." He stops to watch Anastasia M. pose mid-air en arabesque. Her right arm stretches forward, her left back, as she extends one of her legs behind her at a perfect right angle.

"Do you *see* that? Do you see the simple beauty of the arabesque?" he says as he clasps his hands together. "The dancer creates the longest possible line from her fingertips to the tips of her toes." He stops and quickly motions in front of his eyes with a tissue. "It's hard to believe, but after all these months, even at rehearsals, Anastasia has the peculiar ability to make me cry when she dances."

I look over at him, inspecting him for tears. There are none. He nudges my side with his elbow and says, "Put *that* in your book!"

"It's not *my* book," I tell him. "It's *her* book. I'm more of a catalyst."

"Sure! Of course! But, no. Although…" He pauses for a moment and rocks back and forth, as if he has a secret inside him that is about to burst out.

"What?"

"No, no—nothing. It's just that I'm sure there are some things that Anastasia won't tell you. Won't be *able* to tell you," he says as he arches his back with a deep sigh of a breath.

"She's told me so much already," I reply. "Anastasia is eager for the project to be published. She's pretty forthcoming."

"Let me tell you something about dancers. Something no dancer will admit to."

"What is it?" I ask.

The choreographer leans in, puts his hand on my shoulder, and says, "They are the personification of narcissism. No, really! Why are you laughing? It's a fact. They are notorious for that!"

"They are?"

"I'm serious. They have to be. That's what makes them so good at what they do! They spend their days in front of a mirrored wall, watching themselves dance, obsessed with their every movement. Every twist of a leg. Every slight gesture of a hand. Every curve that carves out space. A dancer lives for her own reflection," he says. "Her vanity is what drives her."

nine

MOM PASSED AWAY WHEN I was in college. Just a year before I met Leo. Sometimes I feel as though my grief has two faces. One cries up into the sky from the overwhelming heartache of losing my mother. The other looks down at the floor with tremendous guilt because it's also the end of taking care of someone I love. I feel like I failed at the most important job I've ever had. And someone else suffered the greatest penalty because of it.

Her death took my whole family by surprise. We thought she was going to make it. To beat it. As if it were some battle one could win. As if all you needed were the right weapons—medicine and chemotherapy. But it wasn't that simple. The cancer came and swept her away long before we knew she was gone. It came slowly at first, when I was in high school. It crept into her body as silently as an afternoon shadow. I can remember being fourteen and growing increasingly impatient with Mom for not being able to walk with me in the shopping mall for my back-to-school clothes. "C'mon, Mom, the stores are going to close soon," I remember saying.

"Just a second, Julia," she replied in her soft voice. "I need to sit down and rest again."

Little did I know that her fatigue was only the beginning. Soon there would also be a persistent series of unbeatable colds and flus, fevers, and chills. Little by little, her immune system grew weaker and weaker. But we grew accustomed to going with her to the cancer clinic across town for her monthly blood transfusions. Dad never left her side. He was always there to double-check the doctor's orders, make sure Mom's favorite nurse, Judy, was working that day, and help Mom through her daily anxiety attacks. Mom was just a dainty little thing compared to me and my sisters—five foot three. And a half. Her eyes would get huge when she saw the IV unit and the bag of A positive blood that would replenish her own. She'd start to hyperventilate, and her arms and legs would freeze up until one of us covered the whole IV bag with a sheet or pillowcase. Then we'd massage her hands and feet until she started to feel better and breathe normally again. We were her protectors. "She'll get better," we used to say. "She has us."

But soon the monthly transfusions became weekly.

Then daily.

And then it was too late. The doctor put his hand on Dad's shoulder. "I'm sorry," he said. "She's passed."

That was a few years ago. It's funny how you don't want time to move too quickly when it comes to death. Person after person will try to comfort you and whisper in your ear, "Time will heal your wounds." But you don't want that. You don't want years and years to go by. You don't want to move on. You don't want time to even move—because with every passing strike on the clock, you start to forget something. You start to forget the little things that were your favorite things. How she used to tuck you in at night when you were little. How she'd brush the wisps of hair off your forehead very lightly with the tips of her fingernails. How she'd sit on the edge of your bed with her head on your pillow and make up the most marvelous bedtime story using your pet rabbit and dog and duck as the main characters. And how you'd laugh so hard when she would cast Quacker the Duck as the big hero in the end. You start to forget the jokes. The voices. Laughs. Expressions. Moments. Special little moments that don't have a corresponding photo to ensure their place in your memory.

And so you just want everything to be perfectly still. So still that something that happened several years ago might seem as though it happened just yesterday. And painful memories might seem as though they were just a bad dream. But unfortunately, I just can't hang onto the past. Time has slowly slipped out of my fingers, and the years have already started multiplying on top of each other.

Dad is having an especially difficult time moving on. On top of desperately missing the true love of his life, he has also realized just how hard it is to do those everyday things that Mom used to do.

"You'll never believe what happened to me today, Julia," he said to me over the phone this past weekend.

"What did you do?"

"I went grocery shopping," he said in a defeated voice.

"Well, that's great," I said. And I meant it. I really did. It was a huge step for him to buy his own groceries. He didn't know how to cook, make a sandwich, or even boil an egg. He had trouble finding the butter in the fridge if it was behind the gallon of milk. If it's not out in front, it doesn't exist.

"You don't understand," he replied. "It was a disaster. I just don't get it. I don't know how your mother did it!" He sounded as though he had just been on the frontlines of a war that hadn't gone well.

"Well, what happened?"

"Everything was going fine at first. I had my list, I was shopping—I had trouble finding the ham at first, but some woman helped me, so that was OK—"

"So what happened?" I interrupted.

"It was that damned conveyor belt. You know, the one at the register?"

"Yeah, Dad, I know."

"Oh. OK, so I'm taking my stuff out of my cart and putting it onto that belt thing, and I must have slammed the milk down too hard and the damned thing started leaking all over the place!"

"Oh, Dad," I said sympathetically.

"And so then, as soon I see that the damned milk is all over the place, my watch gets caught on the plastic wrapper of this big pack of toilet paper I was buying."

"What?"

"But I didn't see it right away, so I'm just tearing it open without realizing it, and then the spilled milk got all the paper wet and everything."

"Everything?"

"Yeah, well, then when I saw the paper getting wet, I turned around and my elbow must have knocked that damned milk over on its side. So it just splattered over all the rest of my other groceries too. And it splashed all over this lady behind me. And all over her baby too, I think."

"Wow," I said, not really sure what else to say.

"Yeah, so I just left. I just left everything right there and didn't get any groceries or anything."

"Well, what are you going to do for dinner?" I asked.

"I dunno," he casually replied, "probably just have some cookies. I think I have a package of Oreos."

I wasn't surprised. Since Dad's been by himself, his vegetable-crisper drawer is usually filled with cans of Pepsi and boxes of chocolate doughnuts. The egg and butter shelf are crammed with Snickers and Milky Ways. The entire fridge looks more and more like a vending machine. Dad's admitted chocoholism could soon turn into hypoglycemia.

"But," I began cautiously, "don't you need milk with those?"

"Oh, that's right. Damn it!"

It's become increasingly difficult to comfort Dad. His grief is married to guilt. "I could have done more," he still says. "I could have done so much more." And I want to be strong for him.

When Mom died, I tried my best to cry only in private, when I could be sure that my family wouldn't see or hear me. So I'd cry in the car, on my way to the post office. Or in the shower, when the spray of the water would muffle my sobs. Staying strong is the only thing a daughter can do when she sees her dad, for the first time in her life, cry deeply and painfully. Stay strong.

Dad still lives in Santa Barbara. Same street. Same house. Same everything, except now he leaves his motocross gear scattered across the living room floor and his helmets lined up on the dining room table. And he always tells me that he'll never move. "I'm gonna live in this house till the day I die," he says. "I just couldn't leave it. I couldn't leave the memories behind."

And I don't blame him. It was hard for me to leave home again after Mom was gone. I stayed only a few more months with Dad, and then I had to head back up to school in Berkeley. I visited once every month for a couple of years, but only to make sure that Dad was OK. Dad and I were the only ones left completely alone. My two older sisters had their own families to take care of. Everyone felt the painful absence of Mom's presence, but more so in that house. It felt unnatural for Dad and me to live our lives without her there. Without seeing her glide barefoot through the house in the morning in her long pale-pink bathrobe. Without hearing her softly sing a made-up tune as she planted a row of blue pansies in the backyard. Without seeing her sit in the chair she always sat in at the dining room table during dinner. And one of the most painful things to realize was that for the rest of our lives we would never again hear her gentle voice ask us something as simple and everyday as, "Would you like me to make you a cup of hot tea? With a little milk and honey?"

But things began to change the day I met Leo. Once he stepped into my life, he stepped right into my family. Leo's cheerful and sunny disposition was a comfort to us. We needed his smiles more than he knew. Dad immediately embraced him as a son; my sisters welcomed him as their new brother. For them, Leo was a sweet guy who would laugh heartily at Dad's jokes and try his best to tell his own. But for me, Leo was the shoulder I could cry on. He was someone with whom I could confide and finally release those tears that I had tried so hard to hide from my family. And Leo was someone whose gentle smile would make me feel so much better.

Was he, I wondered, an angel whom Mom had sent down to help me?

ten

THE REASON I BECAME A writer is because I like to stay in bed. Sometimes for days. Sometimes I just want to be alone. And writer is probably the only career that allows for extended, random stay-in-bed days. It's nothing serious, of course. It's just that I tend to grow weary of people. And every so often, I like to withdraw in a quiet solitude in a space of my own so that I can breathe in peace. Just peace. I'll just stay in my bathrobe for days and get out of bed only for meals. No reading. No television. Nothing except for maybe an open window for fresh air in the afternoon or in the dawn. Most of the time is spent just crying and desperately missing my mom. The rest of the time is spent crying about how I'm crying.

There is no release with tears that come from grief. There is no weight that gets lifted off your shoulders after having a good cry.

There is no good cry. There is only a raw, aching feeling, deep in the middle of your chest, every hour of every day, and you do your best not to let it out. You try desperately to guard it. But it's no use. There will always be something that crosses your path and innocently triggers a memory, such as the color of the late afternoon sky or a familiar song on the radio or even a single word, and that terrible feeling inside you will come gushing out in a flood of tears.

Once you begin crying, you can't stop. The strength of that terrible feeling is far too great. The tears keep coming, one after another after another, and you keep crying. It is frightening to hear those wild, screaming sobs come from your mouth. Frightening because you can't control it. And you want so badly for it to stop because you can't breathe and you come close to choking, but the tears keep coming. More and more. Until the only reason they stop is because your body gets exhausted and you fall asleep. It is a harrowing experience; afterward you vow to never let that feeling out again.

You promise yourself to keep that raw, painful feeling deep down inside, where it can never escape. But that never works either, for that terrible feeling doesn't go away. It grows bigger and bigger if you don't it let it out. It weighs you down, so that it becomes difficult to walk. It fills your chest and your lungs, so that it becomes difficult to breathe. You start to wonder if it's really a poison inside that is slowly killing you. So then you go into an empty room and shut the door and cry all over again. The feeling must always come out.

Perhaps it's those times of solitude that keep my grieving heart from exploding. Perhaps those moments spent in bed really do replenish my spirit and keep me going.

eleven

I FIRST SAW ANASTASIA M. IN Barnes & Noble. On the shelf, that is, in the most recent issue of British *Vogue*. Her wide doe eyes serenely gaze at the camera. A light is cast gently against the sharp contours of her face, while a black leotard and tutu veil her svelte figure.

This morning we're sitting across from each other at a minuscule round slab of a table at a Russian café on Franklin Street. It's our third meeting. I'm sipping a cappuccino and pulling apart a croissant because I was so sure that those are what beautiful ballerinas eat for breakfast at ten in the morning on a Sunday. But it's not. Anastasia M. has opted instead for a can of Diet Coke and a cigarette or two. Or five. She has only one hour before dress rehearsal and a half-hour until *The Chronicle* interviews her for the front of its Arts & Entertainment section.

The ballerina is draped over her chair as dreamily as can be. Her long legs are wrapped around each other, and her toes are tapping at hyperspeed while her chin perches against the back of her hand. Anastasia M. is wearing a thin, extra-long angora scarf around her neck and doesn't even care that its feather-like fringe is brushing against the sidewalk as she speaks.

"Tell me, Julia...what deed you think about rehearsals of last week?" she asks in her thick Russian accent.

"Oh, I thought everything was lovely!" I say, unable to temper my gushing, "Your dancing is mesmerizing! Oh, and I even had a chance to talk to the choreographer. We were standing next to each other and—"

"Ah...the choreographer! Such a wild man, don't you think?"

"Well, yes...he has so much passion for ballet."

Anastasia M. bursts into laughter. "He's a genius, that man...a genius. But he is a little...you know...a little...," she says as she waves her hand in the air.

"What?"

"He is...how do you say...very oddball?" she asks.

"Is he?"

"You know, his latest mission is to choreograph an entirely..." Her brow furrows. "Nakeed?"

"Naked, yes. Or nude."

"Yes! Nude!" she screams out. "He wants to choreograph a...a completely nude ballet! It's shocking, no? In Russia people would laugh! But he's serious, this man. He's serious."

We laugh until a waiter interrupts us with the check and the ballerina lights another cigarette. I feel so glamorous sitting next to her. I want to tell everyone who walks by that I'm sitting next to the star of *Swan Lake*. The star of *Kingdom of Shades, Coppélia*, and *Sleeping Beauty*. But instead, I try to maintain my focus and get back to my notes.

"So, Miss M., at what point did you know that you wanted to be a dancer?"

Anastasia M. takes a long, thoughtful puff and then dangles her new cigarette ever so gracefully between her slender fingers.

"Well, you know, in Russia, girls develop more slowly; unlike Spain where a girl suddenly…poof! The girl becomes a woman at just thirteen."

"I mean, when did you start really enjoying being a dancer?"

"I start at eight years old. Most girls start the ballet anywhere from eight to twelve years old. You see, before eight years old, the child's legs…they are…they are—how do you say?" she says as she waves her cigarette in the air. "The legs are not strong enough. It's very hard work, you know."

"Right, right. Their little legs aren't strong enough to bear such physical intensity."

"Exactly!" she says excitedly. "You're good! Ah, it's good to talk with a writer!"

"But when did you know? Did you always know that you would become a dancer?"

"I don't know. I just became…obsess? I became obsess with dancing. Right away I love it. It made me feel like a bird." And her eyes close as if her soul has been transported back to the stage. "I love the flying," she says, her eyes still closed, "I have always loved flying. To tell you the truth, I'm in little bit of surprise when my feet land back on the ground."

twelve

I'M ALWAYS AMAZED AT HOW fast the red comes out of my hair. It's been only a few weeks, but already it's a weird brassy blonde. It's as if the dye just doesn't agree with my hair. Or maybe my hair doesn't particularly care for the color. But winter is here and red it must be. So I'm walking around our apartment with my hair completely saturated in colorant and pinned in a big mess on top of my head. Twenty minutes left and then I can rinse.

"Is that my shirt?" Leo asks.

"Yeah," I reply, "I didn't want to get dye on my blouse. Besides, this is one of your old ones."

"Are you kidding?"

"Don't worry, this is one that we were going to throw out anyway. Or cut up and use for rags or something—"

"You're serious? But I love that shirt! It's my favorite one!" he pleads.

"Honey, it's stretched out. It has holes in it. Look! Here's a huge one at the side. You can't wear this outside." I point out the gaping hole at the seam.

"No, no, you're gonna make the hole bigger! Leave it alone, leave it alone," he says, "I'm not throwing that shirt out, I love it. It's so soft. It's perfect."

It is soft. I'll give him that. But it's so thin from years and years of washing that it's sheer. A few crucial threads are the only things keeping this shirt from evaporating into thin air.

"Honestly," I begin, "it's not even a shirt anymore. It's barely an idea of a shirt."

"I can wear it at night. To bed. When I get cold. Don't throw it out, please," he begs.

"OK, OK," I say, taken aback by his love of the T-shirt. "I won't throw it out. I'm sorry. I'll wash it after, I promise, sweetheart."

Leo looks at me suspiciously, as if I'm going to tear his precious T-shirt into shreds the moment he turns away.

"Don't worry."

"Well, just—OK…so what color are you dyeing your hair?" he asks.

"It's called Red Penny. Fifteen minutes left."

"Hmm. That sounds nice. Wasn't it already red? Oh—I almost forgot. I just picked up the mail. There's a letter on the table for you."

I rush over to the corner of our living room that's designated the dining room and flip through the mail on the large desk that we call the dining room table. There are six letters for me. All from publishers. I hold my breath as I open them, one by one. This is the most excruciating, stomach-churning, nail-biting part for a writer.

The dreaded replies.

About nine months ago, I sent out nearly fifty queries to various publishers across the United States for my very first novel, *Alice's Dream*. Queries are polite little letters that a no-name writer sends to publishing houses and literary agents to pitch her manuscript. In one critical letter, you're supposed to convince the publisher that not only are you a remarkable writer, but that your manuscript is so original and amazing that they absolutely *must* read the entire thing. An editor spends two seconds glancing at the letter before she moves on to the next query in the gigantic slush pile of queries on her desk. No pressure, right?

I was so proud of myself when I finished the manuscript. It had taken me years to write it, and I expected publishers everywhere to fight for the rights to it. But that was hardly the case. Replies trickled in. *"No, thanks." "Not right for us at this time." "We're not accepting material." "Sorry, no." "We handle only transgender erotica."* I soon realized that I was doing what a million writer-wannabes were doing. I also realized that I was going to have to grow a thick skin if I ever wanted to sell the rights to *Alice's Dream*.

OK, no big deal. I'll just open this envelope and not care one way or the other. Oh, who am I kidding? This is from that big publisher in New York. I really, really want this one!

Dear Writer:

Thank you for your inquiry. We are sorry that we cannot invite you to submit your work or offer to represent you. Moreover, we apologize that we cannot respond in a more personal manner. We wish you the best of luck elsewhere.

Sincerely,

R.W. Publishing

thirteen

I'VE SEEN AN EXTRAORDINARY oil painting of the Muse Terpsichore
by Nattier, the famed portraitist of eighteenth-century France. Muses
are the most captivating figures of Greek myths; they serve to inspire
and protect musicians, artists, and writers. Some say that the Muses
are goddesses born of Zeus and Mnemosyne, the goddess of
memory. Others say that the Muses were created from a sacred swan
or that they sprang from a mysterious river of milk and honey.

There are nine Muses altogether, and each caters to a different
specialty in art or science. Terpsichore is the Muse of dance and is
nicknamed The Whirler. Nattier painted Terpsichore with a long,
flowing robe made of gold and white gossamer that freely floats over
her alabaster skin. He also gave her a wistful expression on her soft,

delicate face. And in her dark wavy hair, upswept in a bun, are several feathers: yellow, silver, blue and peacock.

I viewed this stunningly large painting last year at the Legion of Honor, which is where I am this afternoon. I wonder why I haven't been here since then. After all, it's my favorite place in the city. The museum looks like an enchanted palace, cast under a spell and preserved only by magic. Outside, looming rows of columns enclose a large courtyard with eerily quiet grandeur. But inside, mysterious echoes continue to sound long after the last footfall against the Napoleon Grey marble floors. It makes no difference whether there is a crowd of visitors or not, for it always feels as though I'm the first to step inside it for hundreds of years.

Actually built in 1924, the majestic Beaux-arts structure is a three-quarter-scale replica of the 1788 splendor in Paris, Palais de la Légion d'Honneur. Set among equally gigantic, wind-shaped Monterey cypresses, the museum sits on a tranquil hilltop in Lincoln Park. The grounds of the museum have the most dramatic, contemplative views of the Golden Gate Bridge and the Pacific. Any strolls I take along the nearby cliffs must be brave, for biting ocean winds can sometimes sneak up on me and knock me down if I'm not careful.

I was surprised when the ballerina wanted to meet here. I had expected our next meeting to take place in some smoky jazz club like Café Du Nord at two in the morning or somewhere mysterious. But here we are, seated in the elegant outside patio of the Legion's café, surrounded by olive trees and silver sunshine. It couldn't be a lovelier winter day.

Anastasia is on her fourth cigarette and in the middle of recounting the past loves of her life.

"I have been the mistress for many men," she says, "but there was one man. An atheist. From Paris. He was my first fall from grace."

"How old were you then?" I ask.

"Just a child," she replies in between puffs, "Fifteen. Maybe sixteen."

The air around us is intensely quiet as she speaks, as if the olive trees were listening to her story. "He seduced me the way all French men seduce their women. With the dark poetry and the dark philosophy. Baudelaire and Nietzsche," she says, "You know them?" With a dainty flick of her finger, her cigarette is tossed to the ground.

"He was so excited about the existentialism and attacking everything I held in my heart," the ballerina continues, "I hate him— hated him at first. I hated him so much." She stops to laugh a little. "It was the first time someone made me question everything! I was just a simple dancer then—traveling with a small ballet company throughout Europe. We first met in Copenhagen—the Parisian and I. Have you been? To Copenhagen? He was older. In his twenties. My mother hated him and that, well, naturally...that made things interesting. Even when things were horrible."

Anastasia M. rises from the bench. She walks around and stretches one leg up awkwardly against a nearby stone balustrade. Wild animals often behave differently when taken out of their natural habitat. So, too, does the ballerina. On her days off, her seemingly floating, graceful walk transforms into a sort of flat-footed waddle now that different shoes are worn. Black, orthopedic-looking sneakers that look a whole size too big. The overall style of attire is much different, too. What once was tight and fitted to showcase a perfect form is now loose, relaxed and rebelliously slouchy. Track pants. Big sweatshirt. Long puffer coat. Her knit, army-green scarf looks enormous wrapped three times around, as if its only purpose is to hide that lovely swan-like neck. Even the bun atop her head has yielded to a long, tousle of undone waves. Still, the ballerina does not appear messy. She simply looks small, almost child-like, in those oversized clothes and hair.

"On my days off, oh…it's just that the last thing I want to be is…perfect," she told me when we first began our talk, as though she could read my thoughts of surprise when I saw this most different ensemble. "It's the only time I don't have thousands of eyes doing the watching and judging of every bit of me. I can just be…invisible."

Like any other athlete on her day off, the ballerina is sore and stiff. She briefly mentions the spasms in her back and the pain deep in her knee, but then dismisses it all when I show concern. "It will be fine tomorrow," she insists.

And now her frumpy black sneaker slips off the balustrade and throws her off balance, but she waves off the stumble and laughs. Still, the persistence of the ballerina has not taken a day off and she kicks her leg back up, this time higher and leaves it there as she muses.

"He was very dark inside," she continues as she leans in to a stretch, "very dark. He had no faith or creed, but he told me I was his angel. I was so young and already I had become a man's religion. I was too young, too…naive? I was too naive to understand that I was his everything. Such a pedestal he put me on. Such a dark mind. But his kisses, oh! They tasted like the black cherries. Really. I'm saying the truth. It wasn't long before we began our affair."

"He was married?" I ask.

The cold ocean winds begin to blow, and the leaves in the olive trees are trembling. Those leaves are making a beautiful rustling sound, swishing carelessly against each other and their branches, just like the sound a child makes when he strikes all the keys of a piano— up one side and down the other.

"No, no. I was. To the ballet. All my *other* loves have been affairs."

She returns to the bench, takes out another cigarette from a pocket in her gray Chloé bag but then decides against it, and takes out a big bottle of magnesium pills instead. She promptly swallows four.

"It's good for swelling," she explains. She sits beside me yet her lips are still pursed in thought. She has perfectly curved Cupid's bow lips that remind me of Nattier's painting of Terpsichore. Anastasia M. is quite the muse. She must be *someone's* muse. I start to wonder if she keeps feathers in her dark hair at home.

As I watch her brush a rebel wisp of hair from her eyes, I realize all the strange details I've already learned from this ballerina about her life. Of how she ices her feet at the end of every day and cleans them only in alcohol because water softens the feet. How she refuses to wear open-toe shoes or sandals—ever—because ballet has ruined the appearance of her toes, as it does to all ballet dancers who work hard enough and long enough. And I've learned about all those years of painstakingly hard work it took to achieve that deceptively simple illusion of hovering in midair as her toes skim across the stage. Or the years spent learning to be demure and glamorous at the same time; like a tiny sparrow assuming a grand image of royalty. Yes, I know of the struggles behind her ease of movement. The tears behind her poise and beauty and clean, classic lines. The guileless elegance. And I know of the serene competitiveness that dwells inside her, as if she knows that she was born with a spectacular destiny.

Anastasia M. is a ballerina—a prima ballerina, in fact—but not every ballet dancer is given such a title. The term means that she is a principal, or leading, female dancer. Only the rarest girl has such exceptional talent that she stands out from the other dancers. But Anastasia M. is *the* ballerina.

"He was so passionate," she says in a broken staccato. "All Parisians are passionate. It was so long ago. He was the one...the only one...who ever made me stop dancing. For one month I gave it up. For him. I lived with him in Paris in his studio, just above a butcher shop. It's funny talking about it now. I thought I could become a writer."

"Really? You write?" I ask.

Anastasia M. nods. "In Russian, yes. But my grammar is not so good, especially in English. I wrote the poetry."

"How unusual," I reply, "a poet-ballerina!"

Her eyes widen and she laughs a lovely, lilting laugh. "Not a real poet, you know," she says casually. "It was..."—she pauses and leans toward me with a mischievous, almost wild, look in her eyes and whispers—"just for fun."

"Oh, I bet it was marvelous! Did you keep any of it?"

"Keep? You want to read them?" she asks.

"Well, I—"

"I have one I'll show you. Next time we meet. It's a dark one. I wrote it the night I decided I would stop seeing the Parisian. I was so young."

"Why did you stop?"

completely lost

She folds her arms against the chill. "What finally hit me," she says carefully, "was not his philosophies. I was naturally, this, you see, a sad sort of girl, so I could deal with that."

"Then what was it?" I ask.

I watch as she tries to light another cigarette in the wind. It finally catches.

"It was his paranoia. That, I could not live with."

After two puffs she throws the glowing roll of tobacco to the ground.

"He would get so jealous. *So* jealous. It was a long time before I realized what made him that way. It was not the other men who would cross my path. It was dancing. He was jealous of the ballet and of how much I loved it."

"You know," I interrupt, "a famous psychologist once told me that there are two types of people in the world—those who are paranoid and those who are depressed."

I feel so proud that I finally have something interesting to say to my worldly expert. But Anastasia M. just looks up at me with a curious expression.

"Well, that's just ridiculous," she says.

"Is it?"

"There *are* two types. This part it is true. But the types...they are so...so false."

"What would you suggest?" I ask.

"I would say, if you really are honest about it, there are two types of people," the ballerina says: "those who live for the past...and those who live for the future."

She wraps one of those long arms around my shoulder and leans in, as if she were divulging another juicy secret that she didn't want even the trees to hear.

"I can just tell it about you," she whispers.

"Tell what?"

"We are the same, you and I—we both love living for the past. That's why you write, no? To write what has happened? That's why I dance. I'm dancing a ballet that has been danced for centuries. It's intoxicating. And I'm in love with it."

fourteen

IT'S FOUR IN THE MORNING AND I can't sleep. I'm exhausted but my eyes are wide open. I've been tossing and turning for the past two hours. I can hear every strike of the clock. Clocks. We have three different clocks in the bedroom, all ticking and tocking to their own time. Leo is deep in dreamland. Snoring. He always snores when he's exhausted. Or maybe he just always snores.

Sleeping is the last thing on my mind. My thoughts are spinning—wandering in and out of our apartment and San Francisco and back through the pages of time. I wonder who started it all. Which phantom of the literary night was the first ghostwriter? Did Winston Churchill have one? Or Confucius? Whispering rumors have it that Shakespeare had one. And T. S. Eliot. But no one knows for sure. It's one of the mysteries that writers and publishers and everyone else in the business take to the grave. Maybe it was Plato who was the first to ghost. Maybe he spent years and years ghosting, and then once Socrates kicked the bucket, Plato reclaimed his glorious, ever-precious byline.

I can't keep doing this. I can't lie in bed with my mind racing in circles. Carefully and quietly, I slide out of bed—although I know that I could jump on the mattress for hours and Leo would still be sound asleep. I walk over to my desk (really just a small, black fold-out card table that I call a desk, with a tablecloth over it that is really just my French grandmother's ivory shawl) and look over my notes for the project with the ballerina.

At the top of it all sits the mysterious poem, handwritten by a very young Anastasia M., and freshly translated by an older Anastasia M. I wanted to save it for tomorrow night at the War Memorial Opera House while I wait, but my curiosity couldn't hold out for that long. Paper clipped to the front of the moody, tormented, very Russian poem is a note:

Dear my ghost Julia,

Here is a copy of poem I spoke of. I translate it yesterday from Russian. Enjoy!

Yours,
Anastasia

Phantom
by Anastasia M.

Mysterious phantom,
you scour
the amaranthine night,
Feeding me bleeding kisses,
swallowing my every sensation.
You fly,
cascading
down through the lonely sky,
past shadows of yourself.

You come swiftly,
drawing deep
this blood…
Drifting
at your leisure
through my endless dreams,
pouring delusions
into my dizzy head,
teasing me with fatal fantasies…

Poisonous tears
you stream down to my eyes,
burning me with your salted sorrow.
Influx
of triste lunacy…
With that appetite for ecstasy
You are cool in your power,
so tranquil

in your journey for my passions.

You have no body,

no form…

your presence transpires as the wind;

filling my lungs with delirium.

Mistaking your erotica

for my insanity—

I run…

Frightened and perplexed,

I flee.

But still, I am captive.

You, the cryptic vision,

seizing me

with your hunger.

Yet your cruelty lends pity,

and you spare me

Ashamed of your craving—

you fly

back into the restless night.

Somber phantom,

now drifting

in silence, beyond the horrors—

searching for another

to drown happily in your mouth,

drinking the rich wine from their pulse.

Mangling their heart's fallacious notions

with every taste.
You search.

Living in the twilight of solitude,
You call me—
Aching for frenzy,
you beg for me.
Cataclysmic desires,
What cruelty!
Falling downward, swirling weakness...
Forever soaking in this dismal savagery,
you die.

Perishing in grief,
alone in the dark
voices
of sorrow surround you...
the spectrum of terror claws
at your core.
Looking upward,
you try to fly—
but heavy anguish prevents you.

Alas, I hear your desperate cries,
and I return...
saving you
with the warmth
beneath my torn flesh.
Your lips,

wearied,
bathe in my blood—
you regain strength.

Mysterious phantom…
You fly
back
into the gloom of night
staining the sky
red
with your eternal
thirst.
Sanguinary refuge.

fifteen

TONIGHT IS THE OPENING NIGHT performance of *Swan Lake* for the
country's oldest professional ballet company. It's supposed to be a
gala of some wonderful sort and I'm backstage with Anastasia M.
while she stretches. There is a nervous energy in the air that you
could practically squeeze in your hand to feel its charge.

Everything feels and looks like magic at the War Memorial
Opera House. The dressing rooms are filled with orchids. The air is
clouded with face powder and wafting champagne fizz; though
curiously not a glass is in sight. Yet. Filling the hall are racks upon
racks of the most gorgeous costumes made of shimmery, ethereal
layers of tulle and satin. I can hear the orchestra tuning their
instruments below the stage.

Anastasia M. moves to a bench to carefully wrap her toes in lamb's wool. I sit quietly next to her. I hear her hum along with the orchestra's tune.

"It's almost time to *live*," she says in a vibrant voice as she slips her pointe shoes on and patiently ties the long satin ribbons up and then crosses them around her ankles.

She looks perfectly calm and completely immersed in a delightful déjà vu.

Part 3 The Chef

How light the strain when, decked in vernal bloom,
Thalia tuned her lyre of melody.

~James Gates Percival, "An Ode to Music", 1823

sixteen

IT'S AN AWFUL DREAM. I'VE HAD it fifteen, maybe twenty, times already. It's a simple dream really and it always unfolds the same way: I'm at the kitchen table at my parents' house in Santa Barbara. I'm sitting next to my mom and she looks beautiful. It's just us. She's smiling while we watch the sparrows fly and flutter outside the window.

I feel so happy with her as she tells me about the vacation she just returned from and how much fun it was. "There was swimming and there were beaches and oh, it was so much fun!" she says. I interrupt her to tell her how distressed I was, how we thought she had died. She looks at me with such a serene expression and says, "I'm fine. I'm right here." Then she walks out to the backyard and starts watering the plants. I tell her about the funeral, but she doesn't hear me. The sun is shining and birds are flying all around her. I follow her around the grassy yard, begging her to sit back down. "Shouldn't you rest?" But she shakes her head as if she doesn't understand what I'm saying. And then I just watch her for a moment before I walk closer to give her a hug. But as I wrap my arms around her, it's morning. My dream is over.

In those first few precious seconds, I feel exuberant. Those fleeting moments where my body is awake but my mind is still sleeping and my mother is still alive.

I turn on my side and think about what a lovely dream I just had and how I should call Mom on the phone and tell her about it. I open my eyes to find myself back in bed, next to Leo. And then…slowly…I wake up completely. And I start to remember.

It's the saddest moment of my day when I wake up and realize she's gone. It's as if every time I wake up from that dream, I feel like she dies all over again. Waves of pain and sorrow wash over me as I realize that I can see Mom only in my dreams now…brief dreams. That's all I have.

But I can never tell my father about this. I must keep it to myself, locked away from my two sisters. I don't really know why. I think I just want to protect them from my grief. I have to stay strong for them.

I talked to my dad on the phone earlier this morning. He called me to ask when Leo and I would be driving down for our next visit.

"I'm at the diner on 24th Street," he said, "but God, the waiter here is a complete moron. He's definitely one sandwich short of a picnic, you know? He's got one of those damned earrings in his ear. I don't think his elevator goes all the way to the top." He started to laugh. He always laughs at his own jokes to get the momentum going for his listeners. I laughed right along with him to avoid any awkward moments.

"So," he continued, "maybe if you and Leo come down next weekend, we could—"

"Oh, sorry, Dad, Leo's mom is coming to visit us this weekend. Maybe we could come down the weekend after?"

"Well, yeah...OK.... No, that would be great too! And maybe we can all go to dinner together. I'd like to take you kids out," he says. His voice sounds funny. Nervous.

"That would be really nice, Dad," I reply. "Thank you."

"And maybe Olivia could go with us? She really wants us all to get together."

My heart sank into my stomach, and then my stomach dropped down to the soles of my shoes. I had to sit down. I didn't know what to say. My mouth was open but I couldn't think of a suitable response. I had known this question would come sooner or later, but I desperately wished it would be later.

Olivia Q. is the woman my dad has been seeing. He doesn't call her his girlfriend, but I think that's just for my benefit. She's about fifteen years younger than my dad. He met her several years ago, I think, but started spending time with her about six months after my mom passed away.

It all started casually. At first Dad would call to tell me that Olivia had dropped by to bring him some chocolate cake to cheer him up. And then he'd call to tell me that he'd taken her to lunch so that he wouldn't have to eat alone. Later he'd call to tell me that he was glad to know Olivia because she was someone that he could talk to about my mom and how much he missed her. I learned to bite my tongue whenever I felt the urge to scream out, *But it's too soon! What about Mom?* Instead I just tried to be supportive. But it was hard. Before long, Olivia became my Dad's topic of choice for most of our conversations. Everything was Olivia this, or Olivia that, which soon turned into, "Well, Olivia thinks that you should do this," or "I talked to Olivia about your symptoms, and she thinks that…"

I know that he meant well and that she probably did too, but there's something inside me that just isn't ready yet to talk about her out loud. My dad must have picked up on my uneasiness because he started to get nervous and began to babble, talking speedily: "And we could go to that steakhouse downtown—it's Olivia's favorite—we go there every Wednesday and she always orders a glass of wine— merlot—and she knows that I drink only iced tea, so she always orders that for me—and I don't like lemon in my water, and so she always takes the lemon out of my water and puts in her water—isn't that funny? I think it's funny and—"

I hiccup. I always hiccup when I get nervous about what to say. Sometimes the hiccups last all day, like a big frog buried inside my stomach, with echoing ribbits. And they're more than awkward or uncomfortable. They're downright humiliating.

"That'll be fine, Dad," I managed to say between hiccups. "We can visit you."

"Really?" His voice was as excited as that of a kid who'd gotten permission to eat ice cream for breakfast.

"Yeah," I replied (through more hiccups). "I'll have to check with Leo, but I think we can come down next weekend."

"That's great! Oh, and Julia, I was talking to Olivia last night, and I told her about the multivitamin you take and Olivia really thinks you should be taking extra vitamin B. Olivia researches everything up this way and that way, you know, so she really knows this stuff."

I hope that Dad will move on to another topic, but he doesn't.

"Olivia thinks that vitamin B will really help with your headaches. And Olivia said—"

"'K, Dad, well I'd better get going. Lots of work to do."

There is a part of me—somewhere in the back of my brain, I imagine—that is genuinely happy for my dad and doesn't want him to be alone. Or lonely. But the other part of me—the louder part, the one that screams its opinions in my heart—doesn't know how to handle The Olivia Situation.

But at least I don't have to worry about that right now. It's a breezy March afternoon in Napa Valley, and I'm walking side by side with an even breezier French gentleman. His name is Bruno M.— Bruno to me and Monsieur M. to most others. He is the chef and owner of one of the most acclaimed restaurants in Napa. He's also my latest expert.

Mister X informed me that Bruno M. had already gone through four ghostwriters—all of whom were fired before the first month was finished. Today marks the first day of the second month that I've been ghosting his project, so I take that as a good omen.

The project is supposed to unlock the mystery behind his cuisine. Mixed in with the revelations will be some artful narratives about Bruno M.'s life that reflect his philosophy on food and eating. In other words, my job is to write about whatever Bruno M. talks about long enough for me to write it down. Mister X had warned me right away of Bruno M.'s notorious reputation for fiery outbursts and obsessive insistence for perfection, but I've yet to see anything but a warm, generous man with a disarming sense of humor.

There's something special about Napa Valley at this time of year. Everything is much quieter because most of the tourists and oenophiles come late in the summer and in the early fall. It's gorgeous out this afternoon. The rainy season has passed, and the vines are just starting to find their leaves again. Even the wind smells sweet from long days spent sweeping through the bright-yellow carpet of wildflowers that cover the Napa hills every spring. We're strolling through a large indoor-outdoor market, just off Highway 29, as Bruno M. shops for some last-minute ingredients.

"Ah," he moans, "these tomatoes. Ooh la laa…spec-tac-u-laire!"

His voice is deep and resonant, and his accent *français* transforms this ordinary errand into an utterly titillating experience. He picks up a plump tomato and inspects it with such tender care that I wonder if the tomato is actually made of a delicate glass.

"Look at this, do you see this? Do you see how smooth and shiny is the skin? It is a luscious red, no? And look! Do you see how firm the flesh? But not too firm. Ah yes. This one is *parfait*. Perfect! Of course, it won't be as flavorful as the darlings in Provence, but…eh."

I nod, unable to add to his passionate description of the tomato. He shrugs. Bruno M. is in his mid-forties and tall for a Frenchman—just over six feet. His eyes are expressive and softened with an innocence that immediately puts you at ease. He has a round face and rounder cheeks, and his mouth curves into a slight smile, even when he is serious or contemplative. There is something mischievous in all his expressions. His mustache curls a bit at the ends. His nose wiggles whenever he finishes a long sentence, as if speaking makes it tickle.

"But do you know how to *really* tell?" he asks in his deep, rolling voice that makes it impossible for me not to smile.

"How?"

"Use your nose. You have to breathe it in!" he says just before he raises his arm high in the air as he takes a slow, theatrical inhale. It's as if he were a wine connoisseur breathing in a swirling glass of pinot noir. "There should be a fresh aroma coming from the stem of the tomato…almost a peppery fragrance…ah…like this one! *C'est jolie.* It's beautiful. This one. It will have much flavor. Superb!"

Bruno M. is dressed in a simple, yet impeccable way. Navy slacks and a light cashmere sweater in camel. Atop his dark, wavy hair sits a tweed cap tipped slightly to one side. I'm holding two baskets for him. One is filled with strawberries and various hard cheeses, the other with fresh baguettes. Crusty and still warm.

The chef speaks more in gestures than he does in words. And he saunters, patient and slow. We've already spent nearly half an hour just looking for vegetables.

After meticulously (and joyously) finding a dozen perfect tomatoes, he makes his way to the bunches of radishes (he calls them "jewels"), the mushrooms ("wild chanterelle, shiitake, and oyster mushrooms only"), and then over to the small bin of brown and bulbous, gnarled-looking things called celery root (to be later cut into thousands of identical matchsticks).

In all of our meetings, Bruno M. has never worn a watch nor has he ever asked for the time or even glanced up at a clock. It's as if he has absolutely no care or desire for the concept. And today is no different. I am beginning to wonder if he even owns a calendar or a planner at all.

"It smells like spring, no?" he asks as he roots through the bin of large stalks of fennel. "Summer is more difficult. But you'll see, Napa is different then. Ah, but it's California, so you can find anything at any time!"

"Well," I begin, "the project should be finished by then."

"Ah well, you never know," he says lightly.

"No, it should be fine," I insist. "We're on schedule."

He drops the fennel and eyes me haughtily.

"Is that important to you? To be on schedule?" he demands.

"Isn't it for everyone?" I regret the words as soon as they come out of my mouth. I bite my lip and hope that my work ethic doesn't drive him into one of his famous tirades. I start to hiccup.

He raises an eyebrow and hesitates. His hands are both in the air but he doesn't speak. I'm holding my breath the best I can. All of a sudden, the chef crinkles his nose, leans back, claps a paisley handkerchief over his mouth, and lets out a muffled but still thunderous sneeze.

"*Pardon*," he mumbles.

Waves of relief swim over me as Bruno M. continues his search through the fennel. My hiccups are gone. I feel that a major disaster has just been averted. But Frenchmen are not so easily distracted.

"Sometimes perfection takes a little longer, no?" he says, gesturing with a bunch of fennel. I want to tell him that this is what I do. What I've always done. It's my method. But I know I can't upset the expert. Especially not this one.

"I suppose it will take as long as it needs to," I reply.

"Exactly!" he says sharply. "There is a precise moment for everything. Everything! It can't be rushed, no?"

"No. I mean, I agree."

"*Bon.* It is the same for cooking, no? Every good cook knows this. Pretend you are cooking a sauce. A light, delicate sauce."

"All right," I reply.

"There is a single, precise moment when the *full* flavor of that sauce is released into the air. You have to seize that moment! If you jump in too early, or let it go for a second too long, that flavor will disappear like…that!" he says excitedly with a snap of his fingers, which sends his bunch of fennel flying.

I bite hard on the tip of my tongue to keep the hiccups from coming back.

"If you care about something," Bruno M. continues in a serious tone, "you must respect every second you put into it. You cannot rush time. It moves the same with or without you."

Bruno M. grabs more bunches of fennel and then makes his way to the wine seller a few doors down. He scans the shelves up and down as he shakes his head.

"This is when I miss France the most," he says in such a subdued voice that I wonder if he's talking to himself.

He holds up a bottle of wine with an elaborate label and says, "Eh…voilà, this will do."

"Is it hard to find wine that you like?" I ask timidly.

"In Napa. *Oui.* Drinking wine from Napa is…eh, how do you say, eh, it is like dating a girl without ever kissing her. Without ever holding her in your arms and feeling the warmth of her. *Comprendre?* You understand?"

"But what makes it so different?"

"It has to do with the terroir. The earth. The soil. The terroir in Napa is not rich enough. It's just too new."

"What do you mean by that?" I ask.

"Well, France is very old, you see? Like a family that can trace its ancient ancestors. France is so old that every single thing that has ever been planted leaves a memory behind in the dirt. And everything that grows there grows with those memories coloring it. Flavoring it. Adding to it. Because in a family there is no escape! It is same with the grapes in France."

"But not here?"

He frowns and grabs another bottle.

"There's just not enough history in American soil. Something is missing," he says, "something is missing inside it. Things were grown here for a long time, sure, but what? Who knows? Eh, there was no care."

seventeen

LEO'S MOM, LILLY, HAS JUST arrived at our apartment in San Francisco. Even though she has just finished a three-hour, traffic-filled trip in her car, she looks refreshed. Her hair is perfectly coiffed in an elegant bob that just barely grazes her shoulders. Every hair is precisely where it should be. Her royal blue blouse is neat and pressed. Her dark red Revlon lipstick is freshly applied, and her sapphire earrings are sparkling—as are her matching sapphire necklace, matching sapphire bracelets, and matching sapphire ring (not to mention her diamond ring, pearl ring, and plain double gold bands as well). Her green eyes somehow seem extra-green, and even her perfume is at attention; its potent melon and cassia aroma instantly invades our two-bedroom apartment.

I, however, am sporting a much more "near-death" ensemble right now. My hair, unwashed, is a tangled mess. No makeup. Dark circles under my eyes. Mysterious stains decorate my Cal T-shirt (which is the same shirt I wore to bed last night). I haven't even brushed my teeth yet. And I smell like bleach. And maybe a hint of pine.

For you see, there is nothing in the world that motivates a woman to clean her home more than an imminent visit from her mother-in-law. We're not likely to admit it but it's true. And this wasn't just your average dust, mop, and vacuum sort of cleaning that had to be done. Oh no. This was your full-on, get down on your hands and knees and scrub-scrub-scrub and wash-wash-wash with a big red bucket of Mr. Clean and a handy can of Ajax at your side. This was business.

I spent four hours making our home immaculate for her visit. Every corner, every nook was swiped down. Every crevice was gleaming. Potpourri was set out. Pillows were fluffed. Bed sheets were ironed. The toilets were dazzling. Luminous, even. And every dust bunny was completely obliterated. I even set out the French-milled cucumber guest soaps, along with fresh guest towels for her (thanks to a mad rush to the drugstore an hour earlier).

Yes, I did my best to thwart any of Lilly's efforts to critique, suggest, or even hint.

But I should have known she would arrive an hour early. She either comes an hour early or an hour late. I have a suspicion that it's her crafty way to keep everything—along with everyone—on *her* schedule.

Lilly has just walked through the door and is exchanging kisses and hugs with Leo.

"Jules," she sings to me as her eyes shift down to the stains on my shirt, "it's so *nice* to see my daughter-in-law!"

I'm not sure when it started, but Lilly will sometimes call me Jules, not Julia. It doesn't really bother me. To be honest, I'm just glad she doesn't get confused and call me Sylvia—the name of her pint-size Pomeranian pooch, which she carries with her. Everywhere.

Leo stands behind me and whispers, "She brought that damned dog! I told her not to bring that friggin' dog. Damn it!"

"Leo, would you do me a favor?"

"Sure, Mom. What?"

"Would you take Sylvia out for a walk? Poor little thing, she hasn't gone at all today! And do you have some bowls for her water and food? No, you need to pick her up down the stairs. She's tired, can't you see?"

Fortunately, I'm the only one who can see Leo grinding his teeth as he reaches for Sylvia's leopard-print leash. I look over at Lilly, and now she's fixated on my hair. I can practically see the wheels turning in her head as she tries to find a nice way to offer me her travel hairbrush.

"I'm sorry I haven't changed yet, but I was just—"

"Jules, it's so nice to see you!" she says again. "I brought this little gift for you. For both of you. It's a housewarming gift for this…uh…this…*charming* little place you have here!"

"Oh, thank you! That's really sweet of you," I reply as I peek through the ruffles of tissue in a shiny red gift bag. Inside it I find a charming old-fashioned-looking bottle of olive oil, with colorful slices of oranges and cranberries artfully arranged inside. I give exaggerated oohs and ahhs as I set it out on display on the kitchen counter.

"This is lovely!" I say. "Thank you so much! You really shouldn't have."

Lilly takes a step forward and puts her hand on my shoulder.

"Well," she begins with a songlike sigh, "I know you don't have a mom…" She adds a second hand to my other shoulder. "You know, she's not here to get you things like this. So I thought I would."

I feel hiccups welling up in spasms inside me as I fight the urge to tell her that I really don't need the *reminder*. I can hear a little voice shouting to me from somewhere more rational; it's telling me not to be so sensitive. Leo throws me a *Please don't get mad at her—she means well* look from across the room. The only reply I can muster to Lilly is, "Oh, thanks."

And before Lilly even sets her purse down, she walks halfway through the kitchen doorway, turns back promptly and, with the tip of her finger, slides it up high across the very top of the fridge. The one spot in our whole place that I didn't clean (maybe ever). Upon examining the dirty residue on her finger, I hear her say to herself, "*hmmm*."

She then walks over to our living room and stands in front of the sofa. She's facing the wall with her head cocked to the side. Her eyes are squinted. She stands quietly for a few moments, deep in thought.

"You know, Jules," she says as she turns toward me, "I have a real eye for these things. May I make a suggestion? Do you mind? If it were me…I would move that picture on your wall down just a quarter inch. I think it would really give this room a…*finishing touch*."

"I'm just going to get a glass of water," I reply as calmly as I can. "I have the hiccups."

"So, tell me, Jules, how is your father doing lately? Is he well? Is he still dating that Mary or Louise or Olivia or whatever her name is?"

eighteen

IN ADDITION TO TERPSICHORE, Jean-Marc Nattier painted just one other Muse of the nine—Thalia. The name Thalia translates from the Greek as "to bloom" because Thalia is the Muse of comedy and all that is pastoral and idyllic. She's the playful one of the bunch. Cheerful. Merry. Greek writers and poets often invoked the help of Thalia when they wanted to write satire or comic plays.

Nattier placed her in the corner of his oil-painted canvas, half hidden beneath a gigantic blue velvet curtain on a stage. In the background there are actors performing, laughing and gesturing toward a white-wigged actress. Thalia is sitting by herself in a long, flowing robe; she is a cloud of sapphire in satin and silk with golden ribbons. In one hand she holds a comic mask in bronze, in the other she lifts the stage curtain slightly so she can peek out into the audience, perhaps to watch their reaction to the performance.

Because Nattier adored contrasts, he gave her both innocently rosy cheeks and a surprisingly mischievous smirk.

But not all artists depict Thalia on a comedic stage. Some sculptors shape her as a solitary figure and give her a crown of ivy on her head. Some also give her a shepherd's crooked staff at her side, so she can traipse about meadows and country fields. But they all give her that impish grin. Thalia is the only Muse who is always depicted as ridiculously happy for no apparent reason than for what she observes. She seems to know that the magical key that unlocks the mysteries of happiness, of joy, is to follow her whims. She's found what the rest of us spend our days looking for.

nineteen

IT FEELS COMFORTING TO STAND next to Bruno M. while he cooks. French food always reminds me of my mother. I remember the day she tried to teach me to make tomato sauce. The "special tomato sauce." It was the recipe that her mom taught her and her mom before that and three generations of French mothers before that. It was also some darn tasty sauce.

I was fifteen. It was early in the morning, and she was still in her long, light-pink bathrobe. The one that had bell sleeves, which looked as though they belonged on a princess. The kitchen radio was set on the oldies station. She loved cooking to music. Sarah Vaughan came on. There was an extra-large stainless steel bowl on the counter, filled with several dozen freshly peeled Roma tomatoes. Mom's wrists were buried in the bowl as she mixed and mashed the tomatoes by hand. Her fingers worked carefully to press the juice from the flesh.

"Do you see what I'm doing, Julia?" she asked gently. "You have to mix it very well before you put it in the pot. Hmm. We might even need some more. Julia? Are you paying attention?"

"Yeah, yeah," I replied coolly, "you blend it all together."

"No!" She stamped her foot. "The secret is mixing by *hand*," she insisted. "We don't want to damage the flavor by being harsh."

"OK, I get it. Can I go outside now?"

She looked crushed.

"But don't you want to learn how to make the special tomato sauce?" she asked softly.

"I was going to go swimming," I replied.

"But what if someday you want to make this? What will you do? Hmm? What then?"

"I'll just pick up the phone and call you," I said.

twenty

STANDING IN THE CHEF'S home kitchen is a grand experience. Blue is everywhere. A luxurious, regal blue. The counter. The tiled floor. The walls. And the pots and pans are a beautiful copper and are perfectly polished. Every culinary innovation, gadget, and contraption is within arm's reach. Even the knives hang effortlessly from a large magnetic strip on the wall.

And right now, it smells heavenly. Bruno M. is finishing up chocolate crème brûlée for us to eat while we discuss details of the project this afternoon. I certainly have no objection. *Crème brûlée* literally translates from French as "burnt cream"—that means a rich, creamy custard topped with mouthwatering caramelized sugar.

"I hope you give my book a good, happy ending," he says. "I have always been fond of the happier endings."

"With this food, a happy ending is inevitable."

"*Bon.*"

The desserts look rich and luxurious in their white ramekins and well worth the effort. He spent nearly half an hour meticulously scraping tiny peels from vanilla beans, which, as he said, "is essential!"

"How do you come up with your recipes?" I ask.

"Ah, they are my memories," he replies as he waves a large wooden spoon in the air. "All of them belong to my family. They were passed down from generation to generation. Every ingredient. Every detail. Every technique. All of my recipes are so old, you see…all of them so special to me."

Images of Mediterranean rooftops in terra-cotta and lofty French Gothic cathedrals flash into my head as I breathe in a warm, sweet whiff of vanilla from the brûlée.

"There is something about the past that is so reassuring," he says, "All of my dusty old recipes give me much pleasure."

"I know just what you mean," I say. "A ballerina once told me that there are two types of people in the world: those who live for the past and those who live for the future."

Bruno M. is quiet for a few moments. He nods his head as he contemplates the theory.

"A ballerina told you this?" he asks.

I nod.

Bruno M. bursts into tiny shakes of laughter. "Well," he says as he wipes his eyes, "that is complete shit!"

I hesitate for a moment because his accent made it sound like "complete sheet."

"But—" I begin.

"Your ballerina has got it all wrong. Past, future…pfft! Ridiculous!" he exclaims. His voice is so loud and forceful as he speaks that I could easily mistake it for a heated temper—if it were not for the smile across his face. Do all chefs delight in debate?

"What about the now?" he demands. "The ballerina left that out completely!"

"The now? You mean the present? Well, then what would you suggest?" I ask.

Bruno M. wiggles his mustache a little as he ponders my question.

"It's much simpler than what your friend said. Much more simple! There are two types of people in this world," he says as he takes a little taste of the cream from his wooden spoon. "There are those who live life by appreciating the present moment…and those who don't."

"Can you elaborate?"

"Ah, but it's easy! Listen, some people are aware of all that is around them, and other people are not. They're too busy thinking about tomorrow or yesterday to see what is right in front of them. In the present moment! It's as simple as being awake or dreaming. I like to be awake!"

He hands me another cream-dipped spoon for a taste. It's delicious. I decide not to prod Bruno M. further, for fear of upsetting him.

"Well," I begin, "I'm sure it's a lot easier to value the present when there is a delicious dessert in front of you."

"Trust me," coos the chef as he trickles Grand Marnier into cream, "you will *love* the chocolate crème brûlée! *C'est si bon!* It is so good! You like chocolate, no?"

"Oh yes! It looks wonderful!"

"Because if you don't like, I will throw it away…"

"Oh no, no—I love it!"

"*Ah, bon.* Tell me, Julia, do you ever eat the candy bars? I love the Swiss chocolate. Belgian also. But then the Snickers is good also."

Now I can't help but laugh.

"Snickers? You eat Snickers?" I ask.

"Ah, of course! With the nougat? *C'est délicieux!* It's delicious!" he replies with his arms waving vigorously in the air. "Why do you laugh?"

"No, no…I just, it's just—"

"You know, I never understood that about the United States," he says, shaking his head as he garnishes the crème brûlée with sprigs of delicate mint leaves. "You tell me, why is it the chocolate in public is such taboo?"

"Why do you call it taboo?"

"No one here dares to eat it in public, except maybe children. We should put that in the book. I've never seen anybody outside walking around here in your California with a chocolate bar. If they do, they hide it in their purse or pocket and then gobble it up in shame when no one is looking! American adults eat chocolate only behind closed doors, in the home. It is ridiculous! Why are they afraid?"

We sit down at a small, round table on his veranda. Tall bunches of densely potted lavender decorate most of it, along with gigantic barrels of white geraniums. Bruno M. taps his spoon into his dessert. I do the same. After the first taste, we both grab our chairs to support the magic dancing on our taste buds. The chocolate crème brûlée is delectable. Each ingredient serves a special purpose in a domino-like manner. The fragrant aroma of the mint leaves somehow brings out the smooth orange flavor of the Grand Marnier, which in turn softens the sweetness of the chocolate, making it seem even creamier.

"This…is…amazing!" I declare, between moans of delight.

"Is good, eh?" he replies. The satisfied chef leans back in his chair and takes a deep breath. "Ah. Can you smell all this lavender?" he asks me. "Breathe it in, breathe it in. It's good for you. Relaxes you while you eat. Ah, *regardez la.* Look over there at the sunlight coming through the trees. This is a day *spectaculaire!*"

Only Bruno M. could make such a simple experience so immensely pleasurable. It is indeed spectacular. And serene. The sweet Napa air blows in and out of the veranda, casting a flutter of tiny white geranium petals at our feet. They look more like feathers as they fall, slowly twirling in and out of the air currents.

As I finish my brûlée, I can think of no place I'd rather be. I can barely think at all. There is only this moment. And this moment only.

twenty-one

THERE IS SOMETHING MAGNIFICENT, superb, about butter. But not just any butter and definitely not margarine—it absolutely, with a doubt, must be the unsalted variety of butter. Sweet butter. It's the best kind to use for browning.

I love how sweet butter transforms when you brown it. And it's so simple. Slowly cook a lump of butter until it melts and begins to foam. Most people stop here but if you wait a few seconds more, you will witness mouthwatering perfection. The butter will undergo a scrumptious metamorphosis: The sizzle will stop and the pale pool of butter will turn a rich, golden-brown shade and take on the distinct fragrance of roasted nuts—that's when you know it's just right.

Maybe that's why the French refer to browned butter as *beurre noisette*, which means "hazelnut butter," because it really does gain a profoundly nutty flavor when its color begins to darken. Much more savory and complex. And once you brown butter, you can add anything you want to it and it'll make all the difference in the world. But this delicious magic happens in just seconds. As soon as the butter browns, you must immediately take it off the flame. Even one second too long will turn it to the blackest black, and the flavor will be lost forever.

Leo and I are standing together in our cramped, closet-like kitchen at home. He's helping me chop the ingredients for dinner while I brown butter. Even though he's slicing an onion, he's smiling his contagious smile as he works.

When he finishes, he hovers behind me at the stove. "What are we making again?"

"Tomato sauce," I reply. "I think I can remember how my mom used to do it. Or at least I hope so."

"But why the butter and all this other stuff?"

"Well, before I add the tomatoes, we have to sauté the onion in the browned butter first, by itself. Until it caramelizes," I reply while shaking the large sauté pan back and forth. "And then we add the minced garlic and swirl in some olive oil."

I just know that if he had a tail it would be wagging like crazy right now. Food is Leo's passion. Or, more accurately, *eating* food is his passion. I'm probably the only one who knows his secret fantasy is to become a full-time gourmand.

"Oh, I *love* caramelized things," he gushes. He kisses the back of my neck. I now realize that the frilly lingerie I bought a few months ago was a waste of money—I should have just gone grocery shopping.

Leo and I actually get along very well in this tiny kitchen. Cooking dinner is really our only time spent together. We don't have much free time. If he's not at work, then I'm usually off somewhere working with some expert or sleeping in after an all-night writing session.

I'm always surprised at how patient Leo is with me and my writing. From the very beginning, he's been nothing but encouraging. Even when we were engaged and I was working on my first novel, *Alice's Dream*, Leo was tremendously supportive: "Maybe someday," he'd say wistfully, "you will have written enough bestsellers that I'll be able to retire from my job and become a food critic!" He's also eager to be my on-call editor, which is a demanding, high-pressure job, considering the fact that I'm usually leaning over his shoulder, biting my nails like a madwoman, as he turns each page. "Wait! Why didn't you laugh right there? That was a funny part. Go back and read it again, Leo. I think you're reading too fast."

He doesn't even complain about my ghosting or my ever-changing hair color (right now it's chestnut brown, for spring). While I inevitably indulge in my own moodiness, quirks, and neuroses, Leo remains sunny and optimistic enough for the both of us. I guess you could say he's the calm that balances my storm.

Especially this morning. Before we even got out of bed.

I had just woken up from another one of my nightmares. I could feel the perspiration beading down my forehead and in my hair. Even my pillow felt damp. My heart was thumping through my chest in frightful beats, and the blankets were twisted around my legs.

"Shh, shh…don't cry, sweetheart, it was just a dream. You're OK," Leo said calmly as he caressed my forehead with his cheek, "Shh…"

"She's not coming back," I said between sobs, "she's never coming back."

"It'll be OK, honey. You have me."

"But my mom," I kept saying. "I want my mom. I miss her so much, I can't even explain how much."

Leo held me tight in his arms and pulled the sheets and comforter up over us both. I even felt the sides of his fingers wiping the tears from my eyes.

"I'll take care of you," he said.

But I felt empty. I stared at the walls with a swollen, blank face. Leo gave me another warm squeeze and said, "Let's stay home today. It's Saturday, right? Let's close the curtains and just watch movies and eat snacks all day. We'll have a Julia Day."

I looked over at him, and he was smiling at me with nothing but love in his eyes. I smiled back. Leo always knows just how to distract me long enough to get me to smile. It's as if he sweeps up the clouds that are hanging over my head so I can see again.

Later on, however, he gave me quite a scare. After breakfast (eaten on our nearly forgotten balcony), Leo handed me three small envelopes.

"Here, honey. Mail for you. I think they're all for *Alice's Dream*!"

"Oh no," I said. "I don't even want to look at them. I just can't."

"What? Why?"

"They're just going to be more rejections. I'm not up for it. Not today."

"But there might be a yes! You need only one!" he said.

I held each envelope up to the light and then handed them back to him.

"No," I replied, defeated. "Look how thin they are. They're all noes."

"Well, do you mind if I open them?"

And before I could even answer, Leo was already ripping them open.

"OK, here's the first one," he said. "It says, huh. Well, it looks like your original letter, the one you sent to them. I guess they just sent it back. Oh, wait—they wrote a note. It says, 'Sorry, not right for us at this time. Best wishes.' Well, at least they said, 'Best wishes'!"

"Leo, come on. Let's start a movie. I'm really not in the mood."

"Here's the second one. It says, 'Dear Ms. Clark: We are not taking new authors at this time. Best of luck.' Hmm. Well, they probably didn't even read your letter then, right?"

"Leo, I'm really not up for this," I pleaded.

"Here's the last one," Leo said. I watched as he read it silently. He then looked at me but stayed quiet.

"Well what does it say?"

Leo gave a big sigh and then replied, "Seriously now. It says, 'Dear Author—'"

"OK, OK," I interrupted, "I don't want to hear it. That's a no. Why can't they at least address me by my name? Forget it. I'm going back to bed."

"Wait!" he shouted as he waved the letter in the air. "I was just kidding. It's a yes! It's a yes! They want to publish *Alice's Dream*!"

I looked at the letter and I heard what Leo was saying, but it didn't register. I was dumbfounded.

"It says they want to publish it next year! In the fall!" he said happily. "Wow, honey. You're finally an author!"

Part 4 The Monk

Polymnia…sketched in the air
an image of a soundless voice,
speaking with hands and moving eyes
in a graphic picture of silence full of meaning.

~Nonnus, *Dionysiaca*, AD fifth century

twenty-two

I'M MUCH MORE COMFORTABLE at night, late at night, when the flicker of a tiny candle can illuminate an entire room. I love how at around 2 a.m. the dew begins to gently cascade down from the violet night sky, and if I hold my hand out my window, I can feel a fine mist fall against my skin. And I'm deeply in love with the sounds that only night can bring, such as those mysterious birds that chirp only in the evenings, while the wind blows through the trees a bit more in the darkness. I don't know what those birds look like. But I hear them. They sound different from the cheery birds of dawn. The evening birds give hushed, melancholic cries as they search for one another in the slivers of moonlight. I can hear them delicately hopping around on the branches of the young oak tree near my window. Right now there is just the wind and the birds. And the dry oak leaves brushing up against one another.

Maybe that's why I get most of my writing done at night. The day is for living, the night is for writing. It's not complicated, really. I can just think better at night. Thoughts come easier. Words come easier. There is a flow. Patient and smooth.

It's much quieter at night. The phone doesn't ring. The radio is off. The television is off. No sounds of traffic or of doors slamming or windows opening. There are no voices on the street. I can't even hear myself breathe. There are only my thoughts, which suddenly are inspired.

Writers are obsessed with the comings and goings of Inspiration. Who is she? Why does she go? When will she come? I often wonder if Inspiration is always with us—morning, noon, and night—but we can't always hear her in the midst of the noisy busyness that fills the world. And so we just wait for those few quiet moments in our lives when we have the time (and the patience) to listen. And then we can hear her.

This was how I wrote *Alice's Dream*. I started nearly two years ago. I was still in Berkeley. I would start writing around ten and stay up typing until the first pale shades of morning would appear—four or five in the morning, depending on the season. Night after night. Chapter by chapter.

Right now there is just the wind and the birds and Inspiration. It's a little after midnight on this warm summer night, and I'm sitting near the window working on a manuscript for a Franciscan monk. Brother Jeremiah W. I'm almost halfway finished with the project. I should be further along, I know, but I'm distracted. You see, in addition to those pleasing, inspired thoughts that can be heard only in the wee hours, there are also a few painfully ugly feelings that rear their horned heads exclusively in the nighttime as well. They are the feelings that are too heavy and too dark for the light of day.

There is a particularly ugly feeling I'm grappling with right now. I hate to admit this. I really can't stand the fact that I'm even thinking this. I wish so much that it weren't true. But it is.

I'm jealous of my two sisters.

I've never been particularly close with them. They both were the "let's call all our friends and throw a big party!" sort, while I was the more "let's just all stay in our own rooms and read!" sort. But I envy them because they're nine and ten years older than me, which means that they got to have those extra years with my mom. Those precious years. She was here for their weddings and for the births of their kids. For the late night emergency questions over the phone. But when she died, I was in college. I hadn't even started my life. She's not here to see me all grown up. She wasn't here to meet Leo. She wasn't here for our wedding, and she won't be here when we have our children someday. Who will I turn to for advice? Who will answer my questions about my husband's quirks or how to change a diaper or what to do for the flu?

I feel like a criminal. My jealousy is petty. It's ridiculous and ungrateful. But that feeling just won't go away.

twenty-three

I'LL NEVER FORGET THE FIRST BOOK I ever fell in love with: *The Story of Philosophy* by Will Durant. Nearly 600 pages. I discovered it in the school library when I was fifteen. The librarian was indulgent, allowing me to check it out every single week for two and a half more years until I graduated. It was an old copy, published in 1954 (originally published in 1926). Before I read it, it had most recently been checked out in 1962. And even though its corners were worn and some of its pages were loose and others fell out as soon I opened it (despite my efforts to tape them back in), the book was bound beautifully. It was the kind of book that looked hand-sewn, with thick damp-stained pages set unevenly—but just perfectly—within its marvelous hand-sewn, orange cloth binding.

I loved that book dearly. Outside and in. Durant's prose was fantastic. Lovely and clear. Even funny. But it wasn't his colorful explanation of free will or even his clever criticisms of Nietzsche that moved me more than any other text I've ever read. No—it was his dedication to his wife, Ariel:

TO MY WIFE

Grow strong, my comrade…that you may stand
Unshaken when I fall; that I may know
The shattered fragments of my song will come
At last to finer melody in you;
That I may tell my heart that you begin
Where passing I leave off, and fathom more.

I deeply regret not stealing that book from the library because I have yet to find that particular binding anywhere else. Now all I can find are those awful paperbacks with offensive stripes on the cover and even more offensive typesetting inside that squishes *The Story* into a measly 500 pages. Not even City Lights on Columbus Avenue, the champion of rare and wonderful books, carries my beloved clothbound edition of *The Story*. I'll have to keep looking. I suppose that this search will be one of my life's ambitions. After all, such a noble dedication deserves proper binding, doesn't it?

Dedications are a delicate matter for writers. You must decide not only who means the world to you at that particular moment that you compose the dedication but who you think will still mean the world to you once your book is published. This is why siblings rarely make the cut. The other concern is the matter of keeping your mouth shut. Sometimes it is a year or even longer from the time you type out your dedication to the time your book gets published. Such a long time for such a juicy secret! It's always hard not to tell the person receiving the dedication, but every author knows and obeys the unwritten rule: You must wait and let the person himself read it in the published book. No matter what.

I decided today, after finishing nearly half a jumbo bag of peanut M&M's at around three o'clock, that I will dedicate *Alice's Dream* to my sweet husband, Leo. Maybe it's the sugar talking, but I really believe that he is the most tender, patient husband a girl could ask for.

Wait. Stop everything. On second thought, right now he just said something really stupid.

It's almost eight in the evening, and I'm at the sink, washing our dinner dishes. Leo is standing next to me at the kitchen counter with an especially smug expression on his face.

"I can't believe you just said that to me!" I say.

"What? It's true!" he replies as he shrugs.

I'm so upset that I can't even think of anything to say to him, so I take a teacup filled with warm, soapy water and splash it at him. He ducks just in the nick of time, but the left shoulder of his shirt is wet. He doesn't say anything. He just looks at me severely. And then all of a sudden, he turns around and walks away. Perfectly unruffled. I hear him carefully shut the bathroom door and turn the bath faucet on.

"Are you getting a towel?" I call out jokingly.

No response. Several minutes go by and still nothing. He's probably just cooling off. I'm finished washing the dishes now, so I start to dry them. I look up and see Leo standing before me. He's holding the silver bathroom trash can in his arms.

"No, Leo—don't—"

But within microseconds, Leo swings the trash can back and then forth. I try to turn out of the way, but a wall of cold water crashes hard against my chest. A whole trash can full of ice-cold water. He threw it with such force that my whole body feels slapped. I stand there, stunned and soaked. The kitchen floor is covered in a huge puddle. Leo is smiling.

"Now we're even," he says.

"Even?"

Who wants to be even? I look around for something, anything. I'm so cold that my whole body is shivering, but I absolutely must get back at him. My eyes scan the kitchen counter. The soapy water has already drained, so I take the bottle of lemon liquid dish soap and squirt it against his face.

"Ahh! My eyes! You got it in my eyes!" he bellows. He rushes over to the sink to rinse his eyes with water, but I keep squirting him with the dish soap. I get his neck and his arms and his whole shirt covered in Palmolive.

"Go ahead," he mutters as he rubs his eyes. "Does it make you happy? Go ahead. I don't even care."

Without a word, I accept his challenge and grab the bag of white flour from the top cupboard. While Leo is still hunched over, trying to flush water over his stinging eyes, I douse the entire bag of flour over his head.

The flour, combined with the dish soap and water, does an outstanding job of sticking to his skin and clothes. His entire body is covered in a gummy white glue. Even his eyelashes are white. But Leo stays calm. As always. He slowly wipes the gooey flour mixture off his face and takes a long, deep breath. He looks cool and composed. He's taking this surprisingly well. Or so it seems.

Leo takes another deep breath and opens the fridge. He quietly takes out a massive jug of lemon-lime Gatorade and unscrews its lid.

He looks over at me and raises the neon-green drink high in the air but stops. He lowers the bottle, takes a big swig of the drink, and then screws the lid back on.

Just as I turn around to get a roll of paper towels for the counter, I feel cold Gatorade dripping down my shoulders and back. It's even colder than the water. And now I can feel Leo pressing his muscular body to mine in a tight, awkward embrace. He's not making up. He's smearing that gluey flour all over me. Abruptly he lets go. I turn to face him. Now we're both covered in flour. The entire kitchen is wet. The walls. The cupboards. The table. And even part of the living room is drenched, especially the corner bookshelf and most of the books.

"Now we're really even," he says coolly.

I'm livid. Enraged. Who does he think he's dealing with?

I watch as Leo walks away from me. He enters the bathroom and shuts the door. I hear him turn the shower on full blast. Unfortunately for him, he left the door unlocked.

I quietly sneak in the bathroom. I can see Leo's figure through the frosted glass sliding doors. He's washing the floury glue out of his hair. His white footprints cover the green tile floor.

"I see you," he says in his low, serious voice. "Aren't we done? Look, Julia, I don't feel like fighting anymore. Do what you're gonna do. I don't care! I just want to get cleaned up."

Without a word, I turn off the bathroom light and walk out, shutting the door behind me.

"Oh, nice! Showering in the dark! Not your best work, Julia!" he calls out. But little does he know, I'm not done yet.

I run back to the living room and grab a potted fern from the windowsill. I can still hear Leo muttering about the light. I yank the plant out from the pot and throw it in the kitchen sink. Holding the heavy terra-cotta pot in my arms, I go back to the bathroom, where Leo is still showering in darkness. I grab a chair, place it next to the shower, and stand on it. I start tossing handfuls of the potting soil on his head. Little by little. Without a single word.

"What are you doing?" he screams. "What the hell is this? More flour? Jeez, Julia! Flour is hard to wash out!"

Still I remain quiet. After a few more handfuls, I just dump the rest of the loose soil over his head and innocently say, "Want the light back on?"

After a flick of the light switch, I watch as Leo turns off the water and slides open the shower doors. His body is covered in black dirt, and his nostrils are flaring.

"You clogged the drain," he grumbles under his breath. His lips are twisted in a tight, angry frown. And so are mine. He grabs a towel from the rack and ties it around his waist. We're standing next to each other, and the only noise is the sound of our breathing, heavy and fast, mixed in with the furious grinding of our teeth. We're having a face-off.

From the corner of my eye, I catch our image in the bathroom mirror. We look like quite the pair in that reflection. My mascara has smeared down to my cheeks and my clothes are sopping wet. My newly blonde hair has twisted itself into white and gummy dreadlocks. And Leo looks as though he just stepped out of a giant mud bath. Our chests are heaving and our faces have such wild and crazed expressions that we look like children having dual tantrums. Weird, animal-like children. Leo must have seen it too, because he's starting to smile again. And now we're both laughing uncontrollably.

"What were we even fighting about?" I ask.

140

Leo pauses for a few moments and shrugs. "I can't remember," he says, "I think it was something you said."

"Really?" I ask. "I can't even remember."

"Well, maybe we'd better clean this up," he says, his muddy arms around me.

"Yeah," I reply as I kiss him with my floury lips. "I'll get the towels."

twenty-four

LATELY I CAN'T HELP BUT FEEL as though I'm in a literary limbo. Am I an author yet? It's strange to know that *Alice's Dream* is completely out of my hands now, with still yet another year left before publication. I'm just not so sure where that leaves me.

To make matters worse, I'm afraid I'm growing more weary of ghostwriting with every passing season. I'm sick of hiding behind someone else's name. I want to come out from the shadows, but I'm afraid. I suppose I have to be patient for a little while longer. The promise of getting published keeps me going.

There's something rather spellbinding about the thought of having my name in print instead of hiding behind someone else's. It's as if my name, my very identity, will take on a special permanence somehow. A place in history and one in the future as well. Yet sometimes I wonder if I really am afraid of not being remembered.

Would being forgotten really be so awful? What's so special about gaining a place in the collective memory anyway? In the big picture, does it really matter?

But I can't even ask these questions without my eyes widening with worry. The truth is, I really do care. Maybe all writers do. Maybe all writers are mesmerized by the notion that their names (along with their ideas) will remain in the world long after they themselves depart. It's enticing, really. Life eternal.

In ancient Greek mythology, a Muse could make or break a writer. It was believed that if you were a writer or a philosopher or an artist and none of the Muses sang to you, then you would be erased from the pages of history and forgotten forever. Wiped out. Just like that. And so, shrines were built, and milk and honey were offered to the Muses in exchange for not only divine inspiration but also an eternal home in the collective memory. In fact, a writer who was said to be inspired by a Muse was held in such high esteem in ancient Greece that his reputation rivaled that of a priest. Yes, inspiration and remembrance went hand in hand for the ancient Greeks. Muses decided precisely who would receive the highly respected gifts of creativity and artistic innovation and who wouldn't. For the ancient Greeks, each and every pursuit of art or science depended solely on the Muses' discretion.

And yet the Muses seem to be lighthearted about their responsibilities; They're often depicted singing and dancing in a celebratory circle at the foot of Mount Olympus. All of them wear smiles and looks of cheer. All, that is, except for one.

Polyhymnia, the Muse of meditation, is the most serious of the nine Muses. There are a few different artworks found of Polyhymnia in which she's alone, including one Roman mosaic dated AD 240 that's in Luxembourg. She's always portrayed in the same way. Thoughtful and brooding. She wears a doleful expression on her delicate face, which is often veiled. Some artists have her cross her arms or lean her pointed chin against her hand to suggest her contemplative nature, while others have her press a single finger to her lips. After all, Polyhymnia is the Muse of meditation, the sacred, and the sublime. I myself find that I save little time for the sublime these days.

I'm too caught up in cycles of busyness and exhaustion in a frenzied, white-rabbit sort of way. And when I'm not writing, I'm collapsed on the bed until some inspiring thought for a manuscript wakes me up and forces me into the cycle all over again.

I had a dream last night. I can't stop thinking about it. It plays again and again in my head like a movie. I was walking by myself through a lovely green valley. The kind you'd see in some small, faraway village in the countryside or even in a children's storybook. It felt calm at first. Peaceful, even. The sun, warm and gentle, felt good on my skin. The long afternoon shadows swept across the tall grasses so that the green was cool and inviting. I was listening to the wind softly whisper against the grass when I heard someone crying.

They were loud, pitiful wails that sounded like they belonged to a hurt child, and so I began to search. I ran ahead but there was no one. No matter which direction I looked, there was no one but me. I stood there completely still. The mournful cry sounded close. Very close. As if it were right behind me. I turned around but no one was there. And so I knelt down and began to search through the tall field, cutting through the dense blades of grass with my hands. My fingers burned but still I searched. The sound was louder now, and I knew I was close. I could tell that it was a little girl crying. I searched deeper in the grass, and finally I found her.

I couldn't tell what she looked like, except that she wasn't more than six or seven. She was sitting on the ground with the tall grasses towering over her. Her head was down and her arms were wrapped around her bent knees. All I could see was the curtain of dark blonde hair over her face.

"Shh, shh, don't cry, little girl," I said softly. "It's OK, I'll help you. Are you lost? What's your name?"

But the girl's cries only grew louder and more distressed.

"Are you hurt? What's wrong?" I asked.

The child's head dropped even lower, and I could see the sides of her arms glisten with wetness from her tears.

"My mommy…"

"Yes? Where's your mommy?"

"She's gone."

The wind sang in a low hum through the grasses around us.

"Gone where? Maybe we can find her. Here, take my hand."

"No," she said, "you don't understand. Mommy is gone forever."

She then looked up, as if to help me understand. The curtain of blonde hair parted and I gasped because I finally recognized her.

She was me.

And as soon as I realized it, she was gone, and I was back in bed. Awake. My pillow completely wet.

twenty-five

KATERINA, MY LONGTIME friend, asked me an uncomfortable question yesterday over the phone. After exchanging pleasantries about our latest afflictions, as good friends always do, she asked me point blank, "Now that *Alice's Dream* is done, what's your next book going to be?" I cleared my throat while I tried to think up a reply. But Katerina didn't stop there. She continued, "I just read *The Da Vinci Code*. It was good. Really good. You should write something like that. Some theory about something in history…but about Egypt."

"Why Egypt?" I burst out.

"Egypt is so mysterious," Katerina replied.

And I couldn't help but be offended. Who was she to choose the topic of my next book? Egypt? Was she kidding me? Didn't she realize the pain, the agony, a writer goes through before she decides on a project that's worthy of years of her work? How dare she! Or, more accurately, how dare I...

The truth is, I already do have something in mind for my next manuscript. And the deeper truth is, I'm terrified to go through with it.

Right now I'm spending the weekend at St. Anthony Retreat in a hidden mountain town, Three Rivers. Brother Jeremiah invited me here so that we would have a quiet space to discuss the project. Deep in the lush green heart of the Sierras, Three Rivers is a half hour east of Visalia and a few minutes away from Sequoia National Park.

The Franciscans have owned and operated St. Anthony Retreat ever since 1954, when it was commissioned. Several different religious groups "come to the mountain" but it's the Franciscans who love and care for this secluded place, day in, day out.

Brother Jeremiah W. is a young, handsome man. Much younger and much more handsome than I expected. Although I suppose what I expected was something closer to the short, round Friar Tuck from Robin Hood (the cartoon version, of course). But Brother Jeremiah W. is tall and thin and has a pensive look about him.

He also wears a short beard; I suspect it's because he wants to look older. And he is dressed like the other Franciscan monks here: a dark brown habit tied with a simple white rope at the waist. At the ends of the rope are several knots. But on his feet are white Nike sneakers, not sandals. He casually explains the sneakers: "We might go into town."

Brother Jeremiah W. is the first expert I've had who isn't concerned with the project or how it progresses. Mister X warned me about this: "The guy is a philosopher, but he doesn't even know it," he said. "Just try to see what you can draw out of him. You know, for a *feel-good* sort of book."

Three Rivers really is a soothing, marvelous place. The air smells crisp and fresh. And everything is green. Even in the middle of summer. I spot a small family of deer silently flitting in and out of the tall evergreens. In fact, just about everything out here is silent. Even Brother Jeremiah W. We're hiking down this windy trail before he has to be back for evening services. He walks lightly. Carefully. His arms swing gently at his sides, and his brow is furrowed in a preoccupied, contemplative sort of way. He's been lost in thought for nearly fifteen minutes during our little walk together. Pondering.

Usually silence between me and another person makes me uneasy, but with the monk I feel strangely at peace. Or at least it does at first, before my brain goes in overdrive. His thoughtfulness intrigues me just as much as it puts me at ease. I can't help but wonder about this man. *What is he thinking? Is he praying? Does he sense that I don't pray as often as I should? Should I say something? Should I tell him a joke? Are monks allowed to hear jokes?*

And then I remember. *Of course.* I feel so foolish. I remember reading in a pamphlet that this is supposed to be one of those silent retreats. I was assured by the retreat director that whispering would be OK, just as long as it didn't interfere with someone's "quiet time for the sacred," which must be respected. No blabbing. No gossiping. No chattering on and on. Something about "listening to the self within" or something meaningful and weighty like that.

The monk looks up at me briefly and smiles. Now his silence feels more natural. More understandable. It has meaning. And so we continue our wordless walk together on the mountain trails under the pale summer sky.

Our trail soon splits into a fork, and he leads me up the narrow path to the left. The message on a small carved stone in the grass tells me that this leads to the Stations of the Cross. A few minutes later, we reach it.

The first station is a simple stone statue of Jesus with his hands clasped, his wrists bound in front of him. Another small stone sign stands at his feet. It reads, "Jesus is condemned to death." Bits of Jesus' robes are chipped, along with most of his fingers. Brother Jeremiah W. bows his head for a moment in meditation. His eyes are closed and his lips move to a silent prayer that only he knows. The wind is blowing a little and rustling leaves in the tangle of branches above us. I bow my head as well and try to remember some prayers of my own, but I can't stop watching him. He's so serene.

He can't be more than twenty-eight, I finally decide. Maybe thirty-one at the most. I hear him whisper, "Amen," and we move on to the second station. It's a few yards down, just behind a pair of towering white spruces. The monk stands thoughtfully in front of the next statue, one of Jesus bearing a cross on his back. But before Brother Jeremiah W. can bow his head, we're interrupted by ground-shaking thunder. Lightning soon follows and I wonder if its immense flash could be God taking a picture of us. All at once the sky splits open, and we're caught in the middle of a summer storm.

The rain pours down on us, and we both run as fast as we can back down toward the trail. But now it's just a slippery, muddy mess, and everything looks the same under the rainfall. We're both soaked. My hair is stuck to my head, and even the monk's heavy robes are drenched. More thunder sounds and God takes another picture.

Brother Jeremiah W. points toward another trail. "I think that this is a shortcut!" he shouts.

"I'll follow you!" I call out beneath the downpour. The monk runs ahead and I try my best to keep up. He takes a path that looks like it's been forgotten for some time. Giant manzanita bushes cover most of it, but we run down the path anyway.

I feel my arms getting scraped and whipped by the manzanita's gnarled, crooked branches. I take a sharp corner down a slope, lose my balance, and tumble down the hill through shrubs and old leaves. A bewildered rabbit jumps across me. I look up for a hand to help me, but the monk is out of sight. He's too far ahead.

The rain continues to fall. I start to feel the sting of my scrapes as I stagger upright. My feet slip and down I fall again. But this time a sturdy hand pulls me up.

"Are you OK?" Brother Jeremiah W. asks.

"Just covered in mud," I wearily reply. "I can walk."

"I'm sorry. I should have stayed closer," he says as he gently wipes the mud off my face. "We're almost there."

And he was right. A few yards down, we finally find what looks to be a gardener's shed.

"It's dusty inside but at least we're out of that rain," he says. "We'll wait it out. It's just a little flash flood. It'll be over soon."

We sit down together and watch the rest of the storm crash down. The sound of the thunder echoes through the wooden sides of the shed, shaking them a bit.

I look over at the monk and he shrugs. He says, "Looks like God's pretty busy today," and then smiles.

Even though the sky is falling all around us, the air feels warm and lovely. And despite my new bumps and bruises, I think I love summer storms. The monk seems to be mesmerized by the storm too. His white Nikes are all muddied up now, as well as most of his robe from when he helped me up. His face is relaxed and I can see his eyes focused on the tree in front of us, as if gazing upon it brings him peace.

I can't stand it any longer. I have to ask him.

"Why did you become a monk?" I blurt out. "It's just that...you're so *young*."

Brother Jeremiah W. leans an elbow against one knee and rests his chin in his palm. He sighs and I can tell that his thought process is becoming more and more like a chess game. Finally he looks at me with a serene expression in his eyes and says, "Faith is trust. It is a trust that is discerned by your soul and *not* your senses. The soul knows no age. It just is. For the record, however, I am thirty-eight."

I should be stunned but instead I'm just more curious. "But why?" I press on. "Why a monk? Can't you just be spiritual while living a regular life? Why do you want to isolate yourself?"

Now Jeremiah answers quickly. "First you must ask, What is spirituality? For me, it's devoting a major part of yourself to a higher purpose, a Higher Power. And living your life as such." He pauses for a few moments as he collects the rest of his thoughts and then says, "It's a way of tuning out all the noise around you so that all you hear is nothing but inspiration. Divine inspiration."

I couldn't have dreamed up a better reply. I nod as I try to digest what he just said. And the monk asks, "You like flowers?"

"Sure, of course."

"See," he begins, "it was as if I threw armfuls of wildflowers up in the air one day, and then God handed me the most beautiful bouquet the next day. I just knew. Just like you, right?"

"Me?" I ask in surprise.

"Didn't you always know that you wanted to be a writer?"

"Oh. Yeah, I mean—yes, I suppose so. Ever since I can remember."

"Tell me something. Do you write anything of your own? Or do you only do ghostwriting for poor souls like me?"

His tranquil eyes are smiling at me and I feel completely at ease. The thunder has stopped for good, I think. The only sound is of the rain happily splashing down against the earth, like a child stomping through his first puddle on the way home from school. I've never discussed my personal writing with an expert before. Not ever. But then again, no other expert has ever asked about it.

I take a few moments to gather my thoughts, but I already know what I want to say. I want to tell him about my mother and how she passed away just a few years ago. I want to tell him how I miss her terribly and how recently I've felt deeply compelled to write her story. And I want to tell him how difficult it is. How painful. And I do. I tell him everything.

He listens with a patient ear as he cups his hand over mine.

I say, "It's just that reconciling experience with imagination is a frightening process. Right now I wish I could write about my mom's story…" I can hear my voice trail off as my thoughts cloud up.

Brother Jeremiah W. nods and then asks, "So you don't want to wait? Let things settle a bit in your heart?"

"I don't want to forget anything!" I reply, ashamed of the desperation in my voice. "I'm so afraid of forgetting her. But I'm even more afraid of exploiting her story. I keep asking myself, again and again…how can I tell her story without exploiting it?" I wish I could rewind our conversation and take back my question. "I'm sorry," I say, "I didn't mean to rattle on like that. I don't usually talk about my personal work with experts…"

But the monk just shakes his head and smiles at me. "We're all in this together. Trying to figure out life. We all have dreams. We all have wounds. Maybe the journey of life is really a journey of healing. And maybe the only way you can truly heal your wounds is to have trust in their meaning. Just be honest when you write. Have trust in your words."

The rain slows to a quiet drizzle as soon as he finishes speaking. It's as if God himself, proud of his pupil, wants to listen to the wise young monk.

Brother Jeremiah W.'s words leave me feeling more confident in myself and my writing. And I can't help but wish for a notepad or my laptop computer to write down the downpour of thoughts flooding my head right now. I feel lucky to have been trapped with such an empathetic listener. Even if he is too young to be a monk.

"I suppose there are two types of people in the world," I begin. "There are those who live life by appreciating the present moment…and those who don't. Well, to be honest I never used to suppose that at all until a chef explained it that way."

I look over at him and see him nod. His eyes are steady, wise. But then I see something peculiar. I catch a glimpse of his hands, clasped in front of himself. Something is strange about his nails. They're bitten and chewed. Ragged, even.

And now I finally can see the nervous-looking young man sitting next to me. His eyes are not fixed in contemplation but searching, always searching, for some truth that his heart can believe in.

He clears his throat and says, "One could make that argument, yes."

"Wouldn't you?" I ask.

"It's worth considering. That much is certain. However, if there really were only two types of people in this big world we live in, I think you already hit the hammer on the nail."

"I did?"

"Of course," the monk replies. "You said yourself that you're afraid of forgetting. Perhaps that's the key."

"What do you mean?"

"Well, maybe what makes people different from one another is how scared they are of their memories. Or how brave. Some people, like you, spend their days longing to remember, while others do everything they can to forget."

And then, as if to punctuate his last word, he quietly stands up and walks into the rain.

twenty-six

THE SCARIEST PART IS THAT I don't even know what to say. What *can* you say when your husband is wearing only a towel and standing directly across from you while his blood is just boiling with rage? Is saying nothing best? Do you just get down on your knees with your head down and shamelessly beg for forgiveness? Do you play it cool and pretend to ignore him as you hold your head high and walk the other way? Or maybe you just engage in a heated battle of intense eye-contact combat and try to weaken his resolve. I haven't got a clue. So I'm just going to do what I know best: offer my bottom lip a little and look up at him while I offer the most soulful and sad puppy-dog eyes I can muster.

Damn. It didn't work.

You see, I opened the front door a minute ago, but he's still not saying a word. He's just standing there. Silent. And stoic. Like the statue of David, standing tall and focused in our doorway. And furious. Definitely furious. Maybe steamed up. Or burned up. Actually, I think he's just plain mad right now. Just a good old-fashioned, can't-stand-me mad. His hands are clenched into tighter-than-tight fists at his sides. He's not saying anything, but I know he's upset. I can see it in his steady stare and the tight curl of his lips. I can hear it in the air rushing in and out of his nostrils. But despite what my husband, Leo, thinks, it's not my fault. Really, it isn't. I blame the red toenails.

That's where it all started. I remember that evening perfectly. The Santa Barbara sky had just been briefly lit by a lustrous, dazzling orb of gold as it blushed its way into another sunset, until a cast of various shocking pinks swept away the clouds to illuminate a champagne-colored moon. I was thirteen.

On an evening in September, an Indian summer was passing through. Everything outside seemed to swim in a warm bath of hazy, lazy tranquility. Far more than just a warm spell, the sweltering heat swept everyone into an eyelid-drooping lull. It was too hot to work or rush or even play. All you could do was surrender to the warm winds that blew in from the south. Even the black and bluebirds could barely sashay their way through the air currents. After all, Indian summers demand collective stillness and repose.

But not in our house. Under my parents' Spanish-tiled roof, chaos was always in season. The blades of the ceiling fan spun and pulsated at their highest setting and shook the kitchen ceiling in an endless series of rhythmic thumps. A small portable fan hummed along in the background, and a caged canary sitting on the window sill interrupted every other moment or so with low, rolling chirps that made a frenzied sort of song. But over everything, an emphatic, thunderous voice boomed through the summer air.

Dad was arguing with Mom at the dinner table. Again. My two older sisters and I started clearing the table like those tiny automated wooden people in Swiss clocks. That was what we did whenever a fight occurred—stay out of the way and look busy. It didn't matter that we weren't even done eating or still wondering whether there was dessert. Over the clink of the glasses and silverware, Dad's voice blew from our kitchen through the walls and out to the whole world.

"Jesus Christ, Geneviève—how many years have we been married?"

Directly across from him, her hands folded patiently, Mom just sat there. Unruffled, she murmured softly, "Please don't take His name in vain, Adam."

"Oh, don't go pulling that holier-than-thou crap on me. Not tonight!"

Mom sighed her little sigh and straightened the lace tablecloth.

"You just don't get it," Dad began in his most sarcastic tone. "We've been married for more than twenty years, and you just don't get it!"

"I just thought—" Mom began in a tiny voice.

"What? You just thought what?"

Mom stayed quiet.

"No, tell me! You thought what? That after twenty-two years I would suddenly *love* mustard on my sandwich?"

Mustard. Yes, mustard. They were fighting about mustard.

It didn't take much to irritate him, but mustard was always a hot-button issue with my father. And he was especially suspicious of her French cuisine, as if it were some covert operation left over from WWII. "I don't care if it is called a *crêpe*. I'm not eating those pancakes!" The mere notion of eating fancy cheeses or ratatouille drizzled with olive oil or even dipping a warm, toasty baguette into a luscious yolk of an egg left him weak in the knees. And the stomach. Yet perhaps Dad's inexplicable fear of vinaigrette was legendary in our house. "Vinegar and oil again, Gen? Where's the God-damn-Thousand-Island, for God's sake?"

Of course, Dad was a steak-and-potatoes sort of guy. The All-American. A real guy's guy. He did his best to confront and conquer anything that might, in some possible way, jeopardize his masculinity. Whether it was shouting across the street to teenage boys he didn't know ("Hey, kid, you'd better take that earring out before I yank it out with my pliers, 'cause you look like a fag"), or insisting that he go motorcycle riding in the desert early on Thanksgiving, Christmas, and Easter Morning ("Gen, *all* the guys are going. I can't just not go. It's not an option. Period").

Yet surprisingly, he does actually eat mustard. And often doesn't even realize it. Unless he sees it. Once he spots a little yellow Gulden's or grainy Dijon dribbling down the sides of his bread crust, it's over. That's it. Lunch is over. He'll slam the sandwich down on the plate and take a big, dramatic gulp of water to cleanse his delicate palate before he reprimands the negligent and inconsiderate server of the mustard.

"Do you *like* doing this to me?" he said abruptly. "Do you think this is funny?"

Dad looked away just long enough for Mom to roll her eyes before she could softly say, "I'm sorry, honey. I just forget."

"Well, just make me another one. *Without* mustard, OK?"

"OK, love…"

I wanted to yell at her. "Stand up for yourself!" I wanted to scream. But like my two sisters, I stayed quiet as I shoved the knives and forks into the plastic cage of the dishwasher. Sometimes it's best to just keep your mouth shut. And play it safe. Or else Dad might switch gears and throw some wrath our way. We had to pretend not to hear and try to forget about it. And I did. Most of the time. But later that night, it was different. I would learn something special. I would learn that Mom wasn't a pushover, after all. She was instead a master of timing.

From her smooth olive skin to her almond-shaped eyes, it was obvious that Mom was born and raised along the songlike coast of the French Riviera. Having moved to America in the 1950s, her accent had all but disappeared. But she still walked and talked as if she were the girl from Ipanema. Patient. Serene. And supremely carefree. Mom had what all Frenchwomen have: natural sophistication mixed with effortless style, a twist of delicate self-possession, and just a splash of chicanery. Well, maybe more than a splash of it…maybe the whole damn bottle. Down to the last drop. She knew better than anyone that you don't have to argue to win an argument. You just have to have the last laugh.

Long after the dishes were put away and Dad had finished drinking his nightly mug of hot tea (no wimpy teacups and only black tea, of course, nothing "fruity"), I saw Mom gliding down the hallway with the subtle smile that she got when something absolutely wonderful was about to happen. From around the corner I spied, but all I saw was her opening a top cupboard in the bathroom and then shoving something little in the pocket of her fuzzy pink bathrobe. But what she couldn't hide was her little laugh when I asked her what she was doing. "Julia," she said with a sly look, "I'm just going to have a little fun…with Dad."

"But Mom, he's already asleep. He's going riding early tomorrow, remember?"

Mom shook her head and practically floated down the hall to their bedroom. A thunderous snore resonated from the room, and I wondered if Dad's inhale was worse than his exhale. Mom raised her finger to her lips. "Shh." I didn't bother telling her that the house could fall down and Dad still wouldn't wake up. I just stood there, half-hidden behind their bedroom door. And waited.

"I didn't tuck in the sheets," she whispered. "They're loose." She giggled a little as she carefully lifted the rose-patterned sheet at the end of the bed and exposed Dad's unsuspecting feet. They were a creamy porcelain white since Dad never, ever went anywhere without socks and shoes, even in the house ("What if there was an emergency?"). Even his soles were soft and smooth-looking. Mom pulled the bottom of the sheet up to his ankles.

"So he doesn't like mustard," she murmured. And then, in one swift motion, she reached down in her robe pocket and pulled out a tiny bottle of Maybelline's cherry-red nail polish. It was called Shangri-La Red.

"Well…*this* is what I think of mustard," she added.

Dad's toes wiggled a little, as if they sensed danger approaching. And his arm twitched but the snoring continued in the darkness.

Mom worked fast. She twisted the cap off the nail polish, and within seconds, each of Dad's toenails was painted a color that Vegas showgirls would envy. "There now, isn't that pretty?" she asked as she fanned them dry.

I stood there with my jaw open. I was in awe. Never had I been so proud of Mom. It was genius. When Dad gets heated up, there's nothing you can do or say to pacify his anger. It doesn't matter who's right and who's wrong. The more you argue, the louder he gets. And louder and louder. And louder still. All you can do is what Mom did. Patiently wait for him to cool off, and then, like a cat who's been stalking her prey, wait for precisely the right moment to pounce.

Once Dad's toenails had dried to an undeniably feminine shade of red, Mom's almond eyes sparkled as she whispered, "Now, we wait for morning!" I nodded and left for my bedroom. It was tough to fall asleep. I was so excited and nervous. I didn't know how Dad would react, but I just loved being in on Mom's trick.

The next morning went smoother than anticipated. And quieter. At seven, the sunlight was already beaming through the open windows as warm breezes poured in. Mom was in the kitchen, busy with waffle batter (waffles were Dad's favorite), while Dad had just stepped into the shower.

"He's not mad?" I asked her.

Mom handed me the bowl and the electric mixer. "Hmm? Will you beat the egg whites for me, darling?"

My heart dropped. "But Mom, what about the…*you know*…"

"Just beat them until the whites are stiff. Maybe two minutes," she replied calmly.

"But what about Dad?" I pressed on. I couldn't understand why she wasn't nervous. Had the joke gone awry? Had it flopped?

"Oh, *that*," she replied. "Well, it should be just about time. Follow me."

Mom walked over to the bathroom, where the sound of Dad's shower could still be heard. She knocked on the door a couple of times. "Adam?"

"Yeah? What is it?" Dad's sleepy voice rumbled.

Mom looked at me and tried to muffle her giggles. "Is everything OK?" she asked coolly.

"What? Why?" he hollered.

"Look down."

"What?"

"Just look down."

Through the wall we heard a loud thud. Dad's ignorant bliss ended when he saw his surprise pedicure. And he most definitely did not think it was so pretty. I held my breath and clasped my hands together nervously as I waited for fury to ensue.

Amazingly, however, Dad stayed quiet. A brief moan followed by a long sigh could be heard through the bathroom door, but that was it. No yelling or screaming. Not a word. It was as if the wind had been knocked out of him.

Just then, Mom decided to twist the knife of revenge in a little further. "Breakfast is ready, honey. Oh, and by the way…in case you were wondering, I hid the nail polish remover."

Another sigh. "I'll be down in a second," he said quietly.

And that, decidedly, was that.

By the time Dad came into the kitchen, breakfast was on the table. Mom's knack for dressing an everyday table was unmistakably French. A grand lace tablecloth set the stage for a chipped pitcher-turned-vase filled with freshly cut pink roses from the garden, freshly squeezed orange juice, a dishful of elegantly curled strips of bacon, and an array of perfectly sliced strawberries in between every other round of kiwi. The plates were warmed and the glasses chilled. The jar of warmed maple syrup, which stood next to a stack of fluffy waffles, smelled divine. Yet something peculiar stood out. Next to Dad's place setting was a gravy boat. Complete with a serving spoon, it was filled to the brim with something odd and bright yellow.

When Dad sat down to eat, he grimaced a little. I watched as he took a big breath and closed his eyes. "I'm sorry, Gen," he blurted out in a panic. "OK? I'm sorry!" And just like that, Mom smiled sweetly at him and promptly took the gravy boat filled with mustard off the table and replaced it with a bottle of nail polish remover. The game was over. She had won.

So I was trained by the best. Mom was the undisputed master of the classic, though subtle, housewife's revenge techniques. Maybe she inspired me. Or maybe she just influenced how I handle conflicts.

One thing's for sure—I can't tell any of this to Leo. He's too mad right now. Much too mad. And, truth be told, I'm still learning the charming intricacies of his behavior. And maybe, just maybe, I'm possibly...hypothetically...still trying to test Leo to see how many buttons I can push before he loses his temper. Doesn't everyone do that?

We've been married for a few years now. Just a block or two past Newlywed Lane but several thousand miles from the land of Comfortable Coupledom. We met in college. UC Berkeley. Otherwise known affectionately as Cal. And sometimes known not so affectionately as the school where the kids who received painful rejection letters from snooty Stanford University go. Of course, they would never, ever admit to that. Instead, they flock to the Berkeley campus, proudly wearing yellow or blue "Fuck Stanford" T-shirts.

Leo's parents divorced the same year my mom passed away. By the time we met, we both were dealing with new and confusing dynamics of a wounded family, as well as spending more-than-ever-before time with one newly single parent. As a result, it was a comfort for us both to be with someone who understood what it meant to hear, "I miss the way my family was *before*."

Once we got married, we moved away from the East Bay, traveling over the I-80 bridge to the neighborhood of North Beach in San Francisco. Just half a block from the Gothic twin-towered Church of St. Francis of Assisi. We turned out to be the sort of newlyweds who like to hold hands on the sofa when we watch TV at night, smile sweetly at each other when we wake up in the morning, and fight like cats and dogs in between.

I guess that brings us back to now. And I guess I thought that if I spent enough time entertaining those rambling thoughts in my head that Leo's anger would melt away and all would be forgiven. But he's still mad. Still glaring at me. Still making me feel guilty for what I did. Still wearing only that blue towel with the little yellow ducks on it. But really, it should be me. I should be the one who's too mad for words. After all, I was the one who had to listen to him snap at me earlier this morning.

That was when it started.

We both had just woken up and Leo rolled over toward me and said in between a double yawn, "So, do you want to go out to breakfast with me?"

"Honey," I replied, "I still don't feel well. I was up till 5 a.m. with this migraine."

"That's OK," he said. "I'll just get something on my way out. Maybe at that new place down the street."

I watched him as he cheerfully got out of bed. I was stunned that he showed no concern for his wife's well-being. After a few long seconds of biting my tongue, I blurted out, "Sweetheart, do you think you could pick up something for me too?"

Leo looked at me quizzically before replying, "Why? There's plenty of things you can make in the fridge. I'm gonna go take a shower. Then I'm going to go check out that new place down the street and have French toast. It's my only day off this week—I need fresh air."

"But I really don't feel well, honey. This migraine is driving me crazy."

"Is my white polo shirt clean? I was thinking about wearing either that one or the navy. But I really like that white one. I think it makes me look more buff."

"What?"

"My white polo."

"You care more about your stupid clothes than the fact that your wife is trying to get through the worst migraine of her life!"

"OK, OK. There's eggs. You could make eggs. Or toast or oatmeal," he said as he walked out of the bedroom.

"But I don't feel well," I repeated. "Can't you pick up something for me?"

"Why do you always get so dramatic?" he asked. "Have you even looked in the fridge yet?"

"But—"

"Look," he said in his stern voice, "just relax, don't get worked up. It's just a headache."

It was barely nine in the morning, and already my blood was boiling. It was a Sunday and I knew that all Leo had planned was a Kings game on TV that evening. The migraine was getting worse by the second. My head was throbbing and a sharp, piercing pain had found a home behind my eyes. All I wanted to do was curl up in my bathrobe and stay in bed. But I really was hungry.

"Don't you even *care*?" I asked. But the reply was the sound of the bathroom door closing and the shooting spray of the shower turning on.

Of course, things didn't end there. It was as if a strange little light flickered on in my head. Notions of birthright and red nail polish floated around my brain, along with a little voice with a French accent telling me not to get mad, but to get even.

I had to act fast. Leo's showers usually took ten minutes, and then he took another five for shaving. I rushed down the hall to Leo's closet and opened the white sliding doors. Leo was a notoriously disorganized, and forgetful guy, but this closet was immaculate. He really did love his clothes. I think I'm the only one in the universe who knows that his secret pastime is putting together perfectly matching outfits. His dress shirts were hung ever so carefully. Color coordinated, of course. Stripes together. Solids separate. Winter wardrobe in the back. Spring in the front. And his sock and boxer drawer was arranged just so. Even his folded jeans and khakis seemed unusually similar to the display table at J. Crew. Goose bumps crawled up my arms as I felt like an intruder in his fashion sanctuary. But the clock was ticking, and I knew what I had to do.

So I took a big gulp of a breath and grabbed as many pressed shirts and slacks and wool sweaters as I could. Holding the enormous pile in my arms, braced only by my chin, I scurried back to the bedroom and over to my closet and stuffed everything inside. I made thirteen trips altogether. Every pair of shorts, shoes, underwear, socks. Every single thread of clothing. Work clothes. Gym clothes. Swim trunks. Everything.

I was running out of room in my own closet. Now I was stuffing his clothes into desk drawers, bureau drawers, kitchen cupboards—any space I could find. Some of his scarves were stashed in my bathrobe pocket. Even the dirty clothes in his hamper were tucked away under the skirt of our bed.

My migraine had long been forgotten—I was focused. Methodical, even. Trivial revenge was in my blood. I could feel it.

Finally, after ten minutes, Leo's closet was bare. Just a few meager hangers were left rocking back and forth on the bar. I was so proud of myself. Unexpectedly, I heard the shower turn off. I ran back to our bedroom, jumped on the bed, slid under the covers, and waited. And waited. And waited.

Then I heard the bathroom door open. I could hear Leo's usual bouncy stomp to his closet.

"Julia?" he called out. "What have you done?"

I pretended to be sleeping. I knew it was a useless bid for more time, but it was all I could think of. Closed eyes. Slowed breathing. It wasn't me. I've just been here the whole time. Sleeping. I felt drops of water on my face. I pretended to wake up with a start. Leo was standing directly over me, still dripping wet and wearing only a blue towel and holding a hanger. His face wore his classic "I'm annoyed and you're wasting my time" expression.

"Oh hi, honey," I said. "How was your shower?"

"What the *fuck* have you done with my clothes?" he roared like some cranky lion with a tangled mane.

He didn't have to get that *mad. They're just clothes*, I thought. And an even more devilish plan entered my head.

"I threw them away. Every last thing."

"What?" he screamed. His face went white and he braced himself against the wall.

"Don't be so dramatic," I said. "They're just clothes."

"You…threw them…*all*…away?"

"Yup. Downstairs. In the dumpster."

He grabbed his keys in one hand, his cell phone in the other, and headed for the door. Fear showed in his green eyes. It wasn't a surprise. Our apartment building's dumpsters tend to evoke nausea and repulsion. They're always too full, with garbage bags torn open and spilling out of them. Not to mention the staggering mountain of pizza boxes and decomposing leftovers that accumulate right in front of them. Not your ideal welcome mat for a building's entrance.

But before I could say anything else, Leo was gone. I could hear his bare footsteps pound as he raced down the stairwell. Never mind that he had on only a towel. Never mind that it was nine in the morning and our elderly neighbor, Ms. Starks, was usually outside by now, hunting for a *San Francisco Chronicle* orphan on the front stairs.

I pulled the covers up over me. *Good*, I thought. *He can use a scare. They're just clothes. Am I going too far? Nah…*

The phone rang. Caller ID said it was Leo, but I waited a good three rings before picking up. Partly because I thought it would be funny. And partly because I hadn't a clue what to say to him.

"Hello?"

"They're not here."

170

"Leo?"

"They're not here, Julia. They're *not* here!" Leo shouted, but his voice trembled a little at the end, and I just couldn't resist.

"Are you sure?" I asked. "Look under the boxes in the second dumpster. A big cardboard box. I put everything under that."

There was a short pause. "I see the box," he said. "A keyboard box?"

"Yeah," I replied, "that's the one. Just look underneath that." It was a safe bet. There are *always* boxes in that one. It was the recycle bin.

"OK," he said timidly, "I'm looking under the box. And I don't see the clothes!"

"Oh," I said as calmly as I could, "that's odd."

"What? I can't believe you did this. You went too far this time, Julia. Too far!"

"Well, maybe it's another box then. I definitely put them under a box in the dumpster."

"Julia, I'm looking through everything—they're not here!"

"Hmm, then I guess somebody stole them."

Leo was hyperventilating now. I heard him mutter a little in between the short breaths.

"Relax," I said. "Don't worry."

"How the hell can I relax, Julia? You let someone steal all my clothes!"

"Well, there is a bright side to this," I said.

"Oh yeah? And what the hell would that be?"

I took a few moments and finally said, "At least you'll know who stole everything. Just wait and watch and look at what the other tenants are wearing! He'll be easy to spot in your white polo! Doesn't it have your monogram?"

And that brings us back to now. Back to the miserable, dreadful, dire moment of now. Just a minute after Leo hung up on me and started his walk back up four flights of stairs in that ridiculous duck towel. And just seconds after I opened the front door to find nothing but fury staring right back at me.

And still the questions remain: What do I say? What magical words can slow down and soothe an irate husband? Was there some magic spell the priest forgot to hand over to me on my wedding day? Some fairy dust? A secret handshake? Anything?

I take a step toward him, and he takes a step back, as if I were going to hit him with a red-hot poker.

"I'm..." I begin but I can't finish. I don't know what to say. I hate being in trouble.

But I must admit that I had no regrets about what I had done until now. Until this very second. In fact, I was sort of enjoying myself. Revenge seemed so glamorous. So grown-up. I felt like I was doing something Mom would have done. But seeing Leo so upset has smacked me with a dose of reality. He's really nothing like my father. Leo is a much more patient, easygoing, go-with-the-flow, doesn't-raise-his-voice-except-as-a-last-resort kind of guy. *Maybe I did take it too far*, I think. *Maybe I overreacted. And maybe...just maybe...I was a tad dramatic.*

And seeing Leo's furrowed brow and his scowl makes me wish I had never even woken up this morning. Or at the very least, it makes me wish I could rewind time and just argue with him, like any normal, good-natured wife would do.

And then the perfect words float into my head and fly out of my mouth: "I'm so sorry, sweetie. I didn't throw your clothes away. I just hid everything in my closet. Everything's here."

I'm not sure which part of what I said made Leo feel better. I'd like to think it was the "I'm so sorry" part, but it wasn't until I said "Everything's here" that Leo's face began to relax.

"Everything's still here?" he asks in his smallest voice.

"Yes, everything," I reassure him.

Even Leo's shoulders loosen up, as if he'd just finished a thousand-round bout in the boxing ring. He takes a deep breath and walks over to my closet. I watch as he slides the mirrored door open and sees his business suits hung, carefully squished up in the corner next to my mint-green cocktail dress and polka-dotted pullover.

Leo smiles that same smile that I first fell in love with.

"And my shoes?" he asks. "What about my shoes?"

I lift up the skirt of our queen-size bed to reveal his sneakers, loafers, and flip-flops peeking out. Leo starts to laugh and puts his arm around my shoulder. Then he pulls me close. I stay quiet, fearful that I might still be in the doghouse.

"I'm sorry I wasn't more sensitive about your headache, honey," he says softly and sweetly as he strokes the hair away from my forehead. "Why don't I go down to the café on the corner and pick us up some croissants, OK?"

I can't believe my ears. I smile at him and say, "Seriously though, I'm really sorry for scaring you like that."

"It's OK," he says. "Anyway, I think I'd better get dressed now. I'm getting chilly—I mean cold, I'm getting cold."

And that was that. The crisis was over. The anger had melted away so swiftly and ever so sweetly. In like a lion, out like a lamb.

Still, I can't help but wonder what Mom would think of this. If she'd be proud or skeptical of me and my craftiness. If she'd think it was funny or childish or "very French." But I guess I'll never know.

Either way, I'm not going anywhere right now. I'm just going to swallow two capsules of Excedrin Extra Strength and go back to bed. I'm exhausted.

Part 5 The Musician

Therewith she wailed with exceeding woe,
And piteous lamentation did make;
And all her sisters, seeing her do so,
With equal plaints her sorrow did partake.

~Edmund Spenser, *The Teares of the Muses*, 1591

twenty-seven

I WATCH HER SILENTLY. TEARS stream down her round cheeks. Her petite frame is hunched over. Shoulders slightly slumped. Her hair is in a loose chignon held together with a green pencil. Some strands are falling down a bit on the sides. Her hair is a color somewhere between chestnut and auburn. It's messy but looks soft.

Her once-sparkling hazel eyes look gray now. Tortured. They stare down at the hardwood floor. Her expression is blank, maybe vacant from shock. Her skin is a dark shade of olive, though her cheeks are flushed and swollen from crying. Her nails are bitten down to stubs. Her knees tremble a little beneath her tattered jeans. Her left hand makes a tight fist, clenching a wadded-up piece of blank sheet music. She has a stubborn chin, with a little dimple in the center. She somehow manages to cry, smoke, and talk all at the same time. Her pursed lips blow out a quick puff of smoke as she dangles her last cigarette nervously from her fingers. She tells me her mouth is dry and that there's a lump in her throat.

She sits cross-legged on the floor, with her head down. I can hear her stomach start to grumble and growl. She hasn't eaten all day, she says. She wears no jewelry, except for a delicate silver chain around her neck. It barely touches the collar of her V-necked black cashmere sweater, which is too big for her. And a watch. A black watch that's too big for her small wrist. "It belonged to my brother," she explains. Her lashes, heavy and mascara'd, dutifully hide her tired eyes. They look smudged and smoky. She bites her bottom lip as her toes curl up in her sandals. Her perfume from yesterday sympathetically lingers. Her name is Violet L. She is my latest expert.

Violet L. is a solo pianist. All classical. All original. An international star at only nineteen. From an early age she possessed a mysterious musical genius that caused her toughest critic to once refer to her as a "modern-day Mozart who plays piano like a nightingale sings and composes like the greatest composers in history." And now she's the It girl of the classical world, whether she knows it or not.

Mister X wants me to write her autobiography, despite my skepticism. "What does a nineteen-year-old have to say that can fill an autobiography?" I asked.

"Plenty," Mister X replied. "She was a prodigy at four years old. This girl wrote six full-length symphonies by the time she was ten. With the money she's made, she's probably lived several lifetimes by now."

So here I am, sitting next to Violet L. on the floor of her New York loft. West 62nd. Across from Fordham's Law School. This is my fourth time in Manhattan but the very first time I've been here exclusively for an expert's project. New York is lovely in autumn. Happy, even. But I've been here for two weeks, and already it feels like too long. I should be excited about working here, but the project is turning into a dismal disaster.

Not fifteen minutes go by before the musician bursts into a million tears before me. We're barely on chapter 2 and, to make matters worse, the entire outline looks horrendous. But it's not Violet L.'s fault. Not really.

I wait for the sobs to subside and then tell her, "Well, I suppose there's no rule that autobiographies *have* to start at the beginning. Shall we work backward? What are you working on now?"

Violet L. wipes her eyes and nose with the sleeve of her sweater. "I'm writing a concerto," she says quietly as she stares out her thirty-second-floor window.

"Good! Good, OK, let me get my tape recorder going again," I reply cheerfully. I'm just happy she's started talking to me again. After all, it's not the easiest job in the world for a ghost to work with an expert who is utterly lost in the throes of depression.

My heart immediately went out to the poor girl as soon as I met her. Her constant, uncontrollable bouts of weeping reminded me of myself just a couple years earlier.

When I first arrived here two weeks ago, I was surprised at the simplicity and emptiness of her loft. She's worth a fortune but lives modestly. Meagerly. There is just a single chair in her main room. Brown leather. And a grand piano made of mahogany near the window. Nothing else, really. No works of art on her brick walls. No photos. No table or TV. No stereo. And no rugs on her cold hardwood floor. Even the large windows that face Lincoln Center are curtainless and bare. The loft is nearly empty, but the emotional atmosphere of the place is full of dramatic rises and falls, like something out of a Verdi opera.

The musician's kitchen is filled with half-empty red and white Chinese food boxes, along with a dozen or so half-full glasses of red wine. *Maybe she had a party*, I first thought. But then I saw the mountain of empty prescription bottles lying in the kitchen sink. Zoloft. Elavil. Paxil. Effexor. Prozac. All in the same see-through orange plastic.

"None of them work," Violet L. explained to me on that first day with a stiff, awkward smile. "I've stopped trying to fix it. Everyone keeps telling me to take them, but I've tried everything and nothing works. They just make me numb. They do nothing for sadness. They just make my body feel so numb…too numb to cry. But I *want* to cry. I have to let it out. I just have to."

I soon learned that her older brother had died a tragic death when she was seventeen and that she's never been the same since. Her grieving soon transformed into a major depression. To date she has survived four suicide attempts. "They were attempts at relief," she told me. Or maybe I was just overhearing what she was telling herself.

I also learned that there were days when she couldn't get out of bed, not even to eat. And other days she would spend hours sobbing hysterically in the shower. She stays in her home most of the time. Except when she's forced to leave for a performance somewhere or a recording session. But her empty loft is the only place she really feels comfortable. A certain panic overtakes her whenever she tries to go for a walk or out to dinner. She'll be jumpy with anxiety until she gets home, where she can cry in the comfort of her solitude.

And yet still she turns to her music. Her beloved piano and compositions. She told me that she continues to play despite her sorrow. But maybe she plays because of it. Perhaps it's the piano that lets her transform her suffering into song—or an escape.

twenty-eight

I WONDER IF ALL WRITERS ARE plagued with poor vision. I wonder if F. Scott Fitzgerald had to forever squint over most of his revisions. Or if Agatha Christie had to hold her manuscripts embarrassingly close to her eyes. Those large, tinted frames were Naguib Mahfouz's signature look. Did they all wear glasses? Or at least a monocle on a chain?

My eyesight seems to get worse with every passing season. Nearsightedness. Doctors call it myopia. It's gotten so bad that every morning I wake up surprised to find the world more out of focus than the night before. Anything beyond six inches in front of me might as well be a Van Gogh painting. My ophthalmologist tells me that I spend too much time on my laptop, working on manuscripts without resting my eyes. I often write for six hours at a time without taking a break, so I can hardly argue. But I'm still scared.

My vision first began to deteriorate when I was in the sixth grade. I was in the school choir, and one afternoon our instructor wheeled in a large green chalkboard. Complete lyrics of a new song for our upcoming spring concert were hastily scribbled on it. While everyone else began singing the new words, all I could do was lip-synch. I could barely make out that there was any writing at all on the chalkboard. But that was just the beginning. Before I knew it, I couldn't see the television properly from the sofa or see the numbers on the clock on my bedroom wall. My world was slowly getting smaller and smaller.

When the school year ended, I worked up the courage (and worked down the ego) to tell my mom. She of course whisked me off to the family eye doctor, Dr. Wong, who had treated my grandmother just that morning. On my return visit a week later, I must have left every smile I had inside me in his office, because I walked out wearing nothing on my face but a solemn, grown-up sort of frown and a pair of round tortoiseshell glasses. "They emphasize your eyes," Mom said. I hated them.

It wasn't so much the look of the glasses that made me hate them so—it was more about their limitations. I couldn't run in them without feeling the rims slide down my nose or feeling the sides of them pull on my bangs. And I couldn't lie in bed on my side with them without bending the wire frames. Peripheral vision was out of the question—I couldn't even sneak a good peek at someone from the side. Peripheral vision was out of the question.

By high school my prescription became so bad that the lenses of my glasses were nearly half an inch thick. I started wearing contact lenses. Mom referred to them as my "eyes," as in, "Julia, I want to show you this article. Are your eyes in yet?" To which I'd reply, "I can see up close, Mom. Just not far away." "Well, put your eyes in anyway," she'd say.

And soon I became slave to any wind or dust flying through the air, which would render me incapacitated for at least half an hour. And then there were the times that I would forget to take them out before I went to sleep. I'd wake up the next morning and, for a brief moment, I'd think that my vision had somehow miraculously returned. "I can see! I can see! Oh God, I can see!" But after a few more excitable blinks, I would remember that my contacts were indeed still clung to my eyeballs and that, yes, my vision was still desperately imperfect.

For years now, I've waited for one of my other senses to become heightened. I remember reading something about how the blind usually have a finely tuned sense of hearing, just as the deaf usually have an extraordinarily sharp eye. It's as if the balance of gifts must be preserved.

Unfortunately, my other senses are dull. My hearing is below average, and my sense of touch is not acute. Even my senses of smell and taste are just so-so. As a twenty-something, all five of my senses have already waved the white flag of surrender.

And yet maybe, just maybe, I should breathe a sigh of relief. I wonder if I should be thankful. Perhaps I am one of the few who are blessed with extra-dull senses, which act as a buffer between them and the world. Maybe they serve as a shock absorber for the cruelties and severities of this world. Perhaps I am protected? For just as those with keen senses fully experience the beauty and wonder of the world, they also fully encounter its pain and misery. Perhaps I am sheltered. Protected, indeed.

twenty-nine

I'M WALKING BACK TO MY HOTEL. It's just a couple of blocks away from the musician's loft. My good friend Katerina is supposed to meet me in two hours for dinner. I'm about five minutes away from the hotel now. A cool breeze flies through my hair. Autumn in New York really does live up to its reputation. There's a vibrancy in the air. And the leaves in the tall sidewalk trees are painted crisp reds and dazzling golds—a brave contrast to the towering stone skyscrapers. In the fall, even the rhythm of the city changes from a frenzied pulse to a more mellow tempo.

I was in New York most recently a year before my mother passed away. I was visiting Katerina in her apartment near Gramercy Park, the most elegant park in the city, accessible exclusively to those people, such as Katerina, lucky enough to have a key to its wrought-iron gates.

I called Mom to see how she was doing. Her cancer had moved into remission two months earlier, and the whole family was excited to see her finally healed. It had been two years but the cancer was finally gone. The chemo sessions were finally over and her hair had even started to grow back. She would always laugh a little bit when she saw herself in the mirror because her hair, which was normally straight, had started to grow in tight little curls that looked more like a lamb's wool. Her strength was slowly coming back. She had even started gardening again the week I left for New York. Nothing big, just some little potted pansies here and there. But it was a welcome return to her old way of life.

I knew something was wrong even before she said hello. Maybe her hesitation gave it away.

"Hi, sweetie," she said in a calm voice. And then after another long pause, she asked, "Is Katerina with you?"

"Yeah, Mom, she's right here. Why?"

"Julia, I want you to put the receiver between the two of you, so that you both can hear."

Katerina must have heard my mom say that because she leaned in and put her ear near mine. Next to the receiver. We didn't even question her.

"Can you hear me, sweetheart?" she asked gently. Her pet canary was singing in the background.

"Yeah, Mom. She's right next to me," I replied.

"That's good. I hope you're OK over there and eating enough? I mean I'm sure you are, but I just want you take good care of yourself and not work too hard. Not get too tired."

"Mom, what were you going to tell me?"

"Right, OK. Well…Julia, I went back to the doctor for some checkup tests and…" She paused for a moment that seemed like forever. The canary started singing louder, much louder, just then, with long, clear rolls and flutes.

"Everything alright?" I asked.

"And they tell me that it's back."

I was stunned. My hands went limp and Katerina had to hold the phone up.

"The cancer is back?" I had to press my fingers to my lips to keep them from quivering.

"They said that there were some dormant cells…cells they couldn't see after the chemo or the radiation."

"When did you find out?"

"A few days ago."

Her voice was so calm. It was as if she had known all along that the cancer would return. It was as if she had always known. It was completely silent between us for several minutes. Even Mom's canary stopped his singing.

"Julia, sweetie…," she began. "I didn't want you to be alone when I told you. I wanted someone to be there with you."

I wanted to cry badly. But Mom wasn't crying, so I knew I couldn't either. We both had to pretend that we were OK, so that the other wouldn't get scared.

It feels like it's been a long time since I visited New York. I can barely remember how Katerina gave me a big hug when I hung up the phone that day or how I spent the rest of the evening walking around aimlessly in Central Park until I got lost. Completely lost. I was sobbing like a scared child. It was autumn then, too.

I finally arrive at my hotel and wearily make my way up to my room. Number 327.

thirty

WHENEVER I'M IN New York I always visit Katerina, and whenever she's in San Francisco she stays with me and Leo. She's just a couple of years older than me. She's very pretty and rather petite with shiny blonde hair and dark blue eyes. Her naturally tanned skin always gives her a glow. Her mother is German and her father is American. "Look at the two of us. I'm half German, you're half French; together we're either Switzerland or another world war!" she would say.

Her father was in the Air Force, but Katerina was hardly a military brat. She lived in a charming town in Germany for most of her growing-up years and then came to live in the States. She's famous in the ghosting world for her exquisite translating abilities, especially of German poetry. Now she works full time as a translator for a publisher in the Flatiron Building. She's actually my only friend who is, like me, a ghostwriter.

We're having dinner right now at a dark little Italian restaurant on the corner. She's sitting across from me.

"This looks like a place where couples break up," says Katerina, "Or where mobsters take senators out to dinner. Everyone in here is so Kafkaesque."

"So I came up with a question for you today," I begin.

Katerina leans in.

"All right, so you grew up in Germany but you also spoke English early on too, right?"

"Yes, of course! You already knew that."

"So my question is, what language do you dream in?"

Katerina's tiny nose crinkles for a second and then she shrugs.

"You don't know?" I ask.

"I can't remember that!" she exclaims cheerfully "How could I remember such a thing?"

"Don't you ever have conversations in your dreams? Don't you talk to anybody?"

"I don't know. I really can't remember anything I dream," she replies while sipping on my Campari and soda. (I always order Campari but never drink it because I can't tolerate its bitter aftertaste. But I do love saying, "I'll have a Campari, please," to the waiter. It makes me feel so European.)

"Not ever?" I ask.

"No, I don't think so. Am I supposed to?"

"But that's so weird! Everyone remembers something about their dreams. There has to be *something*."

Katerina chews on a straw. "Let me think…last night, last night…no, I really can't remember anything. Maybe I don't dream? Is that possible? Can't a person just sleep?"

"I wish I could just sleep," I reply. "I'd love it if there were a switch I could flip that would let me turn off my dreams. When I wake up, I'm always exhausted from a night of endless dreaming. And then sometimes it's hard to remember those dreams. I'm left with just the feelings, and sometimes those feelings linger all day. It's hard to shake them sometimes."

"You sound like you need a beer. Waiter? Can we get two beers, please? Do you have any Bitburger? *Bitte ein Bit.* You do? Great. And can you put a little 7-Up in the top, with some lemon?"

"So how are things going with you and Michael?" I ask.

Katerina's blue eyes ignite. "Mike is Mike, you know? Everybody loves Mike. He's just one of those guys that can talk to anyone about anything. And I love him for that. We just seem to fit together, you know? We're talking about moving in together. Maybe even marriage."

"You guys are going to get married?" I ask. "That would be wonderful!"

"Nothing is set in stone yet, but...I do love the guy. What about you? How are things in Married Land?"

"It's...good" I begin.

"I know that sigh!" Katerina blurts out loudly. "Don't tell me you two are still battling it out? Really, Julia, you two have the most passionate fights I've ever heard of."

"No, no, I mean, Leo and I are still working things out. That whole compromise thing is tougher than it sounds."

"It's love," she replies wistfully as the waiter comes with the beers. "Love makes everything more intense."

"He puts up with my writing. I don't know how he does it."

"So how's the new book coming along?" she asks.

"With the musician?"

"No, no—I mean your own book. Wasn't it *Elegant* something or other? The one about your mother?"

"*Elegant Simplicity*," I reply as I try to remember when I had told Katerina about it. "I'm not really talking about it right now. The process is…it's pretty overwhelming."

"But don't you want to write it?"

"I do and I am, but it's so hard. She has such a unique story and I just don't want to screw it up. I'm just afraid, I guess. Writers take advantage of their stories. And I don't want to manipulate this one. I'm just scared of exploiting it."

"Then don't," Katerina says coolly, just as she says everything else. She gets out of her chair and moves it right next to mine so she can wrap her arm around me in a hug.

"Don't what?" I ask.

"Don't exploit it. Don't worry about exploiting it. Just write it down, get it done, and worry about it later. Write it for you. There's obviously something inside you that is screaming to get it out. So write it down. And worry about it later. There's always time to worry later."

thirty-one

I DON'T KNOW WHY I'M PRONE to sadness. I've been vulnerable to it for as long as I can remember. Usually when I feel blue, I have to surrender to that feeling and painfully wait for it to pass. But sometimes, if I'm lucky, I'm able to catch the sadness early enough and actually shake myself out of it. Sometimes going for a long, meandering walk will do it. Or listening to a certain kind of music (Rachmaninoff does it; Chopin makes it worse). But sometimes the only thing that can make me feel better is grabbing a pen and my beat-up, leather-bound journal and actually writing everything all down is what brings me pleasure.

And usually by this point I start to feel better. Much better. Of course, there are times when the sadness is too strong, too powerful, for me to stop or distract myself from it. And not even a silly list of happy things can change that. Those are the times that I wish someone would just sit with me and take care of me and make me feel better. Like my mom. I miss her so deeply whenever I get sad, even if what got me sad has nothing to do with her. Sometimes I wish so hard through my tears that I could have just a little more time with her. Just one more conversation. Just a few more words. Just one more hug. Just one more time to hear her voice.

I wish I weren't so prone to getting sad the way I do. I want so badly to live without it. Maybe I should have been a musician. They always seem to know just what to do with their sadness.

Euterpe is the Muse completely devoted to music. Her name translates from the Greek *Eu* as "delight" or "bringer of pleasure." And she certainly is.

In Greek mythology, she follows her favorite musicians around during the day and at night whispers the most beautiful songs into their ears while they sleep. In the morning the musicians wake up and remember only the heavenly tune. She is said to have inspired the greatest sonatas, the most dramatic overtures, and the most exotic, mouthwatering symphonies. She plays each and every musical instrument with ease and has a feather-light touch, especially with the harp. Some myth-historians credit her with inventing the double-flute, which she is often depicted playing. Sometimes she's painted with her robes adorned with an elegant garland of tiny pink flowers, perhaps a gift from her sister Thalia.

In the Louvre there hangs a seventeenth-century painting of Euterpe and Thalia together. Another Muse sister is there too, but looks annoyed and disengaged from them. Perhaps Euterpe and Thalia were the closest of all the sisters. They are sitting together in the cool shade of the feathery branches of a cypress tree in the mountains. White clouds loom in the light-blue sky, but the air is bright and clear. Euterpe is playing the flute, pretending to close her eyes in concentration, but really she is watching her sister react to the song. Thalia sits at her feet, near a tiny trickling creek. Her body is facing Euterpe, but her attention is elsewhere. She's gazing at a theater mask that she holds in her extended hand. Perhaps she asked Euterpe to write the music for one of her plays. And Euterpe, delightful and polite sister that she is, obliges. The masterpiece was painted by the notoriously fastidious Eustache Le Sueur, a man whose last name looks and sounds similar to *soeur*, the French word for "sister."

thirty-two

IT'S TEN IN THE MORNING, AND I'm supposed to meet the musician in half an hour at her loft. I'm talking to my dad on the phone. He crashed on his motorcycle yesterday and hurt several ribs.

"I'll just have to find some barbecue sauce for them," he says. "That's how I like my ribs."

"Real funny, Dad. You sure you're OK?"

"I'll be fine. Your dad's tough," he replies.

"So what exactly happened?"

"Well," he begins in an excited voice, "I was up in Gorman, just play-riding with two of my buddies. I *was* leading, but, well, one of the guys, Sam, was following too close behind me. So then I go to take a jump, but I realize that I'm not gonna make it, so I just veer off to the side. So then Sam comes up and misses the jump and crashes and lands right on top of me. His bike and everything. His bike landed right on top of my chest. And then the other guy, Nick, came up behind him and did the same thing. He missed the jump somehow and crashed and landed on top of Sam and me. That's what really hurt. The second guy falling on me didn't hurt so much, but that third guy took the wind right out of me."

"Oh my gosh, Dad! You are so lucky that you didn't break something. Are you sure it's just your ribs?"

"Oh yeah. My ribs are *really* sore, but they'll be fine. My damned bike is what got hurt. Now I gotta spend another two weeks fixing those gears again."

"Did anyone else get hurt? How are the other two guys?"

"Oh," he says with a laugh. "They didn't do as good as me. I came out the best."

"What happened?"

"Sam broke his right hand and had to drive to LA to see some big-dog surgeon for it. And Nick broke his leg in two places! Can you believe it? I found out and I said *holy* moly. I wanted to keep on riding after it happened, but those guys said they were too hurt. I didn't care. I just wanted to ride. The dirt was really good that day. Not too wet. Not too dusty. Just right."

"Dad, you'd better take it easy. Do you need to see a doctor?"

"No, no…I'm fine. Listen, now there's nothing you can do for hurt ribs. They just need to heal. It just kind of hurts to breathe, and it really hurts when I sit down or get up. Man, that hurts. It's tough just because I'm alone at the house. It's a big house when you're hurt. Real lonely without your mom here. So anyway…what else, what else. There was something else I wanted to tell you. What was it? Oh, right! Your book!"

"What about it?"

"Didn't you say you were trying to come up with an idea for your next book?" he asks.

"Well, no," I reply. "I was just saying that I'm having difficulty with the topic I chose. It's very emotional. I'm already at one hundred pages. It's about Mom—"

"Because I think you should write a book about computers."

"Really. Computers."

"Yeah!" his voice is in super-fast, high-enthusiasm gear.

"You know, some technical manual for beginners! You could make so much money. They really need people to write those things right now. You wouldn't believe all the business in teaching beginners! And you could even—"

I start to hiccup.

"Dad—Dad, no. I mean, thanks for the idea. I'll keep it in mind. You're the computer programmer, not me. You should write it."

Dad quickly moves on.

"Yeah. That's pretty cool that you're in New York. Are you still in New York?"

"I'll probably be here for another month," I reply. My hiccups seem to be gone.

"What time is it there?"

"It's ten, Dad."

"Yeah, Olivia is from New York. Well, not New York but Rhode Island. It's nearby. She lived there for a long time and then moved to Minnesota."

The hiccups return.

"OK, Dad, well I gotta get going, I'm about to eat lunch, so…"

thirty-three

"I LIKE YOUR HAIR," VIOLET L. says abruptly. "It reminds me of something. I'm not sure what."

"Oh," I reply, a little embarrassed at my hair's purple-black color (it was supposed to be a soft black, but I left the color on for too long). "I change it all the time. Helps me to switch gears for different projects."

"Hmm. I can see that. I can totally see that," she replies.

We're back at her loft on West 62nd Street and standing next to her piano. Violet L. is a little more cheerful today, though still subdued. It's noon and she's in her pajamas—an ex-boyfriend's oversized Yale T-shirt and a long, faded navy robe that belonged to yet another ex-boyfriend. But the silver toenail polish on her bare feet is all hers.

My tape recorder has been on for more than an hour. The musician has been unusually cooperative and open with me today for the project. I might even have enough material for a whole manuscript. Most of it, at least.

"Tell me about your process of writing. Of composing," I say to her.

Violet L. nods and then walks around the room. Pacing. Her hair is messy and matted in the back. Earlier she told me that she hadn't slept the previous night. Not more than an hour.

"When I write," Violet L. begins when she reaches the window, "it is purely instinctual."

"So it just comes to you?" I ask. "Or do you need inspiration?"

"I *feel* what to compose...I *feel* what to write," she replies. She speaks with conviction. "I wait. That's the tough part. Being patient and waiting. But it doesn't mean a vacation, do you understand? No...in waiting...I think and think and work through ideas, through themes...exploring them to the fullest...and if the idea falls flat, if the melody cannot finish in my head, then I let it go, which is sometimes hard to do."

"And what do you do with those compositions? What do you do with the songs that don't make it?"

"I just crumple them up and toss them out my window," she says, pointing to Lincoln Center.

I can hardly believe it. *Musical prodigies aren't supposed to have to work at it*, I think. *It shouldn't be hard for them. Should it?* But I don't say anything. I just nod politely, jot down a few notes, and check the recorder to make sure it's still on.

Violet L. walks over to her kitchen and fills a small glass with wine. Red. She's still talking and I follow her. "Then there are moments when an idea feels so right that my only obstacle is whether my hands can play fast enough…or whether they can write down the notes fast enough. And then I have to decipher what I've written…days, weeks, sometimes years later."

She brings the glass to her lips and stops for a moment, as if remembering something. She replaces the glass carelessly on the counter and doesn't seem to notice that the wine sloshes out of it. The floor is a mess, but she doesn't care.

"I want to play," she says. Her voice quivers.

I follow her back to the main room. She stands next to her piano and caresses the length of the thin music shelf, which holds just a few sheets of blank music composition paper.

"When I was a child I was often called precocious," she says, "but no one calls me that anymore."

"Tell me about your piano," I say.

"Oh, I've loved this old girl for most of my life. She was my grandfather's," she says as she carefully sits down on the bench in front of it. The tail of her robe dangles over the edge of the bench. She lays her slender, calloused fingers on the keys but doesn't play. "It's the only piano I'll compose with. I can't work with anything else. I just can't."

The musician's piano is impressive. It's an old-style Steinway. Grand, of course. Made in 1891, according to Violet L. It's covered with superb detailing—elaborate carvings and scrollwork—making the piano itself a true piece of art. And it has a satiny mahogany finish, which is a very deep black color that holds just a hint of rose, visible only when the sunlight hits certain grains of the wood.

It even has real ivory keys. The faces of the keys sometimes fall off, so Violet L. keeps a tiny vial of glue nearby. "The new ones don't have real ivories…they have plastic keys, which look too perfect. Too flawless. Like when someone's teeth are too white. You just don't trust them." she says. "This piano has a real history and I'll love it my whole life." And without another word, she begins to play.

Violet L. is riding a wave of international fame for her conservative yet dramatic approach to composing. Reviewers rave about the clarity of her compositions and how she knows every instrument intimately. "Her sonatas are pure, intoxicating elegance," said one critic. "She makes thematic transformations with such polish, such panache, that one wonders if the young woman channels Liszt," gushed another.

As the young musician plays before me, I can't help but fall under her spell as well. She's a virtuoso, indeed. Her melodies are mesmerizing and her harmonies are haunting. And she herself seems to be captivated by the warm, lush sound of the Steinway. Her eyes are closed as she plays with a smooth, slow tempo. Her head hangs down, as if in prayer. Her body rocks slightly with every sequence of chords and every crescendo. Her right foot seems to melt into the bronze pedals below. I watch with awe as her willowy fingers reach octaves with ease. They roll over the black-and-white keys with such speed that it doesn't look as if she's touching the keys at all. Her fingers are just flying over them.

She is playing a melancholic tune that can only be described as equal parts grace and complexity. And abruptly, right in the middle, she stops. It looks as though even her hands are surprised as she raises them up in the air, suspended just above the keys. Her fingers are shaking and within seconds her body starts to tremble as well. The air in her loft feels strange now, as if the notes from her song are still floating in the air, abandoned and scared without her. A faint echo drifts in and out.

Violet L. begins to weep. She pulls the robe up over her head and leans her forehead against the piano keys as she sobs. Her head hits the low keys and just stays there. A long, deep hodge-podge of chords resonates through the loft. It sounds like the piano is crying with her.

I'm not sure if I should stay or go. Does she want me here? I should go. I should pick up my tape recorder and let her have some time to herself. Don't musicians need solitude sometimes?

But I can't leave her. Not like this. I take a chance and sit down next to her on the piano bench. And just being beside her in that moment I can feel just how much suffering goes into her music.

"You know, a monk once told me that there are two types of people in this world. Those who want to remember and those who want to forget."

No reply. Violet L. doesn't even look at me. She's just crying. I slide closer to her and wrap an arm tightly around her, just as Katerina did for me when I needed it. Violet L. sobs against my shoulder, and I feel her tears through my blouse.

"He was hung, you know," she says softly without lifting her head. Her words are muffled.

"Who?" I ask.

"My brother. That's how he died."

"You mean he hung himself? Suicide?"

"No."

Violet L. slowly gets up from the piano and walks to her wall of windows. She tries to open a window. She has to use a great lever to push the top of it through, but she finally thrusts it open. A cold wind rushes in and sweeps both of us back a bit. Lincoln Center looks empty except for a few people sitting on a bench, near the fountain. Violet L. steps out onto the wide ledge. One foot in, one foot out. The wind is rushing through her robe, dramatically twirling it behind her.

"I'm giving a concert there tomorrow night," she says. "Will you come?"

"Who killed him?" I ask as I step back from the open window. I have a fear of heights. Well, it's really a fear of falling.

"Some kids. They were just kids," she replies.

As she steps her other foot onto the windy ledge as well, Violet L. tells me the story. Her brother died when he was seventeen. A senior in high school. In Chicago. Violet L. was in Prague that week for a piano concert. He was a couple of years older than she was. He was the quintessential popular quarterback, loved by everyone. On an evening in January, after a football game his team had won, he was murdered. Some players from the rival high school waited outside his locker room. It was already dark out. He was one of the last to leave and they were drunk.

Violet L. explains to me that as soon as the door opened, they punched him and beat him unconscious. By that point he had black shoe marks all over his face from their kicks. They threw him in their truck and drove out to a deserted field, where they hung him from a tree using only duct tape. He died quickly, within minutes, but that wasn't enough for the boys. They stripped him and chained him to the truck bumper. They dragged his body down the empty freeway until there wasn't anything left to drag.

"He was declared missing for days…weeks," Violet L. tells me. "One of the kids who did it finally felt guilty enough or scared enough to come forward."

Her voice is calm and she tells me this without crying again. She takes a deep breath and comes in from the ledge. She's shivering and her lips are pale from the chill. I can smell the salt of her tears. She closes the window.

"I think he was wrong," she says.

"Your brother?"

"No."

"Who?"

Violet L. sits back down at her piano but doesn't play. She just stares longingly at the black-and-white keys.

"I remember now what your hair reminds me of," she says without looking at me. "It looks like ebony. They used to make the sharps—you know, the black keys—out of ebony."

"Who was wrong?" I ask again.

"The priest or monk or whoever he was."

"How do you mean?"

"He was just…wrong," she says. "There are two types of people in this world. There are those who are never alone…and those who are always alone, even when they are surrounded by others. I am always alone."

The musician turns around on the bench and looks up at me.

"Julia? Promise me something."

"What is it?"

She puts her hand in mine. Tears stream down her face. She looks older now, as though she's already lived several lifetimes in her young life.

"Don't write what I told you about my brother. I don't want that in my book," she says. "I want to keep that story mine."

Part 6 The Astrophysicist

How euer yet they mee despise and spight
I feede on sweet contentment of my thought,
And please my selfe with mine owne selfe-delight,
In contemplation of things heauenlie wrought:
So loathing earth, I looke vp to the sky,
And being driuen hence I thether fly.

~Edmund Spenser, *The Teares of the Muses*, 1591

thirty-four

IT'S WINTER. ONE OF THOSE winters that makes you wonder if spring will ever come. The days are short. The nights are long. And the outside air is anything but inviting. These conditions, however, are ideal for writing. No distractions. Nothing but a cup of hot tea and my project. I've been working for months on my manuscript about Mom. I've immersed myself in it. Writing ten to twelve hours a day. I'm halfway through it. Well, almost.

It feels strange to write about her. I have to remind myself to use the past tense. It leaves me in a peculiar emotional state that I can't exactly define. And yet I know that writing this manuscript somehow, in some way, makes me feel closer to her—and further away from her at the same time. It's a feeling that collapses on itself just as soon as it begins.

And I don't know if I'll ever want to get the manuscript published or if I'll keep it to myself; locked away in some memory box tucked under my bed. I just don't know yet. But I do know that I'll keep working on it until it's finished. Until the end.

I don't remember the most recent time I went outside. Once in a while I'll stick my face out the window to breathe in the frosty air to wake myself up a bit. I also can't remember the most recent time I wore an actual outfit—something other than my bathrobe, Leo's gray Cal shirt, and flannel pajama pants. I've almost completely lost touch with most of my friends. I should have returned some of their phone calls, but I really wanted to finish chapter 3 by Friday. And I really, really should have returned their emails, but chapter 6 was such a thorn in my foot. I've also just realized that I barely even talk to my family anymore, except for the occasional voice mail phone tag we've been playing with one another. Even my dad has recently resigned himself to just sending me emails telling me that he misses hearing my voice. It seems that the only human contact I've had this season is with Leo and Sam the mailman. Or is his name Saul?

I wonder if all writers become antisocial when they're knee-deep in the pangs of a manuscript. I'd like to go out with everyone again and maybe have a few drinks or a few laughs, but I just know that I wouldn't have anything to say. I'd just be planning the next chapter or second-guessing a sentence I was so sure of the night before. That's what I tell myself anyway. The real reason, I reluctantly admit, is that I just don't have the patience for people right now. I just don't feel like engaging in pleasantries or talking about current events or even my book. That's the hardest thing, I suppose. I feel so awkward when people ask about my own manuscripts. They are such private things to me that I'm wary of discussing their status with anyone but

Leo or my editor. I'll usually shrug and mumble something vague about how my novel is a mystery (which it isn't) or how I'm turning it into a thriller (which I'm not). Sometimes what makes good conversation isn't what makes a good book.

I've also been busy working on a new project for my latest expert. He's an astrophysicist and he's been quite the celebrity in scientific circles lately, ever since he won a Nobel Prize a couple of years ago. I was hesitant at first because I'm not really a scientific ghost (I prefer the arts and culture titles if I have the luxury of choice), but Mister X assured me that he is interested only in "the man behind the physics" and "the heart behind the brains." So I agreed.

The expert's name is Quincy R. and he's an American. Princeton's pride and joy, as well as NASA's. He has a house in Marin County. One of those modern, spaceship-looking mansions that sits high up on a cliff. I've seen it several times on various drives out there, though I didn't know it was his. But I don't know what he looks like. I haven't met him yet. Due to his recent travels to London, we've conducted the interviews exclusively via email so far. I'm supposed to meet him for a discussion of the first draft in a week or so.

But I don't mind. I've enjoyed being able to stay at home and write to my heart's content or at least until my eyes become so strained that I have to close them, along with my laptop. But lately (today, at least), I've been wondering if there's a price I'll soon pay for indulging my introversion. I guess I'll just have to wait and see.

Right now I'm distracted. Leo and I are arguing again. He's saying something about how I don't listen or something like that. I'm not sure what he said exactly. I wasn't paying attention. And now here we are sniping at each other again, like little kids who are tired and cranky.

"You always do this," I say.

"What?" Leo replies, exasperated with me.

"You always hurt my feelings."

"Well, maybe *you* always hurt *my* feelings!" he shoots back.

"What do you mean?"

"I'm going to take a shower!" he declares. His voice booms through the air like a lion. Even his hair is extra wavy and mane-like.

"Let's talk about this," I say.

"I'm done talking. I have nothing left to say. I'm done! I just want to take a shower, OK?"

He takes off his shirt and throws it on the floor. I stay quiet as I watch his nostrils flare in sync with his heaving chest. He's angry, all right. He turns around and slams the bathroom door behind him. I hear the creaky lock turn sharply.

The shower turns on, the glass door slides, and now I'm the one who's mad. How dare he just walk away! What gives him the right to end our argument so abruptly? Doesn't he know the natural order of things? Doesn't he know that we have to argue at least ten more minutes before one of us can walk away? He's ridiculous, I think. So ridiculous, in fact, that I'd better do something. I'd better get him back. I walk over to his open closet and stare at his nice, neat clothes. An idea hits me.

I rush to the first drawer of his bureau and pull it open. Leo keeps a stockpile of toiletries in this drawer. Extra conditioners (he loves that mane of his), leave-in as well as the rinse-out variety. Extra shaving cream. Extra cologne. And right there, the most offensive bottle of pale blue water stares back at me.

Hugo Boss. I hate that Hugo Boss. To my nose it smells like sweaty shoes and apples. I can't stand it. I don't know why Leo hasn't thrown it away yet. But here it is. Three-quarters full. Left over from his early college days, his pre-Julia days. Now he wears something else, but for some reason he refuses to throw out the damned Hugo.

I grab the bottle of cologne and go back to Leo's closet. If he likes this cologne so much, I'm sure he'll just *love* that all his clothes are drenched in it.

I start spraying his hanging shirts, front and back, as well his slacks and jeans. I even douse his polos. And the inside of his briefcase. I spray and spray and spray until my finger can't press down anymore. The Hugo bottle is half-empty now. And Leo's closet is drenched in an awful sweaty-apple smell. That awful stink. It's so strong that I have to shut the closet doors so that the rest of our apartment is spared.

I go into the bedroom and toss the bottle of Hugo, along with two other colognes of Leo's, into an old shopping bag and stuff it under the bed so that he won't be able to get me back. I lie down on the bed and pretend to read.

A few minutes go by and Leo comes out. As soon as he reaches the hall, I hear him say, "Wh-what have you done?"

But before I can think of what to say, I see Leo rummaging through his bureau drawers. He opens the one at the bottom and takes out *another* bottle of Hugo Boss. And it's full. He runs to my closet at the other end of the hall and starts spraying everything like mad. My dresses. My tops and blouses. Everything. He douses them and even unscrews the top of the bottle and splashes the horrid blue water all over my jackets and coats.

"How's *that*?" he asks as he casually tosses the cologne bottle on the bed.

"You're insane," I growl. "I barely sprayed any on your things. You used up the whole bottle. You're ridiculous!" I jump up and look in my closet to assess the damage. Everything is wet. Really wet. Everything smells musty, like soured mothballs mixed with wet dog. It's awful. Our whole apartment is an olfactory disaster.

Leo looks at me and crosses his arms in front of his chest.

"I'd say we're just about even," he says with a voice full of confidence and a look in his eye that makes me wonder if he's got a third or fourth bottle stashed somewhere else, in case of an emergency.

We stand side by side and look at—and smell—the reeking mess before us.

"Well," he begins as he scratches his unshaven chin, "we'd better air everything out."

I press my lips together and stand there as defiantly as I can.

"It's too late to ignore me," he says.

"Hmmph!" I reply.

"I already know you think this is funny, Julia, so it's too late to be mad."

The truth is I'm really not even mad anymore. I'm just pretending to be mad now. I don't even know why I was mad in the first place. But I do know that I have to see this fight through. After all, I wouldn't want Leo to think that I get mad over nothing. But what on earth was I mad about to begin with?

"Julia?" he asks with his hand on my shoulder.

"You're ridiculous," I mutter under my breath.

"Come on…"

"No, leave me alone," I reply as I turn away.

"Julia, come on, let's stop fighting."

At this point I know I should give in, but I can't. I can't call my own bluff, it's just not in me.

"I'm going to take a shower!" I declare.

thirty-five

THE MUSES HAVE BEEN invoked time and again in the pages of history. Virgil called upon them. So did Homer and Hesiod. And Cicero, too. Even Milton invoked Urania as his own personal Muse in *Paradise Lost*, but politely transformed her into the Christian-friendly Holy Spirit. The mythological Urania was known as the Muse of astronomy and peace, which at first glance seems a peculiar pair of responsibilities.

But really, it does make sense. Urania was in charge of the mysteries of the sky, including the phases of the moon, the eclipses, and the entire cast of constellations. Urania helped humanity to cast not only their eyes upward, but also their thoughts. With her guidance and inspiration, humanity's thoughts could move from the earthly to the celestial, where the inner chaos of minds could find harmony and peace.

Likewise, Urania is usually depicted with a tranquil expression on her fair visage. She is cool and calm. Perfectly placid. A crown of six or so silver stars sits atop her head. In paintings she almost always is dressed in a deep-blue gown and holds a globe or compass in her hand. Sometimes her other hand extends upward toward the sky, one finger daintily pointing.

I, however, haven't seen the sky or even thought about it in ages (or weeks, at least). I've been shutting myself in like a hermit in front of my laptop, painfully extracting and inventing ideas. But a thought occurs to me—I need to live again! Or else I will have nothing to write! A writer can't write in a vacuum, can she? Is it even possible to write well without experiencing? Even the great Thoreau once said, "How vain it is to sit down to write when you have not stood up to live." And now after these lonely weeks indoors, I can't help but agree. How can one even dare to describe the beauty of a shooting star if she herself has not seen such a marvel?

It is both a crucial and intimidating moment for a writer when she decides to put down her pen. I'd better get my gloves.

thirty-six

I DON'T KNOW WHY I DECIDED to ride my bike today. It's much too cold out to be bike riding. Am I going against the wind? I'm certain now that my ears are frozen and will fall off at any second. And my nose, too. Along with my fingers. Why didn't I opt for a simple, easy walk for my first day back out in the world? Why did I have to insist that riding a bike would do me good? Why did I insist that I should ride over to the BART station, which is much too far away on such a bleak wintry day?

I'm gliding down a side street off of Haight Street. My knees are shivering and even my feet are too cold and numb to pedal. I'm just coasting. And waiting for the biting wind to chew my skin off completely. I'm riding a mountain bike. It was my dad's. He gave it to me several years ago, as soon as we found out I'd be attending Cal.

The lever to adjust the seat has rusted, so my seat sits a little too high. And then some.

It really does feel like the "dead" of winter today in San Francisco. It's two in the afternoon, but a sea of fog is drifting along the ground. White, billowing fog. There's not really any sunlight out—more of a brightness of a blindingly white sky, which blends in with the all-consuming fog. But still there are a few tiny drops of life splashing about. A few pink magnolia blossoms are just starting to unwind from their buds. They are the only color I see at all through this endless blanket of fog.

I'm steering the handlebar with my knees so I can blow warm air on my fingers. At least they look like fingers. They certainly don't feel like them. They don't feel like anything at all. Just ten trembling little stubs. The fog seems to be rolling in quick now, almost cascading across the street. The winds are moving it along.

My mom knew about the winds. She knew their different names and how the Ancient Greeks personified the winds as gods, winged deities, each with a temperament that corresponded with his direction. After we had said our daily Our Father and Hail Mary on the long morning drive to school, Mom would explain the wind gods to me.

I remember only two. Zephyrus, the west wind. He was the young and friendly one, the god who brought humidity and kept flowers in bloom. And Boreas. His wings were dark purple and his breath was bone chilling. He was a difficult fellow, notorious for his dramatics. He was the north wind and therefore the strongest, coldest wind. His hair was curly and he wore a long, angry beard, which was always off to the side, as if it were constantly in jeopardy of getting blown away.

Boreas must be here today. The winds are so cold right now that I can barely stay on my bike. The street is strangely empty. No cars. Hardly any people. I think I see a few birds flying, soaring up high above me, but they might just be leaves. I'm embarrassed to admit this, but I always ride my bike on the sidewalk. I think I'm the only person, except for the occasional five- or six-year-old, who rides her bike on the sidewalk in San Francisco. Armies of bicyclists have taken over the streets of the city, and proudly so. But I don't care. I have to do it. I'm just too scared to ride on the street. Leo would laugh at me if he found out. Sometimes I think that he could ride his bike on a freeway during rush hour without flinching.

I guess I'm just not used to riding alongside cars. It's just too scary—cars speeding past you, just inches away. Zooming. Whooshing. Zipping by. And so I just leisurely ride along the sidewalks of San Francisco. Next to mothers pushing their strollers. Next to the elderly pushing their walkers. Passersby look at me with a mixture of surprise and contempt, as if I were intruding on their exclusive territory. But not today. The streets are almost empty. No one shakes his head at me or frowns. Today the sidewalks are mine.

thirty-seven

I'M SITTING ON MY BED RIGHT now. I know I should get more work done on *Elegant Simplicity*, but I just don't feel like it. I don't feel like much of anything.

On Thursday I was hit by a car on my way to the BART station. I was walking my bike in the crosswalk when I heard a terrible screech. I looked to my left and there was this dark-colored car coming straight at me. I was so scared that I couldn't move. I just stood there—half my body wanted to go right and the other half was trying to go left. All I could do was turn slightly to the side, but maybe it was the wind that pushed me.

The car hit my right leg, and my body rolled over the hood in a tumble. I even saw the driver's eyes. They were light and wide with fear. I fell to the ground. The car sped off.

I think I landed on my left arm. But I'm all right. It was really quite frightening at the hospital though. I kept thinking about Mom and missing her so much that I had to bite my lip to keep from crying in front of the doctors. At first they thought I had neck damage, so they kept me on a gurney for more than five hours. That was probably the worst part. It was like being strapped to a board so tight that you can't even wiggle yourself into comfort. You just have to remain in the precise position they put you in from the start. It bruised my tailbone and gave me an awful headache. But the nurses were friendly and nice.

Everyone, including the doctors, was surprised that I had made it out OK. No bruises on my leg where the car hit me. Not even soreness on my stomach or ribs from where I rolled over the hood. It's just my arm that's hurt from the landing. The doctors told me that, according to witnesses who spoke to the police, the impact threw me twenty feet across the street. And that the car was going fifty-five in a fifteen miles per hour zone. They were certain that I had internal bleeding. But I had none. They ran test after test but found nothing. There wasn't even a scratch on my bike.

"This is quite out of the ordinary," one doctor said.

"To be perfectly honest, you shouldn't even be here," another doctor chimed in. "Not after being hit at that speed. It's as though someone came and just lifted you right up when it happened."

"Extraordinary," said the first.

"You're a lucky girl," said the second.

"Very lucky," said the first.

Now my left arm is in a splint and my fingers are tingly, but I'm OK. Tonight I just feel sad more than anything. I tiptoe around the notion of wondering what would have happened had I not moved—but let the speeding car hit me at full impact.

It doesn't scare me to think that I could have died; it frustrates me to know that I finally had a chance to see my mom again and that I let that chance slip away. I don't want to kill myself. But I'm not afraid of death. I long for it. I want so much to be in my mother's arms again and feel her hug me. Oh, I miss her so much!

So now I'm sitting here on my bed in my light-pink bathrobe (it was my mother's), ashamed of my tears. I wonder if they are selfish tears. Sometimes I'm afraid that I don't know if the feelings I have are even real. I just feel heartbroken.

Lately I've been saying prayers to my mom. I ask her to come to me in my dreams. And sometimes she does. Then I get a little scared and she leaves, but I wish she would stay. I remember a time when I was sixteen. It was a gray, wintry day like today, unusual for Santa Barbara. I went out in the backyard, where my mom was hanging up wet clothes on a line between the birch trees.

I was so sad then. A deeply depressed teenager. I told my mother to stop hanging the clothes and to listen to me. She put the clothes down and said, "What's wrong, sweetie? Are you alright? Did something happen?" And I told her that I was seriously thinking about killing myself. I ached inside. I didn't want to live anymore.

And then Mom told me something that I know I'll remember for the rest of my life. It gave me a reason to live. She looked at me with her almond eyes, wrapped her arms around me, and said, "If you killed yourself, I wouldn't want to live either." And then she started crying. It was the first time I saw my mom cry because of me. I comforted her and told her I was sorry and that everything would be fine. And that was that...

But now she's gone and I'm still here. And I miss her so much. I wish I were in heaven with her. But I'm not and so I feel helpless. It makes me so sad that my entire body goes limp upon thinking about it. It makes me cry a long cry so deep that it paralyzes me as tears pour down my face.

If I ended my own life, as I learned back in Sunday school, then I would not get to heaven. So all I can do is wait. Just wait for a happy accident that will claim my life and send me home to my mom.

thirty-eight

"ARE YOU SURE YOU can drive with that...thing?"

"It's fine, really."

"Because I can drive for you, if you'd like. Just pull over."

"No, no," I reply, "it's fine. It's just a sling. No big deal."

I continue driving south on the 101. My latest expert, Quincy R., is sitting next to me. Fidgeting. Every time I glance at him, he keeps touching his fingertips to the tips of his thumbs. One by one. Again and again. I picked him up from his weird spaceship house on a cliff in Marin, and we're driving to a restaurant in San Francisco to discuss the latest draft of the project over lunch.

"It really wouldn't be a problem. I wouldn't mind," he says.

"No, it's OK. Thank you but no," I reply, trying to hide my annoyance.

"It's just that I'm not comfortable being driven by a woman. I like to drive," he says.

"But you don't even have a car," I say.

The astrophysicist clears his throat. "Correction, I *do* have a car. And it's a very nice convertible. It's just that I keep it at my other home in Princeton."

"Well, this is *my* car, and I think I'm doing just fine driving it," I reply, keeping my eyes forward. I crack open my car window to let some fresh air in. Quincy R.'s cologne is best for open spaces. It smells just like the Hugo Boss disaster. It's so strong right now that I wonder if the astrophysicist bathes in it.

"Fine," he says with a huff, "fine."

I don't normally feel hostile toward experts, but Quincy R. is an exception in and of himself. He is a very curious man.

Quincy R. has a slight lisp and uses his hands a lot when he speaks, with his pinkies outstretched. He has a pudgy, childish sort of face, with delicate features hiding behind his round, rose-gold spectacles. His hair is colored an unnatural shade of blond. Perhaps he colors his hair because of the press his latest work has received. His skin is quite tanned, complete with the little white goggle circles around his eyes from the tanning booth (even though he insists they are from skiing). He's in his early fifties and just under five feet seven inches with a soft body and skinny arms. And his walk is noticeably out of sync with his limbs. On the three occasions we've met for the project, the astrophysicist has worn the same thing: faded blue jeans that are a couple of inches too high up his legs and a short-sleeved silk Hawaiian shirt (despite the fact that it's the middle of winter).

His insistence on refinement is also surprising for someone in physics. His nails are well manicured, his hands are well moisturized, and his eyebrows are plucked just a little under their arches. On our second meeting, he confided that the only soap he uses to wash his hands is the round blue kind that he orders from a store in Oregon. "They're *divine*," he said, waving his pinkies. "Goat's milk and sage!"

But it's not his la-di-da nature that is strange. It's his alarming, paradoxical resolve to act like a complete chauvinist. He is unabashedly flirtatious and positively wolfish. A pinky-waving womanizer.

As we cross the Golden Gate Bridge into San Francisco, Quincy R. fumbles through the pockets of his leather attaché. Out of the corner of my eye, I spot a Shiseido eyelash curler inside.

"I must make a notation," he mumbles. "Where is my pen?"

"I have some pens in my glove box," I offer.

"No, you don't."

"I don't?"

"No. I doubt very much that what you have is a Montblanc. And I must write with my Montblanc," he says. "It's fabulous. It writes like a dream."

He shuffles some papers around and finally moans with glee, "Ahh! I found you! I thought I'd lost you!" But as the astrophysicist waves his beloved pen in the air, his fingers turn into thumbs and he drops it.

"Oh, darn it," he says, "it fell by your foot. Near the gas pedal. I can see it."

"Just a sec," I reply. "I need to watch for our exit and then I'll get it. It's coming up any second now. Everyone is driving like a maniac today."

"Oh, don't worry. I can get it. Let me just unbuckle my seatbelt."

"Really, just wait a second. Once we get off the bridge, I'll—" But before I can finish my sentence, Quincy R. has reached completely over to my side of the car and is now fumbling around my feet.

"I've almost got it," he says.

"Look, I said I'll get it."

I can feel his fingers glide over my ankle.

"*Cute* shoes!" Quincy R. says. "And *very* cute ankles. You should really be wearing a short skirt because those are great knees. I've never seen a better looking knee." His voice is now a low, deep murmur. I can feel his hand slowly moving up my calf.

"What the hell are you doing?" I scream.

"Oh!" he screams back. "My cell phone! Is that my phone?" And in a microsecond the astrophysicist is back in his seat and digging into his jeans pocket.

"I don't hear any phone," I mutter as I get off the bridge, even though what I really want to do is throw this astrophysicist out my car window right on his astro.

"It's on vibrate," he assures me.

"Of course it is."

"This is Quincy. Hello? Hello? Can you hear me?" he says into his tiny, black-lacquered cell phone.

He pauses for a few moments and furrows his freshly exfoliated brow.

"Veronica," the astrophysicist says in that low, soft voice, "I thought I told you not to call me at this number. I'm *working*! I'll call you when I get back to Marin. Did you get the orchids I sent?

Fabulous. What? What? OK, my phone is cutting out. I'll see you tonight. OK, good-bye."

He leans back in the seat and stretches his back as he puffs out his chest.

"Here's your damned pen," I say.

"Excellent," he says with an amused laugh, "but, I think I forgot what I wanted to write down."

"I thought your wife's name was Florence?"

"Oh, it is. But she's out of town for a few days," he explains.

I parallel park the car as I grimace.

"You know," he says with nonchalance, "I can see your underwear when you turn sideways. Do you always wear white panties?"

thirty-nine

I DON'T REMEMBER MUCH about my mom's funeral. The memory is fuzzy now, as if it were a movie that I watched long ago or photographs that I had seen. I suppose that's for the best. What I do still remember, however, are the moments right *after* her funeral. After the burial at the cemetery. It was foggy then, too. The thick sort of fog that creeps along the ground and your feet and makes you feel as if a little bit of heaven accidentally fell from the sky.

Everyone at the graveside huddled around what was left of my family. There must have been half a dozen hands on my shoulders. And then, one by one, everyone came up to us with swollen cheeks, runny noses, and offered sympathetic words. They all said basically the same thing. "Things will get better. You'll see. Time will heal your wounds."

They all said this with such conviction, so matter-of-factly, that I wanted to scream at them and the whole world, with my fists in the air, *Things will not get better! My mother is dead! Time is not going to change that!* But I didn't say anything. I couldn't even speak. I just stood there silently, my tears brushing off on their cheeks as they hugged me.

And yet, as much as I hate to admit it, the passage of time really is starting to heal my sadness. But this fact *horrifies me.*

Healing is not all it's cracked up to be. With every passing day, month, and year, my mom seems further and further away from me. The more time that goes by, the more I heal. And the more I heal, the more my mom becomes just a distant memory. It's this "healing" that leaves my heart trembling.

I'm so afraid of forgetting the little things about her. The things I cherished but took for granted. Those little lines on the back of her hands. Her eyelashes. The color of her hair and how it changed from toffee-brown to soft gold whenever she was out in the sun. The way her mouth pursed to one side when she was too polite to tell someone no. And her voice. I'm so afraid of forgetting how she sounded. She had the softest, most soothing voice. I don't *want* to heal, damn it!

But I can't stop time. No matter how hard I try, it moves on— chipping away at my heart, little by little. Second by second. Things keep changing. I keep changing. For the first year after she passed, I used to cry every day whenever I was alone. For hours. I would cry and hurt so deeply that I'd end up hyperventilating and passing out. And then I'd wake up and cry some more. It was as if every song on the radio and every cloud in the sky reminded me of her and how much I missed her. The color of a blue pansy or the fallen petals of a daisy would set me to sobbing. Sometimes I'd look in the mirror and burst into tears because all I would see were the features I inherited from my mom. Her nose. Her French eyes. Her olive skin. Her cheekbones. Her soft eyebrows.

But then, slowly—very slowly—things began to change. I'd start to go days without crying. And then weeks. I still desperately missed her, but it seemed as though time was stealing her very memory away from me. Or parts of it, at least. And then the grief transformed into guilt. I felt so ashamed that I wasn't crying every day anymore, as if I were wrong not to mourn her every hour of every day. And then I'd talk myself into crying. It would be an angry cry. Angry at myself. Ashamed that my pain was diminishing. I'd lock myself in the bathroom with the shower on full blast so no one could hear me, and I'd cry and scream in turns.

And now, things are different still. It's been years and I rarely cry anymore. I think about Mom often but her memory sends me into a sort of mindless zone. A blank stare. I have to shake myself out of it to continue with my day or with a conversation, whatever it may be. The times I do cry for her are when my body has been shaken to its core—when I'm sick or overly tired or injured. Those are the times when all I want is my mother to take care of me.

Maybe that's why I want to write her story. Maybe that's what keeps me going. I'm so afraid of forgetting her. Losing my memory of her would be like losing her all over again. If I write everything down, everything I can remember, then at least I'll know that in a sense she is eternal, even in this world. A part that I can see, feel, and hold in my hands. A part that I can read and remind myself to cry.

forty

"BUT HE'S NOT LIKE that, Julia."

"You're not listening to me."

"This is absurd. Can you understand that?"

"But—"

"Look, I've met him. I've talked with him. Believe me, I know. You're getting worked up over nothing. He's totally harmless."

I'm on the phone right now with Mister X, threatening to quit because life is too short to spend it with an utterly annoying astrophysicist.

"Julia, you've never quit a project before. Why start now? Are you just burning out on me? Is that it? Look, I'll give you an extra month, how's that?"

"First of all, I was next to him when he spoke with his mistress. And second—"

"What? He's married?"

"Yes, of course."

"To a woman?"

"Yes!"

"No, that's impossible. I mean, I just assumed…anyways, maybe it was his sister? How can you possibly know the whole story?"

"He's a pompous pig!" I blurt out. "I don't want to write for a pig! I don't want to write for anyone anymore. I'm done. I'm just done."

"Just give it another shot. Give it a week. He's just…eccentric."

forty-one

I'M PLAYING WITH THE NOTION of using a pen name someday. A nom de plume. Something glamorous. Maybe Lucy Lisieux. No. Something more serious. Avery Birch, perhaps. Or maybe Something Swan. That would be a pretty last name, wouldn't it? My mom loved swans. They were her favorite. She collected tiny glass swan figurines as well as oil paintings and postcards and things. "Look at how graceful their necks are," she would say with a long sigh. "Doesn't it make you feel wonderful to just watch them move? They bring me such peace."

No one talks about pen names anymore. They seem so unfortunately antiquated, like writing letters by hand. So many of the great ones had pseudonyms. Lewis Carroll was really Charles Lutwidge Dodgson. George Eliot was Mary Ann Evans. Voltaire was

François-Marie Arouet. And O. Henry was in fact William Sydney Porter.

It's easy to see why they used pen names. There's something enchanting about the practice. You give yourself away publicly and yet still keep a part of yourself private. Deliciously locked away. There's a freedom in that as well. The freedom to say and write whatever you please without having your own reputation on the line. To write without regrets. Without looking back.

I should really get back to work now. I need to focus. I need to pay attention. I need to stop daydreaming about pen names and start listening to what this schmuck beside me is saying. Of course, daydreaming really is the only way to stay sane when you're forced to work with Quincy R. Even if it is at the San Francisco Museum of Modern Art café.

"So you're saying that you can split everyone in the world into one of two types: those who are *never* alone and those who are *always* alone, even when they're surrounded by others?"

"That's right," I reply wearily as I stir some honey into my hot tea.

"And some musician told you that?" he asks, his eyebrows arched as high as the Botox will allow. He's wearing a different silk shirt. Peacock blue. And a different pair of jeans. Still too short. This time he's wearing motorcycle boots. Brand new. He tells me he's breaking them in because he wants to buy a motorcycle next week, although I can't picture Quincy R. riding anything but a moped or a sidecar of a motorcycle.

I start to laugh as I wonder what my dad would think of him. He'd probably tell me that "this guy's elevator doesn't go all the way up to the top" or that "he's one feather short of a duck."

"Are you laughing at the way I talk?" the astrophysicist demands. "Are you laughing at my lisp?"

"Oh—um…no. I was just thinking about my dad. I'm sorry. You were saying?"

"I asked a question," he replies hotly, with his arms crossed.

"Oh, right. Yes, a musician told me. Do you agree with it?"

He remains quiet—a defiant silence—as he turns his head away from me and turns up his nose.

"Hmmph!"

"Sorry, I was just thinking about a joke my dad told me about ducks. Forget it—it's not funny. I'm sorry." I don't know why I feel the need to apologize to this rude little man but I do.

"As I was saying," he begins in a carefully enunciated voice, "it's well known that there *are* two types of people…"

The astrophysicist pauses. I'm not sure what to say or do. Is he gathering his thoughts? Or did he just ask a question and is waiting for my response? Should I say something?

Without a word, Quincy R. leans back in his chair and takes off his round, gold glasses. He opens his mouth, breathes heavily and theatrically on his lenses, and then wipes them clean with the bottom of his silk shirt. His face is expressionless. I watch him sip the rest of his vanilla soy latte (half-caf-light-foam-extra-vanilla, no-that's-too-much-vanilla-start-over).

And just when I think he's about to say something, he swings his legs to the side of his chair, swoops down to the floor, and adjusts the buckle on his boot. I catch him staring at the scar on my knee. My impatience gets the better of me and I declare, "Well, I think the musician's theory is rather insightful."

"I wasn't finished!" the astrophysicist cries as he sits back up in his chair. "Tell me, how does it feel to wait for a response from someone who isn't paying attention? Does it feel good?"

Before I can think of a retort to quash the astrophysicist's power trip, he continues, "I have my own theory. I think there are two types of people. There are those who get lost inside themselves…and those who dare to step outside themselves."

I want so badly to object, but I must agree with him.

Part 7 The Billionaire

Begin thou, unforgetting Clio, for the ages are in thy keeping, and all the storied annals of the past.

~Statius, *Thebaid*, AD first century

forty-two

SOMETIMES I WONDER HOW things would be different if I were to make it as a real, honest-to-goodness writer. Would I ever use a ghostwriter? The Nancy Drew series was mostly written by a staff of ghostwriters. The Hardy Boys too. And a lot of famous authors have names that are so big they don't write a solitary word themselves anymore. They'll never admit it, but they use ghostwriters. They have to. They're just too busy. And so are politicians. Hillary used a ghostwriter. Bill did too. And so did Houdini. Is it any wonder that a magician would hide behind a ghost? Or politicians, for that matter?

No, I doubt I'll ever want a ghostwriter for myself. I *have* to write. I'm *compelled* to write. It's as if I have no choice but to write. Recording my thoughts and musings is as involuntary to me as breathing or scratching my arm when a mosquito bites. I could never relinquish that power to another writer…a ghost. I just couldn't.

Sometimes I even wonder how my experts do it. They never seem to mind that I'm the one who writes their autobiographies. How do they hand over such intimate parts of their lives to me? So easily? So trustingly? I used to think that either they were too busy to write or they just couldn't write. It had to be one of the two. But is it that cut-and-dried? Some of my experts (such as the ballerina) are fine writers, and others (such as the astrophysicist) have oodles of time to waste. No, I think it's something more delicate. It's something that's shrouded in mystery or perhaps swimming in complexity. A psychological Jenga trap.

Or maybe not. Perhaps it's something simple. Could it be that some experts are just too scared to do it on their own? Could that be it? Is it possible that they are overwhelmed at the idea of creating a book that secures their place in history?

After all, history is a demanding mistress. Even more so than solitude. To enter the dusty realms of history is to reconcile yourself to vulnerability. Once your story is published, it is out of your hands. Out of your power. Out of your protection or defense. It must stand alone and speak for itself.

Once your story is published, it really isn't your story any longer. Even if it's the story of your life, your childhood, your hopes and dreams—it's not yours anymore. Instead it is the property of others. The readers. It's theirs now. It's theirs to read, to understand, to question. To love or hate. As they hold your story in their hands, they decide whether another page will be turned. And another. And another. It is up to them to decide if your story is worth their time. Their reflection.

And so upon publication you must release your tense, white knuckles from your story. It takes a certain fearlessness, a bravery, to go through with it. You need valor and pluck. Perhaps that's why Clio, the Muse of history, is also the Muse of heroism. It takes a copious amount of courage to willingly take your place in history. It takes a certain moral fiber that can hold up to the stinging winds of criticism and self-doubt.

It is the Muse Clio who is credited with inventing the alphabet and pouring it into humanity's memory. Usually portrayed holding a tablet or parchment scroll in her arms, Clio inspires all that is intellectual. Ironically, she is also known as the youngest of the Muses, as if the collective wisdom of her sisters had been passed down to her. Or maybe she just listened, her eyes and ears always wide open, as it is with the youngest sibling of every family.

It's even said that Clio is the most demanding of the Muses; she expects the most from those she inspires. But is it any wonder? Clio's inspiring whispers result in wisdom and fame. Her name translates from the Greek as "to make famous" or "to proclaim." It is the unlocking of all those secrets of the past that ultimately allows us to catch a glimpse of our future.

forty-three

"SO I SAID, 'SCREW HIM! I'll do it myself!' I mean, how hard can it be to plan a safari in Africa?"

"A real safari?"

"Oh yeah. It's the real deal. It's not like I'm going to one of those reserves where they take you around to sightsee on a damned tour. No way. This shit is for real. I'm basically getting dropped off in the middle of nowhere. Pure wilderness. I'm paying for a tribe, bodyguards, a guide. The works."

I'm having lunch outside with my latest expert, Conrad H., at Lark Creek in Walnut Creek. Conrad H. is a billionaire. He's tall with a lean, muscular build. Long and lanky. Some people walk with a cool swagger, but Conrad H. somehow discovered how to sit with swagger. His legs are sprawled out under the table, as if they've grown ten or twelve inches in the past minute. His face is expressive yet placid. Clean-shaven. Short, dark hair. Dark eyes. A Roman nose leads his small but determined chin.

The billionaire is young for his reputation. Twenty-nine. I'm sitting with my chin buried in my hand so my jaw doesn't drop as he divulges his plans. I'm also just happy that he's actually stayed on topic for the past two minutes without another distracting tangent.

"You're *paying* for a tribe? What does that even mean?" I ask.

"Well, you have to pay for a license to hunt there. That's why they get so mad at the poachers over there," he replies.

"I thought they got mad because endangered animals are becoming extinct," I say hesitantly.

"Hell, no! Are you kidding me? They're pissed because those poachers go in there and hunt without paying for a hunting license! Those licenses cost over twenty grand, so it's a big deal."

"Really?"

"Oh yeah! The poachers sneak in there and kill those animals and then they just skin 'em or take 'em and the poor tribes don't get any of the meat."

"You're telling me that the tribespeople actually *want* hunters to come in and shoot those animals?" I ask.

"They *love* it! God, do you know how many people an elephant would feed? Or how many lives are saved if a lion is killed? If you kill any of the big five, they pay you!" says Conrad H. His eyes are lit up, but so are every other pair of eyes in the room. It seems that the whole restaurant is on the very edge of their seats as the billionaire tells his stories. Some people have stopped eating so they can hear him better.

"You a real blonde?" he adds.

"So, the big five. What's that?" I ask as I nudge my tape recorder closer to him.

"It's the grand slam."

Conrad H. takes another giant bite out of his mahi mahi, which is his third entrée (the full rack of barbecued ribs were gone in a few minutes flat, and the honey-glazed prawns practically flew off his plate). He holds out his hands and counts on his teriyaki-sauce-drenched fingers as he names them, one by one: "There's the lion. The leopard. The elephant. The rhino. And the buffalo. That's the Cape buffalo," he says with his mouth full.

"That's the big five? What about a hippo? Isn't that bigger than a leopard?"

"No, you've got it all wrong," he says, his mouth still full and his hands sticky with amber glaze. "It's not about the size of the animals. It's about the difficulty of hunting them. Anyone can catch a hippo. But the Cape buffalo? That sucker is tough."

I've been working with Conrad H. for a little more than a week now. Mister X has been trying to get this book deal for the past three years. He even joined Conrad H. in Argentina this past spring just to get chummy with the fearless billionaire.

"So you're going completely alone?" I ask.

"I'm going with just one other guy," he replies. "He's a real nice guy, one of the guys that I went to Argentina with this past year. For dove hunting. You know, your boss went too. It was hilarious. He was too scared to shoot at anything."

"So this guy, does he go all the time? Or is it his first time too?"

"Oh, he goes just about every year. But the guy that went with him last year got eaten by an elephant. Some elephant took a bite right out of him."

"You're replacing *that* guy?"

"Yup."

Conrad H. stops eating for a moment and stretches his back. A loud pop sounds from between his shoulder blades.

"Ah. That feels better," he says as he rolls his neck.

"How long will you be out there?" I ask.

"Two months. Maybe three. God, it takes friggin' three weeks just to trap a lion."

It's a lovely day out today. A calm summer day. Breezy, sunny. A weatherman's dream. Just as pleasant as could be. Even our table is set underneath the branches of a gigantic oak tree.

"I'm afraid to ask but...how does one trap a lion?"

"Well, first you have to kill a caribou or some small animal like that. Skin it. And then hang the body in a tree and wait for the lion to pick up its scent. Like bait."

"That's awful! People really do that?"

"Fuck, it's the only way! Otherwise you'll never find a lion."

My stomach starts to churn and Conrad H. leans over to me and asks, "I have a question for you. Do writers read?"

"Do they *read?*"

"Yeah, like, what does a writer read? Do those Pulitzer people read? Or do they just, you know, write stuff all the time?"

And just as I'm about to reply with a fuzzy answer that starts with "Probably," he moves on to yet another topic.

"So I got this idea for a book. You know, after we finish my autobiography. I want it to be about relationships. Man and woman stuff."

"Oh?"

"It could be about how they're different."

I want to tell him that I'm obligated to work on only this one book, that I have other projects waiting for me, and that he'll have to talk to Mister X about other titles, but I don't. I'm oddly amused by the billionaire.

"Think about it," he says as his brown eyes dart around at various restaurant tables around us. "Women are like complicated computer programs. PowerPoint, Adobe Acrobat, that sorta thing. They're complete with the alphabet and number keys. And they totally have Shift, Control, and Delete."

"And men?"

"OK, alright, see, men are like the binary code…just 1s and 0s. Their thoughts are nothing but grunts for sex and food, you know?"

"That's interesting, but—" I start.

But Conrad H. isn't listening. He's not even looking at me. He's lost in his own ideas. He shoves the last mouthful of mahi mahi in his mouth.

"Or a book about innovation," he goes on. "Stuff along the lines of…has the rate of innovation decreased? Has it remained the same? And I'd explore it through education, you know? Because creativity is encouraged in kindergarten, but after that, it's all conformity, conformity, conformity. Hey, where's the waiter? Fuck. I really want to try those pork chops. They sound awesome."

forty-four

LILLY IS VISITING LEO AND me in San Francisco for a week. This week. It's early evening and we're all sitting on the sofa right now, having wine with blue cheese and fresh French bread before dinner.

"Do you have any crackers, Jules? Crackers would go so great with this cheese," she says as she takes a big sip of her sixth glass of Burgundy.

"Mom," Leo interrupts, "Julia already bought the bread. It's fine. Will you just relax already?"

"We're out of crackers," I say. "I'm sorry. But this baguette is from this little bakery around the—"

"Trader Joe's makes the *best* crackers," Lilly interrupts. "Out of rye. I always make sure to have at least three boxes of them in *my* cupboard. But I always like to have extra on hand for my guests. But that's just me." At the end of her sentence, Lilly's voice turns to song and goes up an octave. From the corner of my eye, I see Leo rolling his eyes as he sinks into the couch.

"So. I have an interesting question for us to discuss," Lilly says as she daintily dabs her mouth with a napkin before pouring herself another glass of Burgundy. Lilly asks her question slowly, with deliberate pauses in between words, as if she's trying to get the wording just right. "What is your passion?"

Leo straightens up and blurts out, "Food!" He laughs but we know that he's not kidding. He's a foodie. "And learning," he adds, for he really is a boy-Pollyanna, wide-eyed with wonder. "I think learning is my real passion."

Lilly smiles and nods, and just as I am opening my mouth to give my carefully prepared answer—*Writing my heart out*—Lilly beats me to the punch and says in her sing-song voice, "Well, *my* passion— actually I have three—is Pomeranians." She pauses to gaze lovingly at a sprawled-out Sylvia, panting near Leo's feet. "And reading—I just *love* to read. And wine. *White* wine."

If you ask any woman who has been married longer than five years, she most definitely will have some advice for you. Mother-in-law advice, that is. From what I gather, five years is about the time it takes for young wives to stop trying to be nice and start getting smart. It's a simple yet essential move from the defense to the offense. Simple as it may be, it still takes finesse.

I received some wise words from my neighbor down the hall, Bianca, who has been married for fourteen years. Her mother-in-law is quick to hand out criticism but slow to call Bianca by her name.

"She calls me daughter-in-law number four. That's it," Bianca told me one day in the laundry room. "It's always, 'Daughter-in-law number four, can you pour me some more iced tea?' Or it's, 'Why don't you make a different dessert for your husband, daughter-in-law number four?'"

"Even now? After all these years?" I asked.

"Yes. It's just her way. All the in-laws in the family have a number. Do you want to know what I do?" she asked. "I just smile and nod. That's it! Whatever she says, no matter how disapproving she is, I just smile sweetly and nod. Otherwise, I know I'll snap at her, and then things will *really* get ugly!"

"But how do you put up with it?"

"I just learned that I can't change her. No one can. All I can do is keep it together and not let her get to me."

"And smiling helps you keep it together?" I asked skeptically.

"Yes. Well...that and I tend to stay in my bedroom with the door locked whenever she visits," Bianca cheerfully replied as she folds her linens. "I get a lot of reading done that way. A *lot* of reading."

"And she doesn't get suspicious?" I asked.

"She just says, 'Hmm, daughter-in-law number four sure does like to sleep.'"

Loraine, my neighbor on the first floor, had some advice for me as well. Loraine has been married for twelve years, and she always tells me that the first ten were spent crying in the bathroom because of her mother-in-law.

"There comes a point when you just have to stop trying to please her," Loraine told me once at the mailboxes in the lobby. "You have to stop going out of your way for her, because nothing will be enough for a mother-in-law. Ever."

I nodded and replied, "But how can you just stop? Won't she be more critical?"

261

"It'll just roll off your back after a while, believe me," Loraine replied. "If she tells you that the floors are dirty, just tell her to grab a broom! She'll get the idea."

"Oh, I wouldn't dare," I admitted. "I could never—"

"If you let her know that she can't get to you, then she'll stop trying to get to you. You have to put up a brick wall between the two of you. She's got to know that her criticisms don't have any effect. Even mothers-in-law get bored sooner or later."

Of course, my husband, Leo, offers his own sage advice as well. Whenever I hang up the phone after talking to Lilly, even before I say anything or let out so much as a sigh, I'll hear Leo shout across the room, "She's crazy! Don't worry about it!"

If only it were that easy. I wish to God sometimes that I could just turn off the worries in my head. I wish I could just toss them out the window or crumple them up like trash and let that be the end of it. But I can't. There's always something, either explicit or implicit, that Lilly says that hurts my feelings. I feel like a dusty cliché admitting this. But it's true.

When she visits I feel as if an army lieutenant is conducting an inspection. When she calls I have to fight my feelings of guilt and self-doubt as she makes wild accusations: "Why do you and Leo visit your father in Santa Barbara more than you visit me? Do you not like me?" or "You didn't return my phone call this morning. Are you avoiding me?"

And to make matters worse, Lilly says this with a lovely, sweet cheerfulness. Never in my life have I met someone with such juxtaposing parts of politeness and condescension. "Jules," she once told me, "I hope you like this new purse I bought for you. Isn't it nice? I didn't want to say anything, but…the handbag you've been carrying around is looking awfully *grubby*." Her subtle critiques, her nimble jabs, are painful.

And I'm not able to just smile and nod or even give up. The only thing I'm able to do is to thank her and then feel bad about myself for an hour or two. Or four. I really wish I could just not worry about it, as Leo so frankly puts it. But the truth of the matter is that I want to have a mom again. I really do. But every time Lilly raises an eyebrow or sighs disapprovingly at me, I just feel hurt and rejected and abandoned all over again.

She could never replace my mom. No one could. It's just not possible. But sometimes I wish she could. I wish she could just magically morph into my mother and that I could be that girl. That happy daughter who has a mom again.

forty-five

I'M STARTING TO WONDER IF my hair will fall out. No, not from Leo or even Lilly. And no, not from stress. I just wonder if I've overdone it in the color department. When I look in the mirror at my honey-blonde tresses (newly dyed for the summer project), I love how the color brightens me up and gives an "I just got back from vacation" look. But when I examine those individual blonde strands pressed between my fingers, they look almost translucent. It's as if I've saturated the hairs with so much color (and so many different ones!) throughout the years that they can't hold onto any more dye. It's as if that poor, tired hair just can't handle it anymore.

And though my hair doesn't really look brittle, it is. I know that I could just snap any hair on my head in two if I wanted. Any day now, my hair might throw in the towel and scream, *Enough already!* at me.

I promised myself that I would go back to my natural color the day I retired from ghostwriting. The problem is that Mister X doesn't seem to care about the health or well-being of my head of hair and keeps throwing projects my way.

I'm having another dinner with Conrad H. to review the final details of the project. He's the only expert I've ever met who demands that all of our meetings take place at precisely lunchtime or precisely dinnertime. "A guy's gotta eat," he explained.

His skin is much, *much* more tan than it was a week ago when we met for the project. He's bronze now. And it suits him. He also seems calmer and more relaxed.

"I just got back from Cabo," he explains. "Cabo San Lucas. A buddy of mine called me up and said that tuna was just flyin' out of the water, so I hopped on a plane and did some fishing for a few days. Then I bought a house there because I needed somewhere to put the boat I bought."

"You go ocean fishing in Mexico?" I ask, embarrassed at my own lack of adventure.

"That's the place to go. The tuna's ridiculous down there! Yellowfin tuna. Bluefin too. It's wonderful," the billionaire says. "I've got a great crew, too. Those guys are great."

He stares at the menu with a frown and then asks the waiter if he can just have a good steak. Turning back to me, he continues, "Everything's in Cabo. There's dorado, marlin, oh my God, you wouldn't believe the marlin they have down there." His eyes light up. "It's wonderful."

Our entrées finally come. Conrad H. has already gone through two baskets of bread and is asking for another. He eats with such an impatient voraciousness that I wonder if his only meals are all with me.

"So I have another idea for a book," he says intensely as he motions the waiter for another beer. "I want to write a story about how to get rich quick. But not like a scam. I'd teach them the real shortcuts, you know? I read somewhere that if you haven't made your first million by the time you're thirty, then statistically you probably won't ever make a million in your lifetime. Did you know that?"

"But," I say, "didn't you inherit quite a bit?"

The young billionaire stops eating and pauses in silence. And I wonder if it's the first pause he's ever taken in his life. His eyes narrow and I start to hiccup as I wonder if I've overstepped my bounds.

He puts down his fork. He's still not saying anything, and my hiccups start to really get out of control. Now I know I've overstepped my bounds. My shoulders are shaking like some ba-gawking chicken as I try to muffle the hiccups. I try to hold my breath, but my chest is tight and it aches. I can't stop hiccupping.

Conrad H. hands me a glass of water and smiles. He takes a deep breath himself and finally says, "I guess my answer is yes. And no."

He starts eating his steak again, and my hiccups start to subside.

"My dad started the company. He's a concept guy. Genius smart. A visionary. And I love him. But I've taken his millions and made billions with them. More than my dad ever could," Conrad H. says in a serious voice, "because at the end of the day, to do well in business you have to be good with people. And my dad just didn't have that. Instead he just jumped down everybody's throat whenever he got mad. Or fire everyone if he was in a bad mood. I do things different."

"How so?"

"I just…oh fuck. Come on. I don't know. But I do. I guess I just treat everyone like my best friend because I think everyone really is my best friend. And people like that. They want to work for someone like that. They want to buy from someone like that."

"Well, your father must be proud of you and all that you've done," I say.

"You'd think so, wouldn't you?" he replies, his voice full of a fire that comes from his gut. "You'd think that a dad would be proud of a son if the son is successful, huh? If the son makes a damn good living…and if he's made the whole world look at a company that they never noticed before?"

"Well, yes—"

"Exactly. But my dad…" His voice thins out and he's silent for several moments. "He just doesn't see it. He thinks I swindled his business out from under him. He doesn't get it." The billionaire's voice is severe. "He just nitpicks, nitpicks, nitpicks…and all he wants to do is tell me what I'm doing wrong. Hell, that's what I hear every day from everyone else. The world is criticizing me. I don't need my dad giving me shit too."

Conrad H. shoves his plate of food away from himself. He fidgets with his napkin and bounces his knee up and down. As he stares off into the distance I glance at him. He looks different now. Or maybe I'm just starting to notice different things about him. His hair looks a little thin in some places. And those fine lines around his eyes. And the wrinkles that are starting on his forehead. Worry wrinkles.

And I start to think that the billionaire isn't just a fiery daredevil. Or just a courageous dynamo. He's an escapist too. He runs away as far as he can. For as long as he can. So he can catch his breath and keep going. So one day he can hear his dad say that he's proud of him.

"I just want him to be my dad, you know?" he says, still fidgeting, "I just want to hear him talk about normal stuff—TV or the weather or whatever—and not about the business. God, I don't even know why I'm telling you this. I don't want it in the book or anything."

"No, it's OK," I begin.

"It's just that...fuck! It's frustrating. The company was a complete disaster before I took it over. A fucking mess. He could have lost everything. But I got in there. And I saved it. I cleaned it up."

The billionaire looks at me and waits for a response. I don't know what to say. There's so much tension in the air, and I feel the hiccups coming on again. My throat's tightening up. I drink some more water, and then I realize that the tape recorder is still on. I turn it off and throw it in my purse. Conrad H. is still looking at me. His eyes are searching my face for some sympathetic words but I'm at a loss.

But soon I remember.

"An astrophysicist once told me that there are two types of people in this world," I begin slowly. "There are those who get lost inside themselves and those who dare to step outside themselves."

I take another nervous drink of water and pray that my hiccups don't come back.

"What the hell does that mean?" demands the billionaire, crossing his arms. "And what does an astrophysicist know about life?"

"Well, I think he meant that in life it—"

"No, no," Conrad H. interrupts. "I mean, he sounds like a fuckin' idiot, this guy. He's got it all mixed up!"

"You have something better?" I ask.

"Yeah. Yeah, I do," he says with a broad smile. His teeth are big and perfect. "I think there are two types of people in this world. Those who leave their shit behind and those who clean it up."

The billionaire leans back in his chair and orders a slice of banana cream pie. Ice cream on the side and on top.

"You know," I say, "I think you'd really get along with my dad. Do you like motocross?"

forty-six

I REALLY WISH I WERE THE KIND of person who diligently writes everything down in a journal or in a lovely, leather-bound diary with gilded pages and perhaps even a lock. The kind of person who records everything every day. And I try to. I really do, but sometimes it's hard. I suppose I'm afraid of sensationalizing my life for the sake of writing, which is a tough spot to be in. And sometimes I worry that if I write down a day's events that it will make them a little less real, that it will turn them into just a story.

Yet still I try. I'll even do a few consecutive days of journal writing. Not more than four, really. OK, three. And after that I'll just get discouraged. Or worse, I'll start making things up to write in those entries. Bogus events that are more interesting than the actual day. Phony feelings that are deeper than they actually were. And these falsehoods will disgust me, and I'll shove the journal in a drawer somewhere. Out of sight. And then a few weeks (or a few months) later, I'll rediscover that journal and start all over again.

Perhaps the most challenging aspect of journal keeping is deciding to whom to address your entries. Must you always write, *Dear Diary*? Or may you write to yourself? *Dear Julia.* Or, *Dear Julia of the Future.* Do the bold journalers choose instead to face the inevitable question of snoops and write, *Dear Whomever Is Reading This*?

I haven't really solved this problem, so I avoid the issue altogether and merely date the entry and proceed with the topic at hand. It looks rather scientific, really. Or it would if I actually kept it up instead of my utterly dismal average of seven entries a year.

My mother kept a journal. Several, in fact. From the month she passed away up until now, I've found seven of them. Some are from her *lycée*, or high school, days. Others from *université*. There are even a few from the early years of marriage to my father. One is navy blue. One is dark red. The others are black. She wrote daily, detailed notes in her elegant French handwriting. Cover to cover. Every margin of every page was filled and scribbled in with her memories and dreams.

I don't know how I found them. I would always stumble onto a journal's hiding place accidentally, each time when I was visiting my dad. When I was the last one up at night, just weeping and brooding about how badly I missed her. When I cry like that, I find myself walking aimlessly around the house, as if my body were still looking for her…as if she were just around the corner or in another room…as if I just have to find her. And it was always on one of those desperate walks through the house that I would find a journal.

I was quite surprised when I found them. One by one. I had never even known that she kept journals, let alone saved them for years. And I was even more surprised when I actually read them. They were filled with secrets. Wonderful, astonishing secrets. With each page I turned, I learned things about my mother that I had never known before.

Before she was Mom, she was just Geneviève. The Geneviève who saved up all her money to buy a light blue convertible, only to have her younger brother take it out for a spin and wreck it the next day in Grasse. The Geneviève who owned a sea-foam-green surfboard and went surfing every weekend in a yellow bikini. The Geneviève who struggled to adjust when her family moved from Nice to California until she fell in love with a wild and reckless American boy, Adam, in his white T-shirt and Levis, and kissed him all over town. The Geneviève who was so thrilled to get married but so completely devastated to have miscarried her first child a year later.

I learned about things she had never told me, perhaps because she forgot. Or because she ran out of time. Things that made me proud of her and things that made me cry. Through those journals I discovered the woman *behind* my mother. A strong, beautiful, and mysterious woman, who was full of contradictions and endured much in silence.

I could hear her voice again when I read those journals. Her sweet, gentle voice. I could hear her sharing each of the passages as if she were sitting beside me at the kitchen table in Santa Barbara again. Even though my mother was gone, it was as if she were continuing to mother me through her written words. And it brought me pure joy.

I felt close to her again. And it was that closeness that I had so desperately craved and missed. This finding of my mother's journals—discovering her secrets—led to my desire to write my mother's story. I want to honor her life and give her the story that she deserves. I'm almost finished now with *Elegant Simplicity*. Just a few chapters left.

My mother-in-law, Lilly, has a few as well. Days, that is. So far, her visit has been pleasant. Leo says it's the calm before the storm, but I think everything will continue to go smoothly. We're having breakfast together outside on the balcony. Leo has left for work.

"You look very nice today, Jules. I must say I really like you with this new hair, this blonde—er—is it blonde? Yes, it does look blonde to my eye," Lilly says in exaggerated sweetness, "and that's *such* a beautiful blouse that you're wearing. May I ask where you bought it?"

I look down at my crinkled white top and realize that I spilled apricot jam right on the collar. I hold my hand up just under my chin to cover it up.

"Oh, I think I got it at a little shop in Santa Cruz this past summer," I reply nervously.

"Well, it's a very *unique* blouse," she says as she nods her head for emphasis, "although…"

"What?"

"I can't help but notice that you would look more…*complete*…if you had a necklace. Yes, I'm sure of it."

I very rarely wear jewelry, aside from my diamond wedding ring (which was my mother's). I don't even wear earrings, let alone a necklace. At most I'll wear a narrow silver bracelet (also my mother's) when Leo takes me out for an evening. But that's it.

Lilly, on the other hand, makes a hobby out of jewelry. She wears at least three necklaces at once, along with several bracelets on both wrists, which jingle when she walks. Even her ears have three holes each to maximize her earring possibilities.

"A little necklace around your neck would really brighten you up," she adds.

"I just don't wear that kind of stuff," I begin in a tone so apologetic it makes me squirm. "I like to keep things simple."

"Here, I have an extra one in my purse. Just try it on," she insists.

"No, that's OK. Thank you, but I don't really like wearing them."

"But a necklace would look—"

"No, really. I don't like wearing them. They make me feel like I'm getting choked."

"But I think if you gave it a chance," Lilly implores as she searches her bag for the jewelry, "you'd like wearing them. A necklace *completes* a woman's look. And then we could get you some matching earrings and a matching bracelet and maybe a brooch for your collar to cover up that jam stain."

"No, I really don't want to," I blurt out.

And Lilly collapses into a sob. At first I think she has the sniffles, but she's crying. A dainty, lady-like cry that almost sounds like whimpering. I watch as she brings her pristine, embroidered handkerchief to her eyes and then dabs her tiny nose.

"I'm sorry," I say, feeling like a monster. "I didn't mean to hurt your feelings. Here, I'll try on the necklace."

Lilly looks up at me with wet eyes and puts her hand over mine. I can feel her hand shaking a little, and I notice that her normally impeccable red-manicured nails now look like they've been picked at and chewed for days.

"No, *I'm* sorry…I know you don't like me," she says tearfully. "I can just tell."

"But I *do* like you. I love you. We're family," I reply.

"I want you to like me," she says. "I want you to think of me as your mom."

I try to comfort her but I'm not sure what to say so I just nod and give her a hug.

"I've just always wanted a daughter, Jules," she reminds me. "I have five boys, but I've always wanted a daughter."

"You do," I say gently. "You have me."

Lilly wipes her eyes with her head down. She raises her head and a slight shadow falls across half of her face. A clear, bright path of light shines on the other half, making one of her eyes appear a deep and infinite green.

"Jules," she says carefully, "for my whole life, all I've ever wanted to be is a mother. I know I was a good mother—a damned good mother, excuse my French—because I look at my five boys and see what wonderful, amazing men they have grown up to be. Being their mother is the one thing that makes me feel like I have a reason to be in this world."

And I realize that now I have two moms who love me, one in heaven and one right in front of me, weeping out of love for her family.

Part 8 The Diplomat's Daughter

Kalliope, who is the chiefest of them all, for she attends on worshipful princes: whomsoever of heaven-nourished princes the daughters of great Zeus honour, and behold him at his birth, they pour sweet dew upon his tongue, and from his lips flow gracious words.

~Hesiod, *Theogony*, eighth to seventh century BC

forty-seven

I'VE FALLEN HEAD OVER HEELS in love with G. K. Chesterton. I even told Leo so. I don't care if the whole world knows. Sure, G. K. died in 1936, but I'm deliriously happy with my literary crush.

Never before have I felt this way about literature. I was the one who sat in the back of the class (with my legs defiantly perched up on the seat in front of me, no less), sighing impatiently and rolling my eyes while the professor discussed Shakespeare. And I'm pretty sure I was the only one who didn't appreciate Hemingway or Henry Miller. Steinbeck made me tired. Even Jane Austen left me feeling angry at the time I had wasted reading *Pride and Prejudice* instead of *Cliff Notes*. To impress a boy in college, I once pretended that I adored Kate Chopin. But I really didn't. I used my copy of *The Awakening* under my kitchen table to keep a leg from wobbling. It worked great.

With G. K. Chesterton, however, things are different. When I read his essays or novels or even his short stories, I feel a bit weak in the knees and my heart beats extra-fast, the way it used to on a first date. As I pore over his perfectly chosen words, I can't help but feel deeply inspired and impressed.

A year ago at Christmas, Leo gave me *The Man Who Was Thursday*. Chesterton subtitled it *A Nightmare*, but I find it nothing short of dreamy. My copy is less than 185 pages long, but it's taken me more than a year just to get halfway through it. I study it line by line. Word by word. Notion by notion. My absolute favorite part is on page 57 of my modest Random House paperback, where Chesterton describes the color black in such rich detail that I felt I had never truly understood the color until that moment:

> [H]is black seemed richer and warmer than the black shades about him, as if it were compounded of profound colour. His black coat looked as if it were only black by being too dense a purple. His black beard looked as if it were only black by being too deep a blue. And in the gloom and thickness of the beard his dark red mouth showed sensual and scornful…those cruel, crimson lips.

I was lost in that paragraph for weeks. Months, even. I read it again and again, as if each time were the first time. I reveled in Chesterton's clever, straightforward, and take-charge style of writing, a style that maintains a clear and stunning eloquence all the while.

It's not at all like my own writing. Not in the least, unfortunately. I tend to just record my ramblings that run circles in my head—in the naïve hope that they will lead me somewhere interesting. Or profound. But more often than not, my written path leads me back to the lonely spot from which I began.

Perhaps Chesterton was inspired by Kalliope. She was, after all, the Muse of eloquence and epics. Even her name translates as "beautiful-voiced," which explains her bestowing the gift of beautiful language on those who invoke her.

Rumor has it that she was Homer's Muse. And Proust's. And Edith Wharton's, as well. Kalliope was also the Muse of philosophers, princes, and kings. Her gifts of rhetoric and persuasion have been sought after throughout history, and rightly so; with eloquence comes the ability to negotiate heated quarrels and encourage peace.

Known as the most distinguished of the Muses, Kalliope is also the oldest. The big sister. She presides over the other Muses, as well as their various comings and goings. Even Zeus depended on this Muse to readily calm any storm with her words. Along with any catfight between goddesses.

With her violet eyes and long golden hair, Kalliope is usually portrayed with her arms cradling a scroll or tablet. Words are both her instrument and her scepter. The immensely lucky individual who is inspired by the Muse Kalliope is said to receive not only a profound talent for rhetoric but also the gifts of respectability and esteem.

More than any other Muse, Kalliope innately knows the power of words. The right words, accompanied by the right inflection, can spark emotion from a void and split it into a thousand flames. Words can make a difference. They can change a life.

forty-eight

I RATHER PRIDE MYSELF ON being a girly girl. Feminine and such. I try to keep my toes polished and my hair (which is now tree-bark brown) conditioned and curled and lavender sachets tucked inside my chest of drawers. I like shoe shopping and I get excited when I buy fresh flowers and even more excited when they're sitting, arranged perfectly-imperfect, on my kitchen table.

So maybe I shouldn't know what a Honda CRX 250 looks like compared to a 500. Or why getting a holeshot is one of the best feelings in the world. But I do. And maybe I shouldn't know what the difference is between a two-stroke and a four-stroke dirt bike. But I do. And I definitely shouldn't know what a kick start is. But I do. And I also know how to find Yamahas by their yellow, how to spot old Kawasakis by their green, and that a *true* motocross rider will tell you that anyone who rides a quad bike is a wimp, and so are Harley-Davidson owners (whose tiny helmets always produce a wave of snickers and chuckles among passing motocross riders).

When I was six, I used to stand right on the grimy, dusty starting line of all the big motocross races, next to my dad and his bike. I had a tiny broom and my job was to sweep the rocks and debris away from the area in front of Dad's Honda (which was always red, except for a brief time in the early '90s when Honda flirted with neon pink). The sound was beyond deafening as the riders warmed up their bikes, revving them while the race that preceded theirs was coming to a finish.

"If I'm gonna get that holeshot, you're gonna need to get those big rocks outta the way up there, darlin'. You see them?" he would tell me, his voice muffled through his helmet, as he pointed his gloved finger to a spot twenty feet down the straightaway. And I'd run with my little broom and sweep them from my dad's lane into someone else's. This wasn't allowed, of course. But Dad said that I was so young that no one would ever get mad at me. I was happy he needed me.

Motocross was as much a part of my childhood as backyard barbecues, birthday parties, and playing with my dolls. Dad dragged the whole family to the races every single Sunday from as far back as I can remember up until I was in junior high, when Mom begged him to finally stop racing. Whether it was Gorman, Mammoth, or Indian Dunes, we would be ready and out the door by four in the morning, so that Dad could get plenty of practice laps in before his races started at eight. "You have to know the track," he'd say. "Only a moron would race a track he didn't know." We'd watch the sun come up over the plateaus on the track. And we'd stay all day long, watching and cheering him on, until the trophies were handed out at nine or ten at night. Our den was filled with those trophies, most of which were nearly as tall as me. At one point, Dad would just toss them into the trash if they weren't.

On those Sundays, my older sisters would help Dad with his heavily buckled riding boots, my Mom would make sandwiches and snacks for us, and I would be in charge of those damned rocks. Dad would usually come in first place. The only times he didn't were when he crashed and had to go to the hospital instead of the finish line, which felt like nearly half the time.

By the time I was twelve, Mom had stopped going, which meant that I had stopped going, and instead started going to church. She told us that attending Mass was more important than the races and trophies, but really I think she had gotten tired of my dad breaking his legs, arms, collarbone, and ribs. She had nursed him out of comas, out of concussions, and out of wheelchairs, and after nearly fifteen of her years doing that, enough was enough. "I just can't watch you do this to yourself anymore," I overheard her say once. "I just can't. You're too competitive. You only get hurt when you race, Adam."

Even though the family stopped going to the races, Dad kept on racing. He kept on winning and crashing all by himself for another few years. And then Mom got diagnosed with cancer, and he finally promised her that he wouldn't race anymore.

And he did stop, for a while anyway. He got a dual-sport motorcycle (which looks the same as the racing dirt bike, but has a headlight and thicker tires) and went play-riding with his friends up in the hills, just for fun. And sometimes he'd go down to Baja to ride on the sandy dunes of the beaches, just for fun. But a few months after

Mom passed away, Dad started racing again. He even bought five more bikes. And he's racing more now than he has in decades. Three, sometimes four, times a week. But it's different now. It's not the thrill of the speed, the flying jumps, or even winning that keeps Dad racing. Not anymore. He tells me that he wants to ride as much as he can before he gets too old and his knees give out. But I think that's just an excuse. I think he's just trying to push back from the grief.

Right now I'm on the phone with him as he tells me the details from his latest race.

"I can't believe you're already riding again. It's so soon. What about your ribs? Have they even healed yet?" I ask.

"Broken ribs take a really long time to heal," Dad replies.

"What? Broken? I thought you said they were just bruised?"

"Well, it doesn't matter. There's nothing I can do about them." He sounds tired and preoccupied.

"You could give yourself time to recuperate," I respond.

"I did. I didn't race for a whole week. But I couldn't miss that race. It was a biggie. The track was incredible. Not too dry, not too wet. You should have seen that plateau. Besides, I'm fine. I feel good. It just hurts when I sneeze or when I breathe in or something like that. So how long are you going to be in Switzerland?"

"I'm in Geneva for another two weeks," I reply.

"Bring me back a T-shirt," he says. "One that says Switzerland on it."

"I know, I know. A red one."

"You should be at home," he says. "It's too dangerous to leave the States."

"It's just as dangerous *inside* the United States."

"Yeah, but at least I could drive up if you needed me," he says.

"Oh, Dad. I'll be fine. I'm just in the middle of another project, and I really need to be here."

"But I thought you were done with that ghostwriting stuff. Wasn't the last one your last one?" he asks.

"I thought it was, but I sort of got talked into this one. It's actually the most interesting project I've ever been assigned though. I'm having—"

"So I was talking to Olivia earlier," he interrupts, "during lunch. And she just loves music. Boy, does she love music. She even got me and her some tickets to this concert this weekend and—"

About seven million hiccups start jumping out of my throat, and I feel flustered as Dad tells me about the band.

"And Olivia thinks that you really should look into—"

"OK, Dad," I say quickly, in between hiccups. "I'd better get going. To breakfast. It's still morning here."

forty-nine

I AM COMPLETELY AND UTTERLY exhausted. Geneva is nine hours ahead of California, and the cruel, laughing face of jet lag has taken me prisoner. I wasn't really expecting it since my normal schedule is hardly typical, with writing sessions lasting until dawn. But it's hit me hard. For the first three days, I felt somersaults in my stomach whenever I saw the cheerful sunlight of Switzerland. And for the first three nights, I kept waking up at three in the morning with hunger pangs for lunch.

Although I'm finally adjusting to the schedule, my feet are still dragging. I'm sitting alone at a table, and my eyelids are almost too heavy to keep open. I'm dressed in a long black strapless gown with white satin gloves that go up past my elbows. They once belonged to Leo's grandmother. Lilly gave them to me years ago to wear on my wedding day. Now I feel like a princess because I've gotten to wear them twice. But if Lilly were here, I know she would have a heart attack because I'm not wearing a necklace. Or earrings. Just a small magnolia bloom in the side of my chignon. Eliza T. put it in my hair just outside a few minutes ago before we walked in. She picked it off a low branch and plucked off a few of its white petals to make it the perfect size. "This will look lovely in your brown hair," she said as she pulled a bobby pin out from her own hair.

Katerina introduced me to Eliza T. in New York. She was looking for someone to write her autobiography. ("Biographies are always so full of lies and agendas," she told me. "It's the autobiographies that are real.") I told her that I was about to retire from ghostwriting altogether after a project in the summer. "Just give it some thought," she said with a smile. "I need someone who knows how to make a life into a story. Katerina told me you can do it. Just think about it, will you?" And although I shook my head, a couple of months later an exquisitely engraved invitation arrived at my door:

THE DUKE AND DUCHESS OF M.

REQUEST THE HONOUR OF YOUR COMPANY

AT THE

LIVINGSTON GALA BENEFIT

FRIDAY, APRIL FOURTEENTH

COCKTAILS AT 7:00 P.M.

GENEVA, SWITZERLAND

BLACK TIE

I RSVP'd faster than you can say *RSVP*. Who could resist an invitation to a ball? I didn't even know they existed outside of fairy tales. I gave Eliza T. the OK for the autobiography. Mister X nearly jumped out of the phone when he heard the news and hammered out a contract for her in less than a day.

And here I am, an American ghostwriter in Geneva, all dressed up and sleepier than ever.

Like me, Eliza T. is from the United States. Her father is a U.S. diplomat to an African country. I can't say which one, but I can say that she speaks both fluent French and German and is wiser than a twenty-nine-year-old has a right to be. An only child, she grew up in fancy hotels all over the world. Her playmates were usually bellhops and hotel maids, and her playgrounds were hotel elevators. Now Eliza T. is all grown up and a human rights activist for underdeveloped countries. She splits her time between Switzerland, New York, and Africa.

I watch as she makes her rounds in the ballroom among countless black and white tuxedos with foreign service agents and dignitaries. Eliza T. is the sort of girl who reminds me of autumn, even though it's mid-April. She's thoroughly modern and old-fashioned at the same time. She can recite Chaucer at the drop of a pin and then turn around and tell you which country has imported the most corn or coffee this year and who should win the Booker Prize next year.

Her voluminous gown is an iridescent blend of colors, with dark teals, deep purples, and emerald greens. It's made of layers of voile, and the skirt has a layer of taffeta that creeps along behind her with a haunting swish. Its rich, opalescent hues bring out her luminous skin, which is the color of champagne. Her hair is a soft auburn, just above her shoulders, and frames her face ever so gently. Her side-swept bangs barely graze her cheek, just as a paintbrush would a canvas.

But most important, Eliza T. looks like the sort of girl who truly understands moonlight, like those flowers that bloom only at night, once the sun has set. Maybe it's because of the nostalgic look in her hazel eyes, as if something always reminds her of something else and nothing is seen for the first time. Or maybe it's because of her berry-colored lips, which discuss and debate her most passionate ideas for the world.

Draped over the scalloped neck of her gown is her usual long necklace of glass beads from Africa. Eliza T. refuses to wear diamonds. "If you only knew the pain and suffering that go into mining diamonds," she once told me, "you would see the blood in those diamonds that I see."

The diplomat's daughter makes her way back to my table and offers me a drink.

"So who exactly is the Duke of M., and where is his Duchess?" I ask.

"Over there," she replies, "near the fireplace, talking to the ambassadors from Italy and Spain. This is their spring residence. They have one for every season."

"How in the world did you get them to invite me?"

"I just told them that you were my dear cousin from California, that you would be spending the month with me in Switzerland, and that I couldn't bear to attend this without you."

"Ah," I reply. "I feel like a secret agent."

"Well," Eliza T. begins as she declines a waiter's elaborate silver tray of cheeses and canapés, "writing other people's autobiographies is certainly a voyeuristic undertaking, no? People tell you things. They confide in you. And you see things that no one else sees. You're sort of a literary secret agent, aren't you?"

"No, no," I say with a smile. "I'm just a cousin."

A string quartet is playing a Chopin repertoire in the center of the room, but you can still hear the excited jumble of conversation in more than a dozen languages floating through the air, along with wispy clouds of cigar smoke. The ballroom of Babel.

"So Cousin, would you like me to tell you who is who?" asks Eliza T.

"Please!"

The diplomat's daughter makes a loud *swoosh* as she and her elaborate dress sit down.

"Let's start near the door," she says, discreetly pointing her finger toward a distinguished-looking man sipping on brandy. His well-coiffed hair exudes a glossy grandeur. "He's amazing. Really. He used to be an immigration attaché for South America, but now he's heading a center for leprosy. He runs it with a Jesuit priest. He gave up everything for that center. It's in the jungle."

The man looks up as if he felt us watching him and nods graciously at Eliza T.

"And over there, standing next to my father," she continues, "do you see the man with the red carnation pinned to his lapel? He's the ambassador to Bolivia. He's brilliant. Just brilliant."

"Are most of them from the United States?"

"No, no," she replies, "everyone has a different host country. There should be a few from Washington coming tonight, but the Americans are usually late anyway."

The diplomat's daughter then whisks me around the giant marble-floored room in a flurry of introductions for a crash course in diplomatic geography. A couple of agents from the Philippines are here. Canada. And the Netherlands. I lose track of the names, and the faces are becoming a blur of smiles and mustaches and tortoiseshell eyeglasses. Germany. Guatemala. France. Ireland, too. Agents from the Near and Far East. And everything in between. Most everyone here speaks French, but I find a few snippets of accented English that I can follow.

We flutter in and out of a hundred conversations, each their own mix of opinions, as everyone seems to talk at once. "Democracy only works in a country that thrives on its diversity of religions and ethnicities," says the agent from Japan, "but for other, more homogeneous, countries…not so helpful," while the official from Italy casually debates the merits of a united Europe. The mood turns introspective as an agent from Germany dressed in tails (whom Eliza T. knows well enough to rest her arm on his shoulder) says, "It's incredible how naïveté can prevent us from moving forward, isn't it? For example, I often wonder why people who are in the most difficult, life-threatening situations—such as widespread disease and famine—always have children. And a lot of children, at that." He pauses briefly to light a cigar he's plucked from his pocket. "I used to actually wonder, and Eliza—I know you will hate me for asking—but why do they want to bring babies into the world if there is no food? Why would anyone want to raise a child in such miserable conditions?"

I turn to Eliza T., expecting a disapproving glance, but she remains perfectly calm and seems to be almost impressed that anyone would admit such a thing to her. She is rolling some of the glass beads of her necklace between her fingers as she listens. At his final pause, she says, "It's a basic, most natural instinct, of course."

"Sorry?" asks the agent from Germany as he leans in closer.

"It's a natural instinct," Eliza T. repeats, her voice clear and composed, "Don't the animals of the world do this too? Some will even have ten or twenty babies when usually only two or one survive. We are all the same. It's in your blood to pass on your genes, your history, your legacy, your hopes, your dreams, to someone else. It's so that a part of you lives on after you die. Even in the face of poverty, disease, or famine," she continues, "your own blood tells you that there's a part of you that must live forever."

The other conversations in the room fall silent as the only sound that remains is the violins playing a mesmerizing "Nocturne in E-Flat Major." I listen intently as I fill the Cinderella slippers of the diplomat's niece. Ordinarily I would remain silent in such an intimidating circle, but Julia the ghostwriter is in disguise. I can say and do what I please. And so without a single hiccup, I bravely interrupt the heavy silence and say, "You know, a billionaire once told me that there are two types of people in this world. There are those who leave their shit behind and those who clean it up."

Certain I will be snubbed or scoffed at, I grab a flute of champagne from a passing waiter's tray and gulp it down. The sting of the alcohol closes my throat a bit but I look up anyway to face the disapproving reaction. But there are no jeers or even sneers. Instead everyone is laughing and nodding in agreement.

"Well said," says one agent.

"Yes, quite," says another.

Eliza T., however, remains silent.

fifty

GHOSTWRITING IS PERHAPS the loneliest profession. Not only do you work in solitude, you must enjoy the fruits of your labor in solitude as well. No one must ever know of the words you write. No one can ever find out that it was you who wrote that poignant description or that lighthearted prose.

There are exceptions, of course, as with everything. Once in a great while, a ghostwriter will be given the opportunity to peek out from the shadows and reveal her name, if only briefly, to the world. It is purely up to the discretion of the expert, however. It is only the expert who holds the key to every ghostwriter's cage. It is only the expert who can unlock that oh so tricky trap-door of obscurity.

An expert, however, never completely surrenders the byline. Oh no. He merely shares it. Or rather, they share a tiny part of it. This partial credit of authorship is worth far more its weight in gold to a ghostwriter than to anyone else. A ghostwriter will forever savor the fact that her name finally, at long last, is printed on the cover of a book.

Of course, the ghostwriter's name is never in the same size font as the expert's. It's usually half or a quarter its size. And it's never on the same line as the expert's name. It's usually several lines below in a discreet spot that often gets unnoticed by the Reader's busy eye. And a ghostwriter's name never, *never,* ever comes before the expert's name. Alphabetical orders are thrown out the window and left on the curb. Just like the heated word, *and.* The names of an expert and a ghostwriter are never separated by an *and.* Experts consider that word an insulting slap to their famous face. Instead, the ghosted books are always attributed to Fantastic Expert *with* Lonely Ghostwriter, or in some cases *As told to* introduces the ghost.

But most of the time, if the ghostwriter is mentioned at all by the expert, her name is buried in the acknowledgments or foreword, as one of many people "without whom this book never would have been written."

This is why I was so surprised when Eliza T. asked if it would be all right to put my name on the cover of her autobiography.

And the World Was My Home: The Autobiography of Eliza T.
By Eliza T.
As told to Julia Clark

I thought she was joking when she first brought it up. I have never been on a cover in my entire life. All my books have been 100 percent anonymous. And even *Alice's Dream* has had its publication debut postponed for a year because my editor has jumped ship. But the diplomat's daughter was completely serious. "Otherwise, I would be a thief," she told me yesterday evening at the ball, "and I don't ever want to be a thief."

"But you're paying me to write this for you," I said, my heart still in denial. "Are you sure? It's not really expected."

"Of course I'm sure," she replied, without so much as a pause.

Ever since I found out the good news, my mind has been in a million places. Even right now, I'm having trouble concentrating on my phone conversation with Dad.

"Can you hear me?" he asks.

"Yeah, I'm sorry, Dad. I'm just a little preoccupied. I got this amazing news the other day," I reply.

"I hear a lot of background noise. You're sure you can hear me OK?" he asks again.

"I can hear you fine. Here, I shut the window. Is that better?"

He doesn't say anything. My dad always has something to say, but right now he's perfectly silent.

"Dad?"

Still nothing.

"Dad? Are you there?"

The line clicks a few times, and now the phone is completely dead. I redial.

"Hello? Hello?"

"Sorry, Dad. The line went dead. Is this better?"

"Still a little fuzzy," he says, his voice unsure. "Listen, I have something to tell you."

"I have something to tell you too, Dad. I'm getting byline credit for the book! You know, the one for the diplomat's daughter? Hello?"

No response.

"Dad?"

The phone is dead again, and now I hear a Swiss operator's recorded voice. I redial but now Dad's phone is busy. I redial again and again, but it's still busy. I open the window in my hotel room for some fresh air, and I hear an ambulance go by. Ambulances in Europe sound so different from the ones in the United States. European sirens are more human sounding, almost like someone's scream or a desperate, mournful wail. They're louder too, and make your stomach turn into knots as they fly by.

I dial my Dad again, and his phone starts to ring.

"Julia?"

"Sorry, Dad. I don't know what the heck's wrong with this phone. I'll have them switch it out later. It's so frustrating when it cuts out like that."

"Darlin', I have some news," he says. "I'm not sure how to tell you this. I just…Julia? What's that sound?"

"Sorry…I have the hiccups."

"Oh. Anyway, I don't know how to tell you this, so I'm just going to tell you. Julia, I'm getting married. Olivia and I have decided to have the wedding next month. I wanted to wait until you got back from Switzerland, but Olivia said, well, she thought we could have the big party, you know—a reception or whatever they call it—when you get back. Julia? Hello? Hello?"

The phone isn't dead this time, but I hang up anyway.

It is the first time I have ever hung up on my dad. I still can't believe I did it. I stand there, staring at my phone as if it will disintegrate in my hands. Five long minutes go by and it rings. It's him. And I can tell by his silence that he knows the call wasn't dropped on accident.

"I'm sorry, Dad," I manage to say.

No reply.

"I'm sorry," I say again.

"You think this is easy for me," he finally says, his voice the same as when he'd scold me as a child for riding my tricycle in the street. Low and sharp.

My face feels hot with regret. I can feel his words coming through before he even says them: "The person who has it easy is you. It's been easy for you being all the way up in San Francisco this whole time. You weren't here every day. You weren't here for the chemo like we were. Yeah, you visited, a few months, here and there, but you weren't *here*. You don't *know*. I'm the one that's had to deal with everything."

Part of me wants to argue and say that I *was* there. And that I was in high school when it started and that I took a year off of college to be there. But I can't. Because I still wasn't there as much as him. I still didn't do but a fraction of what he did.

"I'm sorry," is all I can say over and over again whenever he breaks for a breath.

"I don't want to be alone anymore," he goes on. "I've been alone since the day she was diagnosed. Do you understand that? I haven't had a life in over ten years, Julia. I stopped counting after that." He stops talking but it isn't quiet. I hear a faint, broken cry over the receiver. And then he hangs up.

Another long five minutes go by. I call him back and tell him I love him. I tell him congratulations and then we both pretend that he never told me how he really felt for all those years.

fifty-one

I'M HOLDING A LITTLE SNOW globe in my hands. It's heavy for being so small. I shake it up and watch the tiny white and silver specks swim around in the water. As they settle, a miniature porcelain version of the Golden Gate Bridge appears. It's painted orange and surrounded by glossy white clouds. It's just a lonely bridge in the sky.

"It plays music too," says Eliza T. "On the bottom, you see? Wind it up, and it plays 'I Left My Heart in San Francisco.' My father took us there when I was seven. I don't think I've been there since, come to think of it."

Eliza T.'s home in Zurich is very different from what I was expecting. It looks like a farmhouse from the outside. It's red with a wide, pointed roof, and it's tucked in the middle of green, rolling hills. I've never seen so much green in my whole life. There are even a few cows meandering about.

"I meant to tell you," she said when I first stepped inside her cottage home nearly an hour earlier. "I don't agree with that billionaire, whoever he is. He sounds like a real narcissist who can't be bothered with reality."

"Hmm?"

"From last week. At the party, remember?" she asked as she took my coat.

"Oh, that. I was hoping you had forgotten. I'm sorry, I guess I was just trying to be funny."

"No, it's not that. I just think there's more to it than that."

"Really? What?" I asked.

Eliza T. slid into a brocade chair and pivoted to let her legs dangle over the armrest.

"Well," she began in a serious tone, "well, I think that it all boils down to just two types of people. There are those who can see and feel for the whole world, and those who can't see past the end of their own nose."

The inside of the diplomat's daughter's home is exquisite in a lavish, natural sort of way. It's a botanical paradise, with green plants and potted orchids everywhere. No matter where you look, there are orchids. Purple ones. Pink and white varieties too. Their long, graceful stems are twisted seductively around dried bamboo stalks. It's as if all her chairs and sofa were set in a decadent garden.

An unusual scent fills this home. Calming and soft. When I ask about it she tell me it's sage, Breu resin, and Palo Santo crushed together in long incense sticks she picked up on her latest travel to South America.

"It's used in healing rituals," she explains.

Marigold-colored velvet sofas take up the center of one room. Giant tasseled pillows made of raw silk perch on them. The walls are painted a pale grayish lilac, with a patina-like finish that looks more like ostrich feathers all sewn together. From the ceilings hang dozens of potted ferns. All of them flourishing. Together they make a lacy green canopy that filters the sunlight that streams in through the skylights above.

Tall lamps, whose shades are layered in black tulle, are scattered throughout the rooms. An old-fashioned spiral staircase leads up to the bedrooms. It's made of a curled wrought iron that looks as if it were dusted in olive-colored gold. I'm sitting on the velvet sofa. The tiny snow globe looks happily out of place on her bevel-edged mahogany coffee table.

Eliza T. is still sitting languidly in her brocade chair. She looks as if she were waiting for an artist to paint her portrait among the orchids. She's eating a plum right now as she divulges some of her stories for the project. My tape recorder is on, but I'm quite positive I would remember each word she says anyway.

"The amphitheater is one of those unforgettable symbols of ancient Rome," she says. "It's where gladiators entertained masses of Romans by fighting to the death. Have you seen the Colosseum?"

"Only in movies," I reply.

"That's the most famous of them. I took an unusual walk around the Colosseum a few months ago, actually. I went there at night, which is really the best time to go."

"To beat the crowds?" I ask.

"Oh, for the drama, of course! On a dark night, just imagine it, Julia, that's when it's illuminated from the inside by these unbelievably dramatic gold and silver lights. It's like frozen fireworks. You see, the Colosseum is at the very end of Via dei Fori Imperiali, which is this great big avenue Mussolini had built for his ridiculous military parades. So there I was on my walk, trying to take it all in. As I crossed the corner of the avenue, I heard echoes of agony and misery. But these were not the voices of tortured souls from the past but sounds of a struggle just fifty yards ahead. More real than my own voice."

Eliza T.'s voice has a soothing rhythm and cadence. I can tell that she's told this story many times before, but I'm on the edge of my seat.

"What was it?" I ask. "What happened?"

"I watched a man double over before collapsing on the ground," she continues. "An angry tourist was beating him senseless. Immediately, a crowd gathered while the savage kicked the man's head, again and again. Muffled whispers were exchanged among the onlookers, all while the man was beaten unconscious. Faster than the gore could escape from his temples, nose, and mouth, the crowd dispersed. People returned to their tour of great Italy and cameras or their ridiculously unfoldable maps. And the man lay there. Knocked out. Alone."

Eliza T. pauses to take another bite from her plum. "We're living in a world fraught with indifference," she continues. "We can't help but witness the devastating plunge humanity has taken in recent years. Our eyes remain shut—stubbornly shut—as the world continues its downward trajectory. But we do nothing. We just watch, if that, and remain paralyzed by the weight of apathy."

"But why?" I ask.

"Maybe we're afraid to help," she replies. "It could be a scam. What if the two men were putting on an act to draw us in and then attack us? A person's got to think of his own safety first, they say."

"So there's not really such a thing as a Good Samaritan anymore?"

Eliza T. smiles at me, or maybe she's smiling at her orchids. Her eyes don't look at me. They never do. In fact, she rarely makes eye contact with anyone, I've noticed. Instead, her eyes always seem to be searching for the right word.

She turns again so that her legs are on the floor. Angling her body toward me, she says, "Society's skepticism is not without warrant, Julia, but we can't help but ask ourselves, *What if a person is really in need? What then?* We can't just turn our heads and look away when there is suffering. We can't just continue to ignore people in need. I think apathy is just as inhumane as inflicting harm."

Her voice is steady. She folds her arms and tilts her head against the wall.

"Sometimes I think that the person I am today is made by no small part from how my father made me memorize two different quotations when I was a child. He told me that they're the most important words I would ever read."

"Do you still remember them?"

"I'll remember them until the day I die. The first one went like this:

Do all the good you can,
By all the means you can,
In all the ways you can,

In all the places you can,
At all the times you can,
To all the people you can,
As long as ever you can."

"Your father sounds like an interesting man," I say.

"Hmm. Some say the theologian John Wesley wrote it, but I could never find it in any of his writings. Dad made me memorize it in grade school. He was so adamant about that. We said it together every night after our prayers. I've always tried to be true to those words," Eliza T. says, standing up, "but, well, tell me something, Julia. Do you think it's even possible? Can kindness really fit into today's world?"

"Well, why not?"

"I think the human mind has been desensitized," she replies.

"From overexposure?" I ask.

"Yes, that's it. We're numb. Absolutely numb to the pandemonium that surrounds us. We've shielded our fragile hearts from the misery of others' lives. But enough is enough," she says. She stands now and paces across the room with her hands waving through the air like a composer. "The old ways have outlived their use. Society can no longer remain oblivious to the reality of suffering; feelings must be expressed, emotions must be accepted, and sorrow must bravely break through our callous façade so that truth can be seen. We have to search deep within our collective core and find strength in our weakness, for we are only as strong as the weakest among us!"

She pauses for some time, but the passion in her voice still hangs in the air from the slight echo between the walls. For the first time,

Eliza T.'s hazel eyes meet mine. They're just as deep as she is, with swirling specks of amber that look like broken glass.

"What was the second quote your dad taught you?" I ask, slightly uncomfortable that I am only one person and not an audience.

She turns her eyes away and blinks hard to mentally change gears.

"It was on this photograph when we first moved to Africa. It was framed in raw pine, and it was a portrait of a starving child, lying curled up on the ground and left to die. And underneath the photo were these words, written by George Bernard Shaw: 'The worst sin toward our fellow creatures is not to hate them, but to be indifferent to them: that's the essence of inhumanity.'"

I feel those words slowly etching themselves into my memory before I can even decide if I agree or disagree. I watch Eliza T. as she walks over to a wooden bureau and opens a small drawer from its center. She takes out a small picture wrapped in a yellow silk handkerchief and hands it to me. It's the picture of the child, complete with the Shaw quote. The photograph is in black and white, and I can make out a small shadow near the child.

"What's that?" I ask, pointing to it.

"That's the shadow of a vulture," she replies. "I used to hang it up, but I think it's more important than just a picture to hang and get lost on a wall. I don't ever want to get used to that image. I don't ever want the shock of it to disappear."

And very carefully, Eliza T. wraps the framed photo back in the handkerchief and returns it to the drawer. The room is quiet except for a few distant moos from outside.

"It's the same with stories, isn't it?" she asks, her back still turned.

"How so?"

She turns to face me. "Well, in a way, all stories are trying to fight apathy. Maybe that's why I finally decided to put out a book."

"I'm sorry, I don't follow," I admit.

"If you really stop to think about it," Eliza T. says, "No matter what story you read, no matter what it is about or who wrote it, every story has the same purpose. They all try to make you feel something, somehow. Whether it's love or hate or even amusement. The enemy is always indifference."

Part 9 The Artist

Come, Erato…stand by me and take up the tale.

~Apollonius Rhodius, *Argonautica*, third century BC

Part Seven

fifty-two

In the Vatican there is a special room called Sala Delle Muse, or The Room of the Muses. The room is shaped in an octagon and filled with pillars exquisitely carved from Italian marble. Elegant statues of the Muses line the sides. It is said that anyone who enters the room will receive inspiration in the arts. As long as the Muses are in a good mood, of course.

In their lighter, more generous, tempers, the Muses can bestow a wealth of talents and inspiration on those whom they deem worthy. Hesiod, an ancient Greek poet and historian, claimed that he actually met the Muses face-to-face while tending sheep on Mount Helicon. Supposedly they instructed Hesiod to stop farming and instead narrate "the present, the past and what is to come." And Hesiod happily obliged and even recorded the happening in his *Theogony*: "He is happy whom the Muses love. For though a man has sorrow and grief in his soul, yet when the servant of the Muses sings, at once he forgets his dark thoughts and remembers not his troubles. Such is the holy gift of the Muses to men."

But in their darker moods, however, the Muses can be spiteful, vengeful, and downright cruel. A veritable "revenge of the Muses," so to speak. Those are rare moments for the Muses, but they leave such a sting that hardly anyone challenges them. Except, of course, for Thamyris. Good old Thamyris. His famous story has circled the nervous whisperings of writers, artists, and poets for ages. It goes something like this: A vain singer who was an even more vain poet, Thamyris (pronounced them-iris) felt so confident and proud of his talents that he dared to mock the Muses. He shook his fist in the air and claimed that his skills were more powerful than theirs. The Muses of course punished Thamyris for his boasting and punished him dearly. But as to how they did so remains a mystery.

Nearly everyone has a different version of the ending. The Greek playwright Euripides writes that the Muses became so annoyed with Thamyris that they made him blind. The Greek historian Diodorus Siculus says that the Muses mutilated Thamyris and then took away his memory so that he couldn't recall any of his beloved poems or songs. Homer takes this story one step further and claims that not only was Thamyris blinded and devoid of memory, but also he was made unable to sing. Thamyris was left to wander the streets with the punishment most feared by all artists; he was left talentless.

How happy Hesiod must have felt that he was in the good favor of the Muses and forgot only his "dark thoughts," with his gifts still firmly intact.

I suppose I'm quite fortunate to have finished the projects with the experts without burning any bridges. And surprisingly, I still hear from them on occasion. Eliza T., the diplomat's daughter, sends me postcards from all over the world, even though our project has been in bookstores for six months now. Most recently I heard that she was in Los Angeles giving a speech at a fundraiser for the Amazon Relief project, which is a charity in South America that gives essential aid to adults and children with leprosy. The billionaire, Conrad H., still sends me an email now and then, which is usually light on text and heavy on attached photographs of his latest adventure. His most recent email showed him standing next to his freshly caught bluefin tuna for the Los Cabos Fishing Tournament in Mexico. In one photo his dad stood alongside him in the boat. They weren't smiling but they seemed to be at least tolerating each other.

And I was more than surprised to hear from Quincy R., the astrophysicist. It was a puzzling telephone call, really, and I wondered if he had dialed me by accident and was too proud to admit it once I answered. After an awkward pause he asked me if I could take him to the airport because he was flying to Honolulu for business. When I said no, he became flustered and threatened to fire me. I reminded him that the project was already at the printers and pointed out that I had already gotten paid.

Violet L., the musician, also rang me. Several times, in fact. I don't think she's left her New York loft once since we finished. She told me that she was retiring. Not from music but from live performances. She had said that she was only going to do recordings of her music and that's it. And at the time we spoke, the entire floor below her loft was being converted to a state-of-the-art recording studio. "That way my music will remain...like your books," she said. "It will be lasting."

315

I also hear from Jeremiah W., the monk. He doesn't call or email or even send me letters. He sends me books. Thoughtful, interesting books by authors such as Thomas Merton and Caroline Myss. And the only thing Jeremiah W. writes is the same brief inscription on the inside cover: "Thought you might enjoy this one." And I usually do.

Bruno M., the chef, also keeps contact with me, though usually in the form of a super-quick phone call in which he asks, "Did you see it? Did you see it? How was I?" He's referring to his brand-new cooking show on the Food Channel. After his book was published, he enjoyed a new wave of popularity in the U.S. market, and now he's the famous face on a line of fancy French salad dressings that supposedly can ignite your love for roasted pine nuts and rosemary.

Of all the experts, I probably hear from the ballerina the most. Anastasia M. still performs for the same ballet company ("I have maybe another year left before they kick me out for being too old," she admitted). Her autobiography won critical acclaim in both the dance world and the literary world. At the very last minute, just seconds before it was sent to the printers, we decided to end the book with her mysterious poem, "Phantom." And it was a big hit. Publishers everywhere asked her to compile an anthology of her poetry, and Anastasia M. was happy to do so. She's working on her second anthology right now.

The psychologist, too, surprised me. Dr. Eleanor B. eradicated her fear that she was stamped with the family expiration date of seventy-nine because she saw her eightieth birthday. Unfortunately, she passed away just three days afterward. Lottie the maid told me that her last words were, "I did it. I made it." And she did.

In a way, these eight experts were my Muses, imparting their delicious wisdom to me—even when it was unintentional. And even when I didn't want it. Yes, I learned something from each of them. Of course, there is still one expert left. And one Muse as well.

fifty-three

THE COLD AIR SMELLS LIKE wood burning as clouds of smoke float up from nearby chimneys. There's something familiar about that smell. Comforting. It's autumn now, and I'm working on the artist's manuscript. This project is taking longer than the others. More than two years now. But I know it's worth it. I'm walking up a drive toward a house that has several potted chrysanthemums leading up to the door. Ruby-tinted mums. They don't seem to mind the cold at all. Their burgundy-colored blooms look like miniature velvet pom-poms that bob up and down in the wind.

I'm in Santa Barbara at the house of the artist. Well, it used to be her house. She doesn't live here anymore. Only my dad lives here now.

But it is her memory that is my Muse. My true Muse. After all, it was my mother who gave me the gift of writing. For my tenth birthday she bought me a book of Greek myths, along with a set of calligraphy pens and an empty journal for me to use to write my own myths. And it was my mother who taught me that writing can be a refuge. Whether I was angry at a friend ("Just write her a letter," she'd say) or depressed for no reason ("Why don't you just write a little story? It'll make you feel better," she'd tell me), Mom taught me that writing was always the answer.

My mother was an artist. She would paint early in the morning before anyone woke up. Sometimes I'd wake up extra-early just to sneak a peek. If I was too late, all I would see was her washing her paintbrushes in the kitchen sink, washing the color down the drain and then scrubbing the sink with Ajax.

Mom had a natural eye for art. She understood balance and rhythm and color on a very innate and intimate level. She knew beauty. Maybe it was because she loved flowers, or maybe it was just because she loved life. She loved every tiniest detail of nature and showed her appreciation in her art, from the veins of an iris petal to the labyrinth of lines on a butterfly wing, the artist's hand had them memorized by heart.

But all of her paints and brushes and things were kept hidden in the drawers of her old oak desk in the middle bedroom (her office). Oil-based paints on one side of the desk, watercolors on the other. Brushes and sea sponges were kept in the center drawer, concealed under a blue swirl-print handkerchief. Sometimes the artist painted on canvas or on heavy paper, but mostly she painted on silk. Nothing too big or tremendous, just small, simple squares of ivory silk with unfinished edges.

As I walk inside, I realize that I haven't been here in more than a year. Not since the previous Thanksgiving. I'm not sure why exactly but the house seems different. And yet still the same. Maybe it's because Dad moved the painting that used to hang in the entryway. It was the loveliest painting of a family of swans, set in an ornate bronze-colored frame. It was the first thing you saw when you walked in the house. But it's gone now.

In its place is a new painting. A close-up of an African elephant. The elephant's face and ear alone fill the canvas. I walk down the hall into the living room and see that the swan painting is in the corner, hung just above the bookcase, next to the fireplace. The swan painting looks darker than I remembered, but it's probably because it's just not getting the same light that it used to.

Hardly anyone knows this, but Mom painted that picture of the swans. She never signed the painting or even added initials, but I know it was hers. She adored swans, often calling them "the most graceful creatures God ever created." She lamented over never owning one. The painting is filled with every shade of blue imaginable. Vibrant yet tranquil turquoises delicately mix with indigos and sapphires.

The scene is of a mother swan on a bit of land, surrounded by water that blends into the blue sky. The swan is holding her long, elegant neck in a gentle curve that resembles half of a heart. She's standing beneath some lacy branches of a willow tree and shielding her three babies with her massive outstretched wings. The brilliant white of her plumage looks so soft and real, as if she were under the spell of a soft sunlight. All of the babies nestle close to their mother, except for one, who is heading back toward the water.

I've always loved the painting. It's the sort of scene that you can gaze upon and get lost in for hours. But it does indeed look darker than before. Almost as if the surrounding waters in the painting have grown colder since my most recent visit. But still the mother swan gazes down lovingly at her babies, even at the stubborn one who is marching away.

Erato loved swans as well. Known as the Muse of love in Greek mythology, Erato is usually portrayed standing next to a swan. In some paintings she is surrounded by them, as if she were leading the flock. But in her most famous portrait, done by Italian painter Filippino Lippi, the Muse Erato is leading a giant swan by a leash of long, gold ribbon. Not much has been written about Erato. It's as if her character were a big secret, but her very name makes historians blush. To the ancient Greeks, Erato was thought to be the divine inspiration behind any love story or romantic sonnet. Likewise, she is thought to be the prettiest of the nine Muses, with the most tender temperament. And yet surprisingly, it is the myth that surrounds her pet swan that continues to pique scholars' curiosity and imagination. It is the myth of the swan song.

Shakespeare references the mysterious myth in several works. But it was the philosopher Plato in ancient Greece who first made mention of it in his work *Phaedo*. According to the myth, the swan is said to sing a song "more fully and sweetly" than ever before, upon realizing its own death is just minutes away. Supposedly it is the most beautiful song of the swan's entire life. As well as its *only* song. And yet the question that has remained throughout history for scholars and philosophers alike is why.

What's the cause behind the swan's unusual "power of prophecy"? What's the motive? For what possible reason does the swan, who never sings at all at any other stage of its life—not even in distress—decide to break into a glorious song when death is just moments away?

Some scholars believe that the swan song is a cry of lament, a farewell song expressing the swan's sorrow over its impending death. But Plato disagrees. He insists that no birds sing in distress, not even when they are suffering, starving or cold. Every nightingale, every swallow, and every other bird sings only when it is truly happy. And so, Plato reasons, the swan song must be an expression of an ultimate joyfulness—that of realizing that although life is about to end, heaven is just moments away.

fifty-four

I HAVE NEWS. BIG NEWS. I'VE made one of the most life-altering, earth-shattering, unabashedly bold decisions a woman can make. I've decided to stop coloring my hair.

No more blonde or red or brunette or jet-black tresses for me. No more changing. Just me. Come to think of it, I'm not sure what my natural hair color even is. I can't remember. I think it was somewhere in between a light ash brown and a dark blonde. In any case, my roots will come in, and the real me shall finally appear.

I came to this decision when I decided to nix my job with Mister X and instead focus on finishing *Elegant Simplicity* and getting it published. This biography of the artist has taken me so long to write. I can't just whip it out in three months. Mom's story means so much to me that I want to do my best to do it right. In some ways, it's another ghostwriting gig. The final project. It really feels like she's writing this book with me—as if she's at my side or behind my shoulder, whispering the words I ought to write. Yes, the artist is the Muse behind Julia Swan.

My mother-in-law, Lilly, is having a difficult time accepting my choice of a pen name.

"So have you decided yet?" she asked me over the phone yesterday evening.

"Decided what?"

"You know. About your book."

"I'm sorry—" I began, "I don't follow."

Lilly cleared her throat impatiently.

"Have you decided yet which name you'll use as your byline?" she asked sharply.

"But I already told you. Don't you remember?"

"That whole Swan business? You were serious? Oh. I thought you were making one of your jokes. I thought for sure that you would use your married name. It has such a nice ring, doesn't it?"

"But it's pretty much already decided," I said gently. "I told my publisher and—"

"Just think…Julie Griswold. I think that sounds so nice! Like a romance author! Yes, Julie Griswold sounds just lovely. Very distinguished. Yes, and then I could tell my friends that my daughter has been published, and then I could see it in bookstores and—"

"Wait, hold on a sec. Why couldn't you tell people?"

Lilly stops for a few moments, and I hear her Pomeranian barking in the background.

"Shh…shh…Mom's on the phone…shh…now then, what did you say?"

"I said, why couldn't you tell people about it if Julia Swan wrote it?"

"Because that would be lying, dear. I don't know any Julia Swans," Lilly replied sweetly.

At that point, I just didn't have the heart to tell her that I hadn't even legally changed my name yet from my maiden name, Clark. Socially I go by my married name, but my official documentation—Social Security, passport, driver's license, and such—are still under my maiden name. It wasn't intentional. I suppose it was just one of those things that I never got around to doing. But if I'm really being honest, I'll admit that there's also a secret, self-indulgent part of it that keeps me from making the change: There's something extraordinary about having the freedom of two names. Or three, counting my nom de plume. It's absolutely liberating. It's like living two lives at the same time. I guess even though I've decided to give up ghosting, I'll never give up the thrill of living as many lives as I can.

fifty-five

JUST ABOUT EVERYONE AND everything has a sworn enemy. Lambs have the wolf. Ladybugs have the frog. Jackrabbits have the owl. Zebras have the lion. Humpback whales have the killer whale. And motocross riders have the bicyclist.

"They're a bunch of sissies. They're in their little bike lanes, and they expect everyone on the road to move over for them, and everyone does. It's ridiculous! You don't see anyone giving motorcycle riders their own lane, do you? Well, *do you*?"

Leo and I are having lunch with my dad right now at the house. Things are somewhat back to normal between my dad and I since our phone call when I was in Switzerland. We're eating turkey and Swiss sandwiches with a side of raving rant.

"No, I guess not," I reply.

"And do you want to hear the stupidest part? Bicyclists don't even pay any taxes for the road! It's my damned road! I'm the one paying extra taxes for it! Do you know that when you have a motorcycle, they make you buy all these special tags for it? They tax the hell out of you. But not the bicyclists," Dad says, switching to a high-pitched, sarcastic voice. "Oh no, don't tax the *bicyclists*. They're helping the *environment*."

My dad's latest bicyclist tirade is the result of an announcement in the news today that another one of his beloved motocross tracks is about to be shut down.

"So what's the deal with that track?" asks Leo. "Is it because of the noise? Were people complaining or something?"

"No! It's just past Gorman. There aren't even any houses anywhere near this track. It's up in the mountains near the Grapevine, miles and miles away from anybody. It's ridiculous."

"So then why are they shutting it down?"

"Because of those damned sissies on their bicycles!" Dad replies. "Some stupid bicycle-activist group talked the lawmakers into preserving that side of the mountain for the environment. But really, it's just so they can have those trails to themselves. They hate us."

My dad is talking with his mouth completely full. He's the only person I know who can carry on a complete conversation without missing a bite of his food. Even if his mouth is full, he somehow finds room on the other side of his mouth to continue shoveling in his food. He's a master of this technique, really. Sort of like a chipmunk or hamster who stores his entire winter's worth of acorns in an extra flap in their cheeks.

Sometimes I wonder if my dad chews his food at all, really. When I watch him eat, I see him take a super-huge bite of his food, talk, take another huge bite, talk some more, and then swallow everything down with a spectacular gulp. Not surprisingly, nearly every meal with my dad consists of him having a coughing fit that turns his face hot pink and forces him to wave his arms up in the air for a gasping…glass…of…water. But after a giant sip from the glass, he'll quickly resume the simultaneous shoveling in of food and talking as if nothing had ever happened. Ah, the cycle of life. Needless to say, he also suffers from acid reflux, which I've decided is just his body's special way of saying, "Slow down!"

But despite my dad's manly man, animalistic approach to eating, his best friend at the dinner table is always his napkin. This is because my dad hates (as in *absolutely* hates) to get his fingers dirty. This translates into my dad not ever starting a meal unless he has his trusty napkin beside him, as well as outright refusing traditional finger foods, unless it's with a knife and fork. Even if it's a steaming slice of pizza, Dad needs his knife and fork. A banana? Knife and fork. I wonder if he secretly eats Snickers candy bars with a knife, fork, and napkin.

And maybe that's why my dad is never too excited about eating a sandwich. It just doesn't work with a knife and a fork. If he absolutely has to eat it, he'll insist that the mayonnaise be in the center of the sliced bread and not too far on the sides because "it will squeeze out and get all over my fingers."

It's hard to believe that my dad has such a dirty-finger phobia, considering that his passion in life is taking apart his motorcycles and rebuilding them. Mud, dirt, oil, grease, and all. But if you're his daughter, you'll know that he always wears white surgical gloves when he works on his bikes. He probably has the cleanest fingernails of any motocross rider who's ever lived.

What's not surprising is my dad's fridge. Like any bachelor's fridge, it's empty. Completely empty. Unless, of course, you count the five-year-old ketchup on the shelf inside the door (it's the industrial size, fit for a company picnic) or the gallon of chocolate milk.

After all these years, my dad still struggles with figuring out what to eat. Firstly because he still hasn't a clue how to cook for himself (he went straight from his mother's cooking to his wife's cooking). Secondly because he gets too lonely eating by himself. Consequently, my dad has become a regular at just about every restaurant, diner, and café within a twenty-mile radius of his house. He knows just about every waitress, waiter, and manager by name, and he has his favorites from every single menu.

Dad's just one of those people that hates being by himself. Even when he leaves his house, he always makes sure to leave a good amount of lights on inside, as well as the television—that way, when he comes home he won't feel so lonely.

Deep inside, I know that he needs someone. But it's hard for me to admit it. I wish I could say that I think he's OK coming home to nobody day after day, or eating alone at the 24th Street café while my two sisters and I have our own families. But I know it's not OK. He needs someone. He really does.

Ever since Dad told me about his engagement to Olivia, I've had no choice but to admit it. Their engagement party is tonight, which is why Leo and I drove down to Santa Barbara. The two of them decided to postpone the wedding a few more months until spring and nicer weather came along, but really I think it was because they realized that everyone was in shock and needed just a little more time. Or at least that's what I'd *like* to think.

Of course, I'd also like to think of Olivia as a future aunt or second cousin, not a future stepmom. But label or no label, it's still going to happen. And it doesn't matter what I think or feel because it's my dad's decision. And as much as it's uncomfortable for me to think about, I know that Mom would want him to be happy again. And deep down, so do I. That's what matters.

fifty-six

I WONDER IF FICTION IS EVER completely fiction. Can there be such a thing as a story purely drawn from imagination? Or a character experienced exclusively in the mind's eye of the author? Can it even exist? Or are all stories based on some set of truths? And I wonder how often an author is defined only by her writing—her personality characterized only by her printed words.

I'm almost finished with *Elegant Simplicity* now. I'm sitting alone in the backyard of my old house in Santa Barbara. The sky always looks different when I'm at home. The porch light is off, and the stars seem particularly bright. Everyone is already asleep and has been for hours. I should be in bed too. But tonight my eyes are wet with tears because I miss my mother. How does a girl live without her mom? Without the one person who truly understood her? My mother is in heaven—the most joyful and beautiful place to be, I was taught—yet I cry and cry, unable to stop. I'm happy that she's not suffering anymore, but oh, I miss her with all my heart!

Sometimes, when I cry like this, I can hear her gentle voice, feel her arm lightly curve around the top of my shoulder, and even smell the faintest hint of iris from her Shalimar perfume. Is it her spirit or her memory? Is this real or in my mind? Is she really up above or is she here with me, right now? The voice tells me that it's her love that surrounds me and comforts me at my bluest hour. "Why? How?" I ask, aloud. The voice says that a mother's love will never die.

My Muses have taught me many things, but it was the artist who taught me that love is what keeps you going. After the tragedies, after the despair, after the loneliness and suffering, there will always be love.

I remember one afternoon with the artist. It was before she got sick. Maybe a year or two before. We were sitting in the backyard at home in Santa Barbara and watching the black and bluebirds fly through the cloudless sky. It was the first day of spring. The air was still cool, but everything outside looked so vibrant, so alive in the sun.

Mom had even moved her caged canary outside on a table in the patio with us to give him some fresh air. And I remember how we laughed as the little canary excitedly hopped back and forth on his perches as he sang his rolling chirps out to the wild birds in the sky. The canary's flirtatious advances were ignored but still he sang. And still the black and bluebirds flew through the air currents until they finally decided to rest on the branches of the old birch tree. We watched them as they weaved in and out of the sunlight filtering through the leaves, as if the shade was still too cold.

Mom leaned back in her chair and thoughtfully pursed her lips.

"Hmm…," she wondered out loud as her eyes took in every last detail of the scene.

"What is it?" I asked.

The artist carefully gathered her thoughts for a few more moments before answering. "You know, Julia," she said slowly as she rested her chin upon just a few of her fingers, "someday you'll find that there are two sorts of people in this world. Those who live in the shadows and those who live in the sun."

And now, I think I have finally grown weary of shadows. I think I'm going to try living in some light for a change. The swan has sung her last song and has long since flown to the sky. The ghost has been freed.

fifty-seven

IT'S ALMOST FIVE IN THE morning. I just can't wait any longer. Leo is still asleep. His nostrils are throwing out hot blasts of air, which would normally wake me up and force me to roll over. But not today. I've been awake for the past hour, trying my very best to downplay my excitement. It's still dark out, but I hear some traffic noises outside. I slip out of bed like a cat slinking out of his owner's arms.

My socked feet skate down the hall so fast they slide right into the doorway, and I stub three of my toes. I open the mirrored cabinet and fumble around for the box. My eyes squint into nothing. I turn on the bathroom light. I find the box. The directions are followed. A tiny oven timer is brought in from the kitchen and turned on. The three-minute countdown has begun.

It's impossible not to watch the blinking number. My eyes fix on it as if somehow the intense power of my yearning could make the three turn into a two…but instead it has the reverse effect and time seems to stop. I become superstitious that my watching has everything to do with it and so I look away. At the tiny hole in the toe of my sock. At the chipped clear polish on my fingernails. At the outline of a snooping pigeon perched on the other side of the bathroom window. At the timer…it's still at three.

The worries begin. What if I didn't follow the directions properly? I pick up the folded leaflet, which fell on the floor, and scan through seven languages of instructions. What will I do if it's positive? What will I do if it's negative? I take a quick breath and try to force my mind onto other subjects, such as guessing the expiration date on the milk in the fridge and whether today is Monday or Tuesday.

A loud, beeping alarm sounds. Part of me wants to shout to Leo to turn the oven off, but then I remember. I turn the timer off, but I'm not ready to look. I sit on the closed lid of the toilet, pull my legs up under me like a child, and close my eyes. I must have reset the timer instead of turning it off because it starts beeping all over again. *It's time!* it seems to say, *it's time! This is what you've been waiting for! That moment is here!* I stand up and walk over to the sink. The test is right where I left it, perched near the soap dish, but everything is different now. I take another breath, look down, and see that little word staring back at me.

My knees become weak and I can barely stand. My legs switch to autopilot, and somehow I find the strength to sprint into the bedroom and leap onto the bed like a giant frog. My hands and knees speed-crawl over to the still-sleeping Leo and, with my face directly over his, I shout, "I'm pregnant!"

Leo's eyelids flutter briefly. His eyes open and then they droop back into sleep as if I were part of his dream. But I don't have to repeat the words. In seconds, his eyes reopen and grow wider than I had ever seen them.

I grin.

"You? I mean—we?"

My expression—an equal mix of excitement and fear—tells him yes.

"We're going to have a baby?" he says. "Oh...oh, I'm so happy!" Leo sits up in bed and grabs my shoulders. "I'm gonna be a dad...and you're gonna be a mom! Can you believe it?"

We lie back down and stare at the ceiling. Neither one of us is able to go back to sleep. I feel the warmth of Leo's hand on my stomach as if he were shielding it. Protecting it from the world. He keeps it there until the sun comes up. No other words are spoken for hours.

I'm barely able to control the restless chatter buzzing in my head. I start to imagine what our baby will look like. If the baby will have Leo's wavy hair. My long nose. His ears. My big teeth. His strong build or my bony legs. Or if there will be a part of the baby that looks like my mom. Like her almond eyes or her dainty hands. And then it hits me that maybe, just maybe, I might see her smile again someday.

The sun has just started to rise. Honeycomb-shaped pieces of sunlight force their way in through the blinds. I rub my hands over my belly. It still looks the same. It's hard to believe that there is a tiny life inside there. Slowly building his or her features. Absorbing bits and pieces of us and our family. Leo turns to me and begins to speak in midthought. "It's like—doesn't it feel like—our lives have been unfinished until now? Until this little baby? We're going to be a family!"

The day goes by quickly. It's late afternoon before I pick up the phone, but it's a long, agonizing ten minutes before I can do anything but make small talk with my dad.

"Oh, so *that's* the name of the town where we used to picnic when I was little," I say slowly, trying my best to buy some time. "I always wondered about that. And what freeway was that off of again?"

"That was the 101," Dad replies curtly. "Look, Julia, my cell phone is almost out of battery, and I was just about to head out for lunch anyways. I'll give you a call later, OK?"

I try to suppress that terrible rising pressure in my chest that signals looming hiccups. So much, in fact, that it begins to hurt.

"Oh, Dad, before I go…oh, now I remember what I wanted to tell you. Can you get your calendar out?"

"Honey—"

"Just real quick," I reply. My fingers start to fidget. They twist and mold a whole sheet of paper into a tightly wound boomerang. "What are you doing in March?"

"What day?" he asks. Then he says, "What was that? You got hiccups?"

"Early March." I twist the paper again, harder this time, into a tiny loop. I can hear him flip the pages of his daybook.

"Uh, nothing. Nope. Nothing. I've got a thing in early April, but nothing going on in March."

"Really?" was all I could say, not sure how to advance.

"Why?" he asks. He sounds half annoyed, and I know he's aware that I'm trying to tell him something. Dad always hated it when I couldn't confront an issue.

Quickly I spit out more words: "How far away is that? March, I mean."

"It's about six, seven, eight...eight months away," he says.

"Really? Are you sure it's not *nine* months away? *Nine?*"

"No. It's eight months."

"I'm pretty sure it's nine months, Dad," I say as I flatten out the paper, trying to return it to its original letter-ready appearance. But it's completely wrinkled now, like an old smoker's face. I keep pressing it, as if my fingers could somehow make it smooth and pristine again. And still it keeps rising up at the edges, as if it truly enjoyed being curled and twisted into new shapes and refused to return to its boring, creaseless self.

"Well, eight and a half," Dad finally says after flipping through the pages again.

"No, Dad. It's nine."

"Well, what's going to happen in March?" he says, now completely bothered and out of patience.

"I'm going to have a baby then. Dad, I'm pregnant."

There isn't any reply. Not at first. The only sound is the sheet of paper crinkling up again. But it isn't mine. My hands are neatly folded in my lap now. It's Dad who is mindlessly crunching the pages of his calendar. I detect another sound, further in the background: the long, tired creak of his desk chair when he leans too far back. I am also quite sure I heard his jaw dropping on the floor before he quickly picks it up and says, "Pregnant? How'd *that* happen?"

"Well...uh...Dad, we've been planning for this...it's what we wanted...and Leo and I are both really, really happy."

I should feel better now that the words are finally out, but Dad's silence weighs on me.

"I don't know if we're having a boy or girl yet, though," I continue, trying my best to just talk more and give him time to take it all in. "It's too early to tell. But I'm really excited. And the baby will be born in early March, Dad...the same month Mom was born."

I can hear his chair squeak again as it comes forward. His voice sounds more relaxed now as he takes a big breath and says, "It's really something. Really something, Julia. Con...gratulations."

Sharing the news with Lilly goes surprisingly much smoother. Leo and I both hold the receiver as I exclaim the words, "I'm pregnant!" to which she immediately sighs with relief and under her breath says, "*Thank* God."

But her first intentionally audible words are sweet: "You both are going to make such wonderful parents! And Julia, I know you will make a truly exceptional mother. I really do. I'm so happy for you both!"

"We're absolutely thrilled," I say, smiling at Leo.

"Can you believe it?" adds Leo. "There's going to be a little baby running around!"

"Now Julia," says Lilly, her tone firming up, "are you taking a prenatal vitamin?"

"Uh-huh," I reply as Leo puts his hand over my belly again, pretending to feel the baby. "The one with folic acid?" she adds.

"Yup, with folic acid. I've been taking it for three months now, just in case."

Sylvia begins to yip and yap in the background, as if she had her own canine advice to add. But Lilly continues, "Oh, good. And you'll also want to drink lots and lots of extra milk. Babies need calcium! Lots and lots of calcium. For their development. When I was pregnant, I drank it in the morning, with meals, and another glass at night. Don't forget!"

"More milk. Got it. Thanks, I'll do that."

"Oh, and rest! Get lots and lots of rest. Take it easy and just enjoy yourself. Really try to enjoy your pregnancy. I have to tell you, and this is going to sound funny, but there's a part of me that really misses pregnancy. I never felt better or closer to God than when I was pregnant. It's so special."

I hear her voice start to crack over the phone. She finishes her thought in a whisper. "I'm just so...so happy for you."

Leo calls his dad next, and then we tell my sister. And then my other sister. And then Leo's four brothers. "Well, I think that's it for family," Leo says, smiling as he puts a proud arm around me. "I mean, we really shouldn't tell any of our friends until we get to the twelve-week mark. Just to be safe?"

"Yeah, that's probably a good idea," I say. "Just to be safe."

He walks into the kitchen and starts to put on a pot of coffee.

"Oh, jeez. I'd better make you herb tea now instead, right? Do you think chamomile is OK for the baby? Or that raspberry women's tea you just bought? Probably chamomile, right?"

I smile and nod as I pick up the phone once more, press it to my ear, and begin to dial the number that will never disappear from my memory. I stop. I want to place the phone back on the receiver but I can't. I want to turn around but I can't. All I can do is just stare at the phone in my hand. Silent. Dumb.

Something is missing. No, not something. Someone. There is still someone I need to tell more than anyone. Someone I can never tell.

I curl my bottom lip in, but it's too late. The teakettle on the stove begins to whistle just as I begin to cry. Leo doesn't hear me. But it doesn't matter. He sees the back of my shoulders slump forward and shake, and he knows.

"Shh, shh, don't cry," he tells me as his thumb wipes away the tears from my cheeks. He takes the phone out of my hand and hangs it back up.

"I just wish I could call her," I say as I turn my face away. I feel stupid, like a child who is too old to believe in Santa but insists on writing the letter on Christmas Eve. Just in case.

Leo holds me tight and kisses my forehead. "She already knows," he tells me.

But it's not the same. I need her. I need her right now—I need her to tell me that everything will be OK and that I'm going to be a good mother and that she's there if I need her, I want to tell him. But I don't. I just stand there silently and let Leo console me.

fifty-eight

I'M STANDING IN THE GREETING card aisle at the drugstore around the block from our apartment. Katerina's birthday was yesterday, and I completely forgot. I've been forgetting a lot of things lately. This morning I put the milk in the cupboard and the cereal in the fridge. Yesterday I accidentally put a red washcloth in with the laundry at the last minute and dyed Leo's undershirts a very frustrating shade of pink.

They tell me pregnancy does that. But that's also what they used to tell me about grief. Same goes for headaches, sleeping problems, and feeling alone and unprepared. And when I get sad and moved to tears, well, apparently pregnancy does that too. "It's just your hormones," people tell me with a laugh. "Pregnancy does crazy things to your hormones!"

The card aisle is empty except for one little elderly woman with a cane, swaying her hips to the easy listening music playing in the background. I try to peer over her blue fresh-from-the-beauty-shop hair as she slides right in front of me and the entire belated birthdays section. And just as she begins to hum off-key along to Barry Manilow's "Copacabana," something else catches my eye. In the bottom row in the middle of the blank section, a card with a very familiar face peeks out from the others. I swoop down to pick it up and quickly turn it over to confirm my guess. "Yup. It's her," I say to myself. Or so I thought.

"It's who?" asks the old lady.

It seems that pregnancy can also make you think you are talking to yourself when you most certainly are not.

"No one," I reply, taken aback. "Sorry."

Secretly thrilled at my random find, I make my way to the register at the front of the store. Of course, it's not until I am in the car that I realize I've forgotten all about Katerina and her belated birthday card. No matter. As soon as I shut the car door, I quickly slide my card from the square of the brown paper bag. I gaze at the pretty face smiling back at me and reread the caption:

By Filippino Lippi. *Erato*. 1504. Tempera on panel. Gemaldegalerie, Berlin, Germany.

There she was. Just as I remembered her. As beautiful as ever. The same patient, smiling mouth. The same crown of pink roses atop her flowing auburn hair. The same pet swan, in all its open-winged magnificence, held only by her leash of sheer golden ribbon. But there was something else. Something peculiar and out of place. At the bottom right of the image, I see two toddlers skipping in the grass. Their cheeks are round and pink from smiling as they try to hold onto one giant wing of the pet swan. The swan looks decidedly unamused and is stepping on one of the careless toddler's toes. In all these years, in all my studies, I have never noticed these children in the painting before. And suddenly it all makes sense. Erato, the Muse of love, is a mother.

fifty-nine

HOW MANY WEEKS is it now?" Leo asks. "Seventeen? Or eighteen?"

"Nineteen tomorrow," I say, barely able to get the words out.

"Nineteen tomorrow," Leo repeats to the triage nurse in the emergency room.

There is a great deal of rushing about. My blood pressure is taken. Signatures are needed. They help me into a wheelchair, and the nurse rolls me down the hall.

"Can you tell me your birthday, Julia?" she asks as she helps me onto a bed.

"Ten years," I reply. "It's been more than ten years since my mother died. More than ten years since I've heard her voice." But the nurse doesn't hear me. I've passed out.

I wake up a couple of minutes later. Leo is standing over me. He is doing his best to sound calm as he rubs his hand over my belly. "You're doing so good, honey," he tells me. I turn away because his face is turning fuzzy again, along with everything else in the room. When the doctor comes in, I hear Leo say, "There was some blood, and she started getting some really bad pains around midnight. And then they just started getting worse. This is too early, isn't it? Well, isn't it?"

The ER doctor asks a few questions, feels around the top of my abdomen, and then walks back into the hall to order an ultrasound and some other tests. Before he leaves, he pulls the curtain across the front of the bed, and Leo and I are alone again.

"Are you cold, honey?" he asks.

My whole body is trembling. My legs are shaking so bad that the small metal bed frame begins to rattle. Leo takes a blanket from the supply shelf and unfolds it over me.

"I'm so scared," I tell him, my teeth chattering. "I don't want to lose this baby."

"I know, sweetheart, but everything will be just fine. We just have to stay calm."

My eyesight is still fuzzy, but I can feel Leo rub the tops of my feet. His touch is tender and comforting, and slowly my vision becomes clearer and his face comes into focus. He looks as scared as I feel.

I can see the room better now. On the front wall is a large laminated poster of the circulatory system of the human body. Beside it is a small yellow flier urging readers to get a flu shot. White cupboards line another wall, each door marked with a tiny label. I break down in tears.

A different nurse walks in. She's tall with short blonde hair, and she's holding a needle. I try my best to stop crying but I can't. Instead I just cover my face with my hand. She sticks the needle in one of the few veins that show, and I don't even notice. She pats me on the head.

"Pregnancy is a journey," she says cheerfully as she tosses the used needle into a bin. "Your body has so many hormones right now, and they're front and center! Trust me. It's just the hormones talking. I remember."

The nurse stops talking as I begin to sob even louder. She connects some wires and the heart monitor to me and quickly leaves the room.

Leo drags his chair across the room until it is right next to my bed. He lays his head beside mine on the pillow and returns his hand to my belly. "Talk to me," he says softly.

Tears roll down my cheek and onto his. He wipes them away from both our faces. "I'm just so worried," I say in between sobs. "I just don't want to fail again."

"What do you mean? You didn't fail. You're doing so good, honey. You're doing everything right. You're healthy, you eat right, you're doing great."

I shake my head. "I have this helpless baby inside me. A whole person who depends on me. I'm trying so hard and I don't want to screw up. I haven't felt this way since I was a teenager taking care of my mom. She needed me and I let her down. I failed at taking care of my mom, and now I'm failing at taking care of this baby. I just don't know what to do…" My voice runs out.

"But you didn't fail with your mom. It wasn't up to you. Look at me, Julia. It wasn't up to you."

353

I shake my head and the muscles in my belly become tense and hard. I scream out. The pain is unbearable. Leo calls the nurse back in.

"On a scale of one to ten, with ten being the worst pain you've ever felt in your life, what would you say your pain is right now?" she asks.

"One hundred."

"OK. And what does it feel like?" she asks.

"Like a dozen knives all stabbing me at once," I reply, panting, as I point to the lower half of my belly.

"So, shooting pain?"

"Yeah, I'd say it was."

She makes a note on my chart, and a dark-haired technician walks in. She's pulling a wheeled cart carrying a small machine behind her. She looks tired. But so does everybody else. It's three in the morning. "Hi, I'm here to do your ultrasound."

Leo stands up but doesn't let go of my hand.

As the technician wheels my bed into another room, I try to prepare myself for the worst. As she lifts my gown and rubs some cold, clear goo on my abdomen, I imagine how she will break the terrible news to me. And as she presses the ultrasound wand over my belly, I look away from the monitor. I look at Leo instead.

He looks worried. His mouth is drawn. The technician flicks the on switch for the monitor. Leo's eyes scan the monitor.

I take a deep breath. The sharp pains are still there as the technician moves the round end of the ultrasound wand across the center of my belly. I grab Leo's hand tighter as I brace for the news.

"This is where it all happens," she begins like a narrator for a silent film. "Here is your uterus. And right here is your baby. And that's the heart beating. Right there."

My eyes grow wide as I immediately turn my head toward the grainy black-and-white screen.

"You can see a heart beating? My baby's alive?" I ask, with my own heart feeling like it's stuck in my throat.

"Yup. Right there," she replies. "See that? That's the heart beating. About 140 beats a minute."

"That's amazing!" says Leo, with his hand on his forehead. "I can't believe we can see the heart!"

"And is that normal? Is 140 normal?" I ask, still worried and bracing for bad news.

"Very normal. Everything looks fine, just fine."

My eyes take a few seconds to make out the picture on the screen, but then everything becomes clear. A tiny heart is beating. I can see a face—even the nose and chin—and a little body. I didn't know I was crying until I felt the tears spill down my face. The pain I felt in my abdomen has disappeared. All I feel now is pure, concentrated happiness.

"Uh-oh," says the technician. Her hands race through a series of clicks with her computer as she zooms in on one portion of the screen.

"What it is it? Did you see something?"

"I definitely saw something."

"What?" Leo and I ask at the same time.

"You're having a boy."

Leo beams. He shoves his hand in his hair and doesn't even care that it leaves every strand standing up. His smile takes over his entire face. I've never seen him so happy.

"Is that the *something*?" says Leo, leaning in closer, just to make sure.

"Yes. Right there. Can you see it?" she says, pointing to a small gray blur on the screen.

"We're having a *boy*!" Leo shouts, just like a lion roaring proudly to the jungle.

"Wow, he's really moving around," says the technician. "He looks like he's having a good time in there."

"See that, honey? Everything is alright," Leo says to me. "That's our baby boy!"

My eyes follow each and every movement on the screen, afraid to see the baby disappear. I watch him do a somersault and move in funny twists and turns until finally he holds his hands up to one cheek like he got tired and is trying to fall asleep. I watch him, holding my breath, until I see his tiny hand reach out and something changes inside me.

I want to take my own hand and try to reach his on the screen. Right away I can remember how to make tomato sauce and what type of tea to make him if he gets sick. I remember what to tell the school office if he pretends to be sick and wants to stay home from school one day. I remember what stories to tell him about rabbits and ducks and the dog. And how I need to teach him about the different types of clouds and winds and how the bougainvillea are really Chinese lanterns. How I want to hold him in my arms and tell him about my mom. His own French grandmother.

And just then I can hear her gentle voice saying, "Instead of Grandma, do you think you could have him call me Mimi?"

Brushing the tears away, I whisper into my pillow, "Yes. You'll be his Mimi. Forever and ever."

"Don't cry, honey," Leo tells me. "Our little boy is going to be just fine."

"I'm just happy," I say, "just really, really happy."

He looks relieved. He leans in for a kiss but hesitates. He asks instead, "Does that mean I can go get a burger from the cafeteria downstairs? I'm super-starving right now."

·

END

acknowledgements

What began as a meandering series of ramblings finished as a story about the everydayness of grief in its more quiet and private moments. This is due in large part to several extraordinary individuals, all of to whom I am sincerely grateful:

To Beverly McGuire in Moss Beach, for her cheerful patience in proofreading; to Kathy Kaiser in San Francisco, for her meticulous work in editing; to Erika Storella in New York, for her support early on; to Jaimie Hunter in New York & Michelle Gibbs in Sydney, for their reads of the manuscript in its early stages and for filling our London years with laughter before we scattered across the globe; to Stella Chung in Rocklin, who was there since the beginning to offer support when it was needed most and whose friendship I cherish; and to David, for his ability to brighten even the darkest cloud by sheer force of optimism.

about the author

Jessica Swan is an American author who left her tiny flat in London for New York to drive cross-country until she fell back in love with California. A former ghostwriter for fifteen years, she holds a rhetoric degree from UC Berkeley. She has published one other novel, *Dear Isabelle* (Harbor House Books, Augusta), and co-authored the nonfiction business book *The Big Book of Motivation Games* (McGraw-Hill, New York). Her articles and column have been published in *Psychology Today* magazine and her co-authored work in *The Behavior Analyst* journal. She lives in Oakland.